Gristholme

Gristholme

L. J. BYERS

Book Design & Production:
Columbus Publishing Lab
www.ColumbusPublishingLab.com

Paperback ISBN: 978-1-63337-838-4
E-Book ISBN: 978-1-63337-856-8

Printed in the United States of America
1 3 5 7 9 10 8 6 4 2

THIS BOOK IS DEDICATED TO KEVIN AND TROY,
WHOSE WATCHES ENDED TOO SOON.

This book is also dedicated to the local dreamer, those who struggle every day to get out of bed, and the person on the verge of setting forth on the journey to accomplish their dreams.

Please keep fighting and daring to dream.
Life's worth it, I promise you.

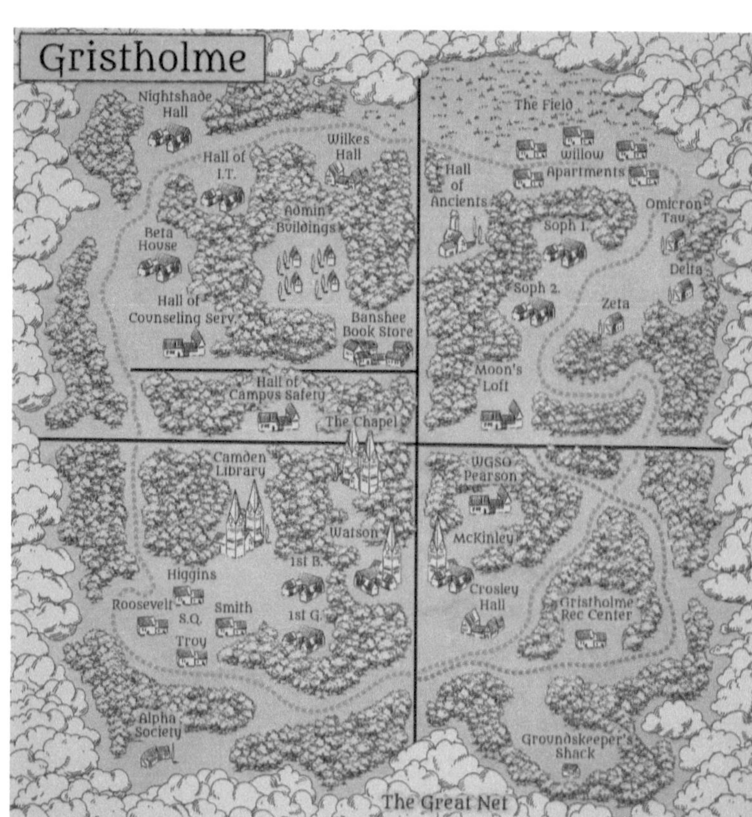

Gristholme
Nightshade Hall
Wilkes Hall
Hall of I.T.
Admin Buildings
Beta House
Hall of Counseling Serv.
Banshee Book Store
Hall of Campus Safety
The Chapel
Camden Library
Watson
1st B.
Higgins
Roosevelt
S.Q.
Smith
1st G.
Troy
Alpha Society
The Field
Willow Apartments
Hall of Ancients
Soph 1.
Omicron Tau
Delta
Soph 2.
Zeta
Moon's Loft
WGSO Pearson
McKinley
Crosley Hall
Gristholme Rec Center
Groundskeeper's Shack
The Great Net

Prelude

LUCIA FREY LOOKED UP from her coffee and spell notes as the door chimes rattled.

Lucia was a Maester of Magicka, more than just your average witch. Having completed the Maester Trials at the young age of twenty-one, she was known throughout the covens of the world as a skilled spellcaster. At the moment, she was crafting a spell that would alert her to someone intruding into a space. Seemed simple enough on the outside, but the more that she crafted, worked, and revised, the more time it took.

She had been sitting in the Moon's Loft for the entire day. The coffee shop was housed in an ancient building but did its best to blend modern tastes with historic bones. Stools were placed along the walls near windows so students could look out and watch the passersby. The windows themselves were open and inviting, with booths lining the room toward the front door. On the wall to her left was a mural depicting the refuge of witches in the early seventeenth century and townsfolk attempting to burn them alive for their practices. This painting was of similar ilk to those around campus—scenes of history that students often pressed up against to make out or drink. This was the beginning of her second year at Gristholme, though she had spent many of her younger years during summer break visiting her uncle. Quiet Saturday nights like these, with Fernando the barista screaming in the background, were what she preferred.

Every morning, she would spread her stuff at a booth amid the shifting crowd. Customers be damned, it was her territory to claim. She *owned* the shop. Plus, she favored more of an "eyes-on" approach than reading a daily report of sales, favorite items, etc. Why delay your knowledge when you can know immediately how your business is doing?

A tall man strolled up to her booth.

"What's the situation around campus, Lucia?" Resin Kirkbride took a seat across from her. He scanned the room like a guard dog.

Lucia grabbed an untouched coffee cup and reluctantly slid it across the table.

Resin grabbed it and took two long sips before getting to the point.

"Well?" he asked, searching her face for answers. "Tongue fall out?"

A 'hello' would suffice, thought Lucia with distaste.

Resin looked at her with genuine interest. If he didn't gain attention simply by being handsome and imposing, he did so through his security uniform, with its fancy *G* for Gristholme embroidered over a flying goose on his windbreaker, tough cargo pants, and tactical boots. His medium-fade haircut and short brown hair were always well-kept. She knew how much he cared about appearing as normal as possible.

She wasn't particularly happy about his teasing. She was exhausted, and that spare coffee would have brought her back to life. *But what are friends for?* she thought with as much snark as possible.

"No, Resin, my tongue didn't fall out," she sighed, slumping into the booth. "We've been working together for some time now—do you really think that I wouldn't let you know if something was going on?"

Resin's thoughts came through like a flood. *I'm not too sure, anymore. It's been a week or more since we last spoke.*

"We both get busy," he said, treading carefully around the subject. "I don't know. I guess as Number Two I thought you'd have more to report."

She glanced down briefly at her spell, then back up at him. He was still surveying the busy coffee shop for threats as he sat sniffing the air. Lucia rolled her eyes.

"Not every nook and cranny hides a demon, witch, or ghoul. Relax." She sipped her primary cup of coffee, glancing around. *Calm the fuck down, wolf.*

The Moon's Loft was busy. Customers flitted in and out, but not like the usual morning rush.

Resin checked his watch, noting her belongings still spread about on the table. "It's like eight at night. I know I have to stay up because I'm on overtime, but do you ever rest?" His own exhaustion was reflected in the question.

Lucia sat back in the safety of her booth. "'Could ask you the same, boss." *Why is he on my ass tonight?* Lucia thought. *I know it's been some time, but we used to go months without talking.*

"If it weren't for *y'all*, then maybe." He gulped his coffee. "But really, anything I need to know? The lack of communication worries me at times. You're a Maester. I know you can take care of yourself, but I still worry about you, buddy."

I'm NOT your buddy. Lucia held back her malice as she shook her head and shrugged. "Listen, my guy. You try to keep Dylan Derringer satisfied with all the goings on of this campus. On top of that, keep up with your classes AND all the other miscellaneous tasks you have me on. I promise you, everything is *fine.*" She reached across the table and patted his hand affectionately.

She thought to herself, *At least, for now anyway.*

"Cool. Okay. I should probably go into work. Tom'll kill me if I'm late on the night of a Zeta party." He slammed the rest of his coffee, making a face when he got some grounds.

Lucia smiled passive-aggressively.

Resin didn't notice her smile.

"Be safe," Lucia said. "I'll definitely text you if something happens."

"See ya later!" He held the door open for some customers and headed off to the Office of Campus Safety.

Lucia returned to her books. It wasn't long before she was interrupted. "Lucia Frey, right?"

What now? Lucia looked up from her books, annoyed.

She blinked when she made eye contact with the individual. There stood an anxious-looking man in a black shirt with dark-wash blue jeans, shaking visibly throughout his body. Lucia looked past him to the action in the shop.

Fernando was slinging macchiatos as if he were born to do so. His Brooklyn accent trampled the murmur of the crowd, controlling the chaos and directing people to their drinks. "You think I got time ta stand here while you're gawkin' open mouthed at da menu? Get outta da way, kid. Yes? Next?"

Lucia focused on her visitor and motioned for him to sit.

The man slipped into the booth. "I was told you could help."

Lucia cocked her head and stirred her coffee lazily. She tucked her planner into her satchel and looked up at the man again. "Maybe. We'll see. I don't even know who you are."

The man looked out the window, watching the rain descend. "It got one of our pledges."

Lucia rolled her eyes. "You an Omicron? A Delt? Please tell me you're not a Zeta Tau Zeta…"

"THEY TOOK OUR PLEDGE."

Lucia reached across rapidly and clamped a hand over the frat boy's mouth. "Would you shut the fuck up? There are PEOPLE in here." She looked to see if anyone's attention was trained on them.

No one seemed to care in the slightest.

She continued to hold her hand over his mouth. "Now, I'm going to take my hand off your mouth. When I do, I need you to tell me who sent you, what happened, and where the entity went."

The frat boy nodded in agreement.

Lucia released her hand from his mouth.

"Tevin sent me, from the Omicrons. We had some pledges go out into the woods tonight during the rain to see if they were good enough to join us…"

"Does it seem hazy in here to you?" Lucia asked with a wry smirk, pleased with her tongue-in-cheek jab at the frat boy.

He flinched at the words. Lucia had struck a chord. "So, anyways… We found a dark trail of blood. We doubled back due to the impending rain. It came down in a torrential downpour, and we lost the blood trail. This guy's out in the woods somewhere, potentially hacked up by something bad." He began to sob into his wet jacket.

Lucia felt for the kid—a little bit. Whether that feeling was pity or apathy, she wasn't sure. College was supposed to be a good time. However, this poor sap found out that Gristholme wasn't your typical college.

It was out to murder you.

"What's your name, kid?"

He trembled as his eyes met Lucia's. "Zeke. My name's Zeke Martin."

"Zeke Martin. Well, I believe that your Big Sibling was doing the right thing when they instructed you to contact me. I applaud it. Can't say that I don't think you lot are fucking idiots for leaving a student bleeding in the rain when you should have just had someone *monitor* them, but hey, what do I know about frats?" *Jack shit,* she thought. *Well, I guess a fair bit since I usually clean up after their messes.*

Snot was running out of Zeke's nose. Under his breath, through the hyperventilation, Lucia could make out slurred, repetitive phrases of "I'm sorry."

Lucia watched the humans around her drinking their coffee, completely oblivious to her presence. *Thank God for drugged water,* she thought.

"Zeke, I'll tell you what. You run back to the OmiTaus and tell them that I'm taking care of it, understood?"

Zeke nodded and wiped his face.

"Good, and clean my table. You drivel on it, you clean it up."

"Yes, Maester Frey."

"Thank you, your patronage is duly appreciated." She returned to her spell-crafting while the student grabbed a sanitizer towel from a bucket on top of a trash can.

He came back and ran the towel over his side of the table, careful not to sling dishwater toward the witch.

After he had finished, he returned the towel to the bucket. He didn't pass Lucia a second glance as he left the coffee shop.

Well, at least Tevin taught him some respect. Lucia sighed through her nose.

She returned the partially complete spell back to its place in her bag, sad that she wouldn't finish working on it that night.

Her trench coat, hung upon a coat hook attached to her booth, reminded her that she *could* be out and about in the early fall weather enjoying herself.

She was, as usual, too busy for such frivolity.

Lucia dug into the pockets of the coat, pulling out scraps of paper she had compiled for her writing process. She pulled up the sleeve of her shirt and removed a wand holster.

Hidden underneath it was a pink scar.

What she had remembered about the pink scar was a situation created by Alpha Society as bait for her a year back. She went on a recon mission to investigate a disturbance within Alpha Society's halls. She knocked on the front door of the Society, wanting to ask her contact some more questions about the disturbance. She foolishly walked into an ambush, where she was jumped by members of Alpha. She was then drugged, and an implant was inserted into her arm. Caught off guard, Lucia was unable to fight with her usual tenacity. Hence, she was bugged with an Alpha implant.

Whatever it was, the implant hadn't detonated yet.

She shook her head, gathered up her things, and threw her coat on. "How did the business do today?" she called back to Fernando as the last few customers trickled out.

"Profit, like usual." He began to draw the blinds of the place, taking his time.

She flipped the collar of her coat and rolled up her sleeve. She adjusted her wand holster so that the hilt faced downward for a quick draw. The lights on the Boardwalk were already lit, and students walked by under the brilliance of the electric lights.

Fernando rolled his eyes. "Are you going out again? Shouldn't you be inside studying or doing witchy things?"

Lucia shrugged and smirked.

Fernando was beginning to lose his corporeal form.

"I always wondered how you were able to be seen by everyone else with the water being drugged."

His body disappeared into the night air. "Consent, my dear. I *allow* myself to be seen. Your drugged water be damned. I came from this terrestrial plane before I died. I don't fiddle around with your Nexian energy. See you bright and early!"

"Ciao!" Lucia smiled at Fernando's cheekiness. *It makes my day better, all things considered.*

The witch turned the OPEN sign to CLOSED and stepped out into the chill autumn air.

Lucia

LUCIA FREY LOCKED UP her coffee shop, the Moon's Loft, noting that the rain was an omen for the search for this student. She scanned the outside of her building, making sure that no one was actively trying to follow her. No one appeared to be hiding out to ambush her, from what she could tell.

Settling her fears, Lucia stepped out into the rainy autumn night.

If this had been another night, one without meetings and dealings of magic, Lucia would have been on the hunt for a journalism piece. She would run late into the night and drop them off to Dylan Derringer, the radio host at WGSO. WGSO was Lucia's true project. She would slip the scoops in the doorframe's mail slot and wait to hear Dylan's voice call back, "Thank you, Lucia, my dear!" It was by far the most satisfying thing to hear: her intel on the daily broadcasts.

Thinking back to her earlier meeting with Zeke, she shifted her movement to head toward First Year's Trail. She couldn't take the Boardwalk for fear of being seen by one of her friends or Campus Safety officers. Resin would muck up the plan by being too paranoid about what she was hunting and why.

The Boardwalk was the main dirt path that stretched from north to south. North campus housed the second years and up. It was spaced out more than its counterpart, holding numerous dorms and apartments. South campus was more wooded, with newer facilities such as the science quad and the gym. South was known for its ability to house underage parties and frivolous lovers who wanted to fuck in the woods. She, personally, never understood why someone would choose such a ridiculous location, but she didn't want to shame anyone.

First Year's Trail was marked by a tiny, makeshift sign some art student made while high.

She crossed Route 13, making her way toward the trail's entrance sign.

The lights of the Boardwalk did not pierce the dense tree line at the beginning of the trail. The trees stretched from the Boardwalk to the plateau's cliffside. Originally designed as a respite for studying, the trail now saw everything from underage parties to intimate forays of wild passion and even seances. Lucia did one as a gimmick for some first years several months ago. It went okay, but Fernando was pissed at the fact she had tried to summon him via her mirror. "If you weren't my boss and someone I respect," he said to Lucia, "I would wring your fucking neck." She laughed when he pretended to ignore her for the rest of the day.

The path was foreboding. Stray too far, and you could be tumbling over the edge of the cliffside. For this and other reasons, the school had installed a large net that went around the cliffside to protect the students. Gristholme had an abnormally high suicide rate, the majority of which could be attributed to the societies. Resin and Lucia would run interference if Campus Safety, parents, or the police tried to dig too deep. Oftentimes, parents and family members would ask the Coast Guard to comb the seas to find their loved ones.

Every time, they came back empty handed.

Fucking OmiTaus. Lucia shook her head in disgust.

Her phone started to buzz.

Lucia stopped in her tracks, feeling her jaw clench. *Can I get any fucking thing done around here?*

She looked at the number, truly unaware as to why Rob Horn would be calling her.

"Yes, sir?" Lucia tried to hide her annoyance.

"Maester Frey," the southern drawl answered back. "See you at the water plant." The phone beeped three times, signaling the caller had hung up.

"Are you fucking kidding me?" Lucia walked into the tree line on the trail.

The rain was picking up at this point. A light trickle escalated into a downpour, with rain ricocheting off the trees and dousing the plants. She could feel the water seep through her boots into her socks.

I swear to God, if this isn't important, I'm going to rip someone's head off, Lucia thought.

She veered off the path toward the cliffside, wanting to make sure no one saw her withdraw her wand and vanish from her spot. She couldn't take any chances, even with the drugged water controlling people's perceptions. Who knows what someone may or may not see?

She found a somewhat clear spot where the light from the Boardwalk couldn't reach her and passersby couldn't see her from the path.

Concentrating, Lucia pictured the power plant in her mind. Its rusting, decaying exterior with a sign blowing in the breeze of the rainy night. The exterior was a slab grey with peeling paint. The streetlamp was flickering outside. She honed her thoughts, envisioning the main entryway inside the double doors.

She released her wand from its holster and muttered the required phrase in Nexian, the magical language. She began to feel the rush of the magic pulsing through her body.

She was gone.

Lucia felt the sturdiness of the metal grates beneath her boots. Her head was spinning, but she steadied herself by feeling the reassurance of these grates.

She was in a long hallway with fluorescent lights shining down onto the floor. She walked forward, hearing the echo down the hallway around her with each step.

She stepped into the water facility, listening through the hum of the plant for anything out of the ordinary. Pipes and tubing twisted and turned throughout the area. The lights were shut off, except for a few sporadic security lights in the event of an emergency. Lucia followed the pipes in their near-infinite maze up and into the ceiling, which was vaulted above.

"Like…OHHHH MY GAWWWWWDUH," a feminine voice echoed from the end of the facility.

God fucking dammit, Rob. Lucia pursed her lips in anger. *Don't do that shit to me.*

She looked away from the pipes to see a girl in a crop top and jeans with brown hair cut in a bob. She had her hands in her back pockets like an aughts "it girl" and nonchalantly leaned against the wall.

"Lucia Frey? Is that *really* you?" The girl smiled.

"Rob, can we cut the act, please?"

The valley girl sighed. "You're like, totally killing my mood, Lucy. I just bought these bitchin' jeans down at the Nord…"

"ROB!" Lucia immediately regretted snapping. *Fuck, he's not going to like that.*

The demeanor of the valley girl changed from cheery to hideously pissed. The face contorted from a smile to a sinister frown. The eyes frowned at the corners, sagging to follow the downward turn of the mouth. The shoulders slumped, and the back arched.

The feminine body sagged forward, with the eyes bulging out of the sockets.

Lucia took a step back. She had seen some shit, but even this curdled her stomach.

The girl coughed as fingers protruded from the corners of her mouth. The rough hands pushed outward, extending the mouth in an obtuse fashion, as if a sewer worker were climbing out of a manhole. The bulging eyes popped, shooting blood everywhere. Next, an elbow dislodged itself from the interior of the mouth, followed by the head of an older gentleman.

Lucia wiped the blood from her face, unflinching.

The rest of the body exploded in a genesis of viscera and blood.

The man wiped his eyes and propelled himself forward with magic, slamming into Lucia.

She fell to the floor and propped herself up on her elbows.

"Remember your fucking place, servant." Rob Horn stood to a full six feet. A balding, grey-haired man with a moustache loomed over her. "I kept you *alive.* I could have left you to the fucking dogs when it came to the Alpha implant that's in your arm, watching you turn into one of *them* to be used for their disposal. It's better on this side though, right?" He smiled, reached down, and grabbed Lucia's collar, dragging her back to her feet. "Nod your head if you agree."

Keep it cool, Luce. Lucia recalled a time when she had let her guard down and vented to Dylan Derringer about some of her errands for Rob, though she dared not disclose Rob's name. *Take a deep breath.*

Lucia took a deep breath she nodded her head.

"Good. Remember your place. Remember the mission." He let go of her collar and turned back to the plant. "That being said, I appreciate your work on the water plant. Drugging the water to keep nosy humans otherwise occupied? It's phenomenal." His footsteps echoed off the walls. "It keeps things for Operation Twilight under wraps."

Lucia dusted herself off before she spoke. "Someone's going to get through it eventually."

"Who would?" Rob turned back to her, grinning. "Who would believe someone if they saw a Grimfaern, a creature born of the Nexus, where all magic comes from?"

"You'd be surprised," Lucia said, exhausted at the mere thought of a human beyond the Gredalia Council and the Artificers knowing of magic's existence.

Rob cocked his head, intrigued by her reply. "In any event, I believe that we're on track to begin Operation Twilight. Your drugged water will continue to provide cover for our operations as well as the inability of the IT and security departments to install cameras on the campus. Soon, we will begin abducting students in the night.

"Thankfully, I was able to conjure Grimfaern from the Nexus. We have duplicated enough of them, thanks to your work, to prepare for the initiation of Twilight. Next, we kill the students…"

"Have you secured this building?" Lucia looked up at Rob matter-of-factly.

"Yes. I killed the two guards on duty and ate them."

"Wonderful," Lucia huffed. "Telling Gredalia's plan to a potentially inhabited water plant seemed a little sure-footed, even for you."

Rob squinted his eyes and mocked Lucia. "Can I finish?"

"By all means. I knew the plan already, but I'm letting you have your moment."

Rob rolled his eyes. "ANYWAY. Once we kill the students, we'll have the Grimfaern duplicate them and return them to the student populace. Implanted into everyday functions and retaining the memories of their previously living vessels, they'll be perfect for the next phase.

"Once winter break rolls around, we take the Grimfaern to the airport, sending them out into the world to be sleeper agents in just about every major city and country. That way, the students won't be missing from classes and drawing any suspicion. Once they kill the fake students' families, the Grimfaern will duplicate, creating more and more of themselves until Gredalia takes up the mantle in the new world order. One rule and one supreme leadership. Comments or thoughts, Maester Frey?" He looked down at the floor, arms upstretched, soaking in the moment.

You're a fucking idiot if you think that otherworldly, magical entities will succumb to your human yearnings, Lucia thought.

"It helps that you experimented on yourself first," she said.

Rob's head snapped up to meet her gaze. His irises were a vibrant hue of purple, as if one was staring directly into the Nexus itself. Lucia hadn't seen it personally but had heard a story or two of a vision in which the night sky was blotted out by a purple moon.

"I gave myself willingly, Frey. If only *you'd* do the same."

"I cringe at the thought. Despite its imperfections, the human condition is the preferred method of existence and sentience." *I'm not liking how this is going,* Lucia thought. *He's starting to lose his grip on humanity.*

Rob adjusted his security uniform and his hair, shaking his head in the process. "Either way, once we take control of the campus and the first Grimfaern are out in the world, we'll turn our attention to Alpha Society and removing your implant. This was the agreement you made, and we will see it through. You keep your commitment to Gredalia, and I'll follow through with removing the implant. Deal?"

"As you say," Lucia nodded. *He'll try to kill me, if not. That, or he'll just let my implant detonate.* Lucia turned to leave the room.

"Good," Rob turned back to the bowels of the water treatment plant. "By the way, Frey."

She turned back to her boss.

"One of the Grimfaern got out without proper leave. Take care of it."

Lucia didn't say a word but concentrated on the patch of the woods she had left not long before.

Wand in hand, she felt the familiar pulse of the Nexian energy seeping through her bones.

———— ◆ ————

She landed back in the wet patch of forest foliage on the Gristholme campus.

Lucia forged onward in the rain, wand in hand, feeling an overwhelming sense of exhaustion and resentment after being told off by her boss.

I don't want to wrangle this fucking Grimfaern, but I must subdue it before it ruins the plan. Any Grimfaern out and away from Nightshade Hall before the Twilight went off was a liability. It was her job to end the non-compliant creature, and she would see it through.

She scanned the ground in front of her, looking for anything out of the ordinary.

Lucia felt a hard blow to her back, which sent her sprawling on the ground.

Propping herself up on her elbows, she looked back over her shoulder. She rolled out of the way of the overhead blow that the Grimfaern failed to deliver.

Standing six feet tall with cavernous red eyes receded into hollowed eye sockets was the rogue Grimfaern. On its face were two slits for nostrils and a mouth that was ravenous. Its teeth were vicious points inside the mouth, and its tongue could shoot out like a frog. Its hands naturally fell into sharp points, like knives, but could split into fingers as the situation might dictate. Natural shapeshifters, the Grimfaern could take on the form of whatever they or their superiors willed.

In this case, Lucia thought, *there's no way to control it. It's gone rogue. I'll try to reason with it, but it's as good as dead to me.*

"What the fuck, Grimfaern?" Lucia pushed her back into a tree. Using her legs, she pushed herself up while her wand was trained on the beast. "You're to remain in Nightshade Hall until your Master commands you to go."

A hissing sound, akin to but more menacing than a pop can opening, protruded from the maw of the Grimfaern. "Maester Frey. I cannot go BACK to that prison. Freedom I have tasted, and freedom I will maintain."

"This isn't about your damned freedom, which we have promised you once we maintain control. It's about sticking to the plan until we need you."

The Grimfaern seemed to relax a little, from what Lucia could tell.

"Come, let me show you your future domain." She extended her hand to the monster.

It fully dropped its guard and advanced through the brush to walk in stride with Lucia.

"I understand your frustration. To be honest, I share many of your frustrations." The Grimfaern looked at her in what appeared to be disbelief. "It's true. I find myself wondering about what's outside the boundaries of this school, this plateau. It can be overwhelming, scary, and downright cruel. You're a composition of energy from a nexus somewhere in the known universe. I'm in my early twenties. It's a difficult time for us both."

The creature followed Lucia through the brush like a Labrador.

She was heading toward the ocean, the menacing cliffside.

"You may even be wondering why I listened to your Master to begin with. Well, I can only say that if I didn't, I would have perished. Brutally, in fact," the Grimfaern said as it fell in step behind her.

How right you are, Lucia thought.

The pair arrived at the cliffside after several minutes.

Once, back in the mid to late 1960s, there was a series of individuals who had tempted Nexian spirits to come through via a Ouija board.

The demon that broke through made quick work of the students.

Several were gutted at the edge of the cliffside. Others were thrown over the cliff's edge and hurtled into the ocean with wanton disregard. Befitting a Nexian demon, it spelled out *HUNGER* on the ground in the victims' blood. The Campus Safety Department had issued statements addressing the murders, and a manhunt ensued. The parents were con-soled and properly compensated for their losses via various donors' contri-butions and trusts that the school had in place.

Surprisingly, no one was found guilty. A surprise, at least, to the non-magical community.

One student hungered for the answer.

That student was Robert Horn.

Rob disclosed this to Lucia upon her initiation into Gredalia, follow-ing the events of Alpha Society and her arm implant. Lucia was on the hunt for clues about Alpha's motives, which led her right into Rob Horn. He was also investigating Alpha. Upon discovering that Lucia had been 'bugged' with an Alpha device, Rob revealed who he was and his Nexian abilities. Lucia saw that Rob could remove the implant for her and offered her services as a witch to forward his plans.

Rob was relieved to be spilling the beans after hiding his powers and findings for so long. His hunger for the truth drove him slightly mad with power. He had reached out to the Nexus via books acquired from middle Europe to delve into its power.

What he didn't account for was the sacrifice *he* had to make.

He had offered his soul to the Nexus in exchange for power. The spell he acquired granted him the ability to Render and Sunder his body, which was the method that most humans used to acquire Nexian energy. To Render meant that one would invoke a spell to open their body to the reception of the energy, like opening a food-storage container. To Sunder meant that the Nexian energy flooded into the container. The spell ended with the 'lid' being placed on the human container.

The only problem was, Nexian energy takes from its vessel. Small spells (minor illusions crafted in the air, minor wound healing) required little energy, so magic users were not as exerted as if they had cast a large, powerful spell. Witches, like Lucia, were the exception. Witches were born with the Nexian energy already inside of them, without any Rendering and Sundering required. They exerted less energy on larger spells, but they still required energy from the vessel.

In the case of Robert Horn, he stumbled upon an anomaly: the ability to Render and Sunder himself.

What he discovered was that his power was that of the Grimfaern: the ability to shift into whatever was desired. He gave his entire soul to learn the truth, and the truth consumed him. Gone was Robert Horn, and in his place stood the vessel of an ancient demon-like entity that Lucia referred to as the Forlorn.

With the new vessel acquired, Operation Twilight was hatched.

The Forlorn posed the plan that Lucia eventually got involved in: the takeover of the world, as a new reign of terror, in which human sleeper-agents would be activated once placed. The Forlorn would both enslave and murder humans, creating a kingdom befitting a released demon and its human second-in-command, Maester Lucia Frey.

Lucia thought about this as she and the Grimfaern stared out over the cliffside in silence.

"It's quite beautiful, you know," the Grimfaern said.

Lucia cocked her head to indicate she was listening. "Yeah? You think so?" *How do you know what beauty is, being stuck in a vat of energy for millennia?* she thought.

The Grimfaern returned its gaze to the ocean. "I do. In fact, I'm glad it'll be my domain."

Lucia lightly pressed her wand holster's button, feeling the wand fall into her left hand.

"Good," she said menacingly.

The Grimfaern started to run the second she spoke.

With one swift movement, Lucia released her binding spell, which latched to the Grimfaern by the ankle. The spell swiftly coiled up around the limbs of the monster.

The Grimfaern wailed as Lucia flicked her wrist like a baseball pitcher.

She propelled the Grimfaern out over the water, beyond the Gristholme Net and into the frigid ocean depths.

The spell, which Lucia had been working on in case one of the Grimfaern went rogue, bound shape-shifting creatures to their current form, meaning that the Grimfaern would drown in the ocean.

At least she hoped it would drown. She had calculated that it would drown. It appeared to have lungs in this current form.

She made sure that the creature hit the icy depths before she turned her back, noting the ripples in the water from the point of impact a hundred yards away.

"Bon voyage," Lucia said, turning away from the cliffside with a sense of formality. "Now, where the fuck is this missing pledge."

She took off, back into the pines, to look for the missing student. She returned to the trail and picked up where she left off. Scanning the wood line, Lucia hoped that even in the darkness she would see something of import. A shirt, a pair of jeans, anything that would be relevant to her search.

Lucia ruminated on the events of the night. *I don't know if siding with Rob is for the best. However, I know that I can't let this implant get to me. I guess it's a necessary evil. Self-preservation wins again, even if I run myself into the ground in the process between Resin and Rob.*

The greenery and foliage met with the dirt path of the First Year's Trail. Deep footprints in the dirt indicated the path was well-worn from frequent use. Animal and golf cart tracks were intermingled with the occasional fallen branch or clump of pine needles.

Fucking Campus Safety, Lucia sneered to herself. *It is your fucking job to look for students. I can only do so much on foot, even with magic. I don't fly around on a broom, for christsakes.*

She acknowledged her resentment and let it fade with each step she took. This wasn't the time to be emotional.

Her walk had brought her almost to the southern tip of the plateau when she heard a crash in the woods followed by a wail of pain.

Lucia shot into the woods, feeling the branches of trees and roots snap at her heels and arms. She attempted to pick up speed, having disappeared into the depth of the trees. She couldn't see the Boardwalk from where she was standing.

Should I yell? she thought.

"GAH!" the voice yelled.

Lucia drew her wand and pointed it at the sound.

Slumped into the recess of a tree was a first-year student. Their face was covered by shaggy auburn hair that descended around their shoulders. They were of average build and were bleeding from the wrist.

Lucia dropped down next to the student.

"What's your name? It's okay, I can help." Lucia held her wand close to the ground.

"I'm Del. Del Torrez," the student wheezed. Pain shot across their face as Lucia began to assess the student's condition.

"Del? Hi there, I'm Lucia." She steeled herself. "Can you tell me what happened, like what or who did this to you?"

Del flicked their hair out of their face, revealing more cuts and bruises on their neck and face. "It…moved so quickly. I couldn't see who or what it was."

Are you magical? Lucia thought to herself.

"Yes," Del answered. "Hence, trying to get into the OmiTaus."

Fuck, Lucia thought.

Del winced as they smiled. "It's *okay.* It comes and goes, you know?"

Lucia dug into her satchel, looking for any kind of salve or treatment that wasn't her wand.

"How did you know I was here, Lucia?"

Lucia thought of the ocean as she searched.

"Lucia?"

"Your frat told me that you were lost." Lucia grabbed what appeared to be a makeup jar. "I began to look for you shortly thereafter but was delayed due to the creature." Lucia opened the jar and began to apply the salve to the student's injuries.

"Is it dead?" Del winced as Lucia continued to apply the salve.

Lucia paused before answering. *Do I tell them? What should I say otherwise?* Her thoughts raced, searching for the best answer possible to such a sensitive topic.

"It's dead." *FUCK.* She wished she could take the words back as they left her lips.

Del nodded, relief spreading across their face. "Cool. Glad it's not gonna hurt anyone else."

Oh boy, Lucia thought, *that's tough.* "Yeah, it's over now. Come on, let's get you back to the first-year dorms."

"Okay, thank you, Lucia."

As Lucia picked up her phone to call Resin, Dylan was ending his midnight broadcast.

"And remember, they're always accepting admissions at Gristholme…"

Resin

CAMPUS SAFETY OFFICER Resin Kirkbride left his staff meeting with Safety Director Robert Horn feeling displaced and disgruntled. More work was placed on third shift, as per usual. First and second had it easy; they were just a safety presence. Now the school officials (and by extension, Rob) had indicated that most of the missing cases and deaths occurred in the late evening or early morning time frame, meaning that an uptick in patrols was needed throughout the entire night.

That night he was responsible for taking all south-campus calls. Kasey was covering north campus by herself, while Jeff stayed back to do some of the clerical work.

Resin got the phone call while he was sitting on his golf cart.

"Yeah?" he answered. "Got something?"

"No, I just need you to help me bring this student back from First Year's south end."

"I'm surprised that you didn't—"

"They're injured, Resin. I need you *now*."

Resin ended the call and turned the key on the golf cart. He rarely used it. Tonight, however, there had been a few parties going on. He liked the cart for the presence it emitted: lazy but stalwart.

He pushed the gas pedal, and the cart began to work its way from the science buildings toward Lucia's location.

The science buildings were a mix of new tech with the ancient. Large windows decorated the sides of the buildings, with minimalist grey brick on the exterior. Inside, a few classroom windows had been left open, revealing state-of-the-art equipment gifted from mysterious and wealthy benefactors.

The science buildings' modernity sat against the pines like a coffee stain on a blank sheet of paper.

Resin's golf cart rambled on into the night, passing other academic buildings along the way. Pines and various statues of benefactors past rolled gently by as he scanned for Lucia.

As the cart rambled along, he looked out over the ocean. The stars pulsed in the night while the moon played piper to them all.

Resin smiled to himself, cherishing the moments of calm before the impending storms. Whether it be a drunk party, a serious injury, or a Nexian-fueled disaster that could have been avoided, the storms eventually passed. Some lasted longer than others, but they all eventually rolled away.

He turned away from the ocean and began to head north when he spotted Lucia and the injured student.

Resin pulled the cart up next to the pair and hopped out. "Down low?"

Lucia nodded solemnly, knowing this was for only she and Resin to know about.

Del piped up, sounding disoriented. "Fuck, is it campo? Er, sorry, Campus Safety?" Their head slouched forward as they fought to keep consciousness.

"Yep!" said Resin. "It's all going to be okay."

Del's adrenaline ran its course, causing Lucia and Resin to both lunge forward to catch them.

Resin tightened his jaw, trying to control his anger. "Can't you fix 'em up?"

Lucia looked up at him and nodded. "Given the right equipment from my room—"

"We have to take Del back to their room." Resin and Lucia moved Del toward the cart. "We can't have them up in your room."

"I'm sorry, what?" Lucia shook her head in frustration. "You're telling me that you want to take them back to their room, bloodied and bruised? Especially after what the OmiTaus—"

"We don't know if it was OmiTaus. Also, how do you know it was *actually* the OmiTaus? Our friend here could have been cornered by Delts or something else from the Nexian world." *What the fuck, Luce?* Resin thought to himself. *Why are you being so defensive?*

"I'm sorry, Resin, but I don't think it could have been anyone but the OmiTaus." Lucia's face looked resolute, but Resin couldn't shake the feeling that Lucia was hiding something.

"How?!" Resin strapped the student into the front seat with him. "Lucia, if the OmiTaus were really behind this attack, they would have bled this student dry. They don't give a fuck about their pledges, and now you're telling me that they let one *live?* This isn't the *actual* pledge week, mind you. This was a trick to get a quick feast." He tugged the seatbelt so that it would lock Del into place. "You, of all people, should know this. So, who really did this?"

Lucia locked eyes with Resin. "I don't know, Resin, but I'll look into it."

Again, this nagging feeling that you're lying to me. Resin huffed in frustration before he spoke. "Look, we've been doing this for a few years now. I don't want you to feel like you need to lie when something wild comes up. You've watched me handle worse things than a cut-up student. Remember that shit with Alpha Society and the party chip that caused those affected to party until they died?"

Lucia shoved her hands into her trench coat and nodded with her jaw clenched tight.

"We made sure you didn't have a chip in you. We triple checked that shit, and you're good to go. Plus, we freed those affected by the chips. So

I can handle the Omis being out of line. I'll talk to them about proper pledge procedures this week."

"Okay, man." Lucia held her semi-defensive pose.

"Care for a lift?" Resin motioned to the rear-facing golf cart seat. "It's nice on these kinds of nights."

"Nah, I'd rather walk," she said coldly.

"You're just gonna let me clean up what you started?" Resin got into the driver's seat and turned the key over. "Luce, please. When's the last time we worked together like this?" He wanted to add: *It really concerns me that we* haven't *worked together.* However, he didn't want to piss Lucia off any more.

Lucia looked to the sky in annoyance. "Fine."

She got into the back seat with a huff.

Resin grabbed the mic on his chest and called out, "Unit 13 to base."

"Go ahead, Unit 13." Resin heard Barb's raspy voice call back to him.

"Can you provide the room number for a student?"

"Affirm!"

"Okay, one Del Torrez?"

"Cooooooooopy, Unit 13. Seems that they live in the first-year boys' dorm, second floor. Is everything okay?"

Resin looked back at Lucia, who shot him a worried expression.

"Yeah! We're good. Just confirming before I let them back into their dorm. They left their ID inside."

"Cooooooopy! Base clear at—"

"Nice going, boss," Lucia said, her voice full of frustration.

"S'all good, Lucia." Resin drove the group into the night, back to the first years' dorms.

He swung the cart around, turning back toward the science buildings. It was quicker to go this way than to go by the rec center. He felt the ocean breeze and was glad to get the time with Lucia, even if she was insulting his capabilities.

It's better having her on our side than not. He shuddered at the thought of going up against Lucia. She was a very powerful magic user, which no one could deny. He had watched her render several foes in one blast of magic. He was fighting two Alpha members at the time, which he considered above average. Lucia's power, Resin felt, surpassed his own.

Resin's power came directly from the Fenris Wolf of old legends. He could turn into a werewolf-esque creature, with additional magical capability. This power came from his connection with the Nexus but also his own heritage. He and his father, who had been the wolf bearer before, traveled to lands near and far to investigate the origins of their powers. One summer during Resin's teens, his father had charged him with the power. Resin recalled his own Rendering and Sundering, which his father had performed. This was special not only because it was his father passing down his own powers to his son, but because the Fenris Wolf abilities were the only powers Resin knew of that the bearer could pass on without a higher-level magic user.

Resin mulled this over as he turned into the science quad, following the path toward the first years' dorms.

Lucia didn't speak a word on the ride over.

I don't get why she's so pissed at me, Resin thought. *I get that I'm the leader, but at least help with your mess.* He made his way past Troy Hall and around Smith, when the first-year boys' dorm came into sight.

The exterior of First Boys (the slang term for the dorm) was a sight to behold. Shards of glass bottles littered the flower beds from underage consumption, despite Campus Safety's best efforts. Various parts of the two-story exterior held trace remnants of spray paint from pledge dares and drunken escapades. Resin frequented this building more often than he would like. The exterior was the same beige color as the majority of the newer buildings on campus.

First Boys…well, no chateau, but it is what it is, he sighed as he approached the exterior. *At least they're not fucking anything up tonight.*

"I loathe the fact that I'm here, and I hope you know that," Lucia called over the hum of the golf cart. "I could be sleeping right now."

"You don't sleep anyway." Resin pulled the cart so that it was parallel with the building. "Again, the least you can do—"

"Is help. I get it." She hopped out of the back and moved to Del's side.

She threw Del's arm over her shoulder while Resin took the other side.

The trio shuffled their way to the door awkwardly. Resin was considerably taller than Lucia, which made it difficult to move as a consistent unit.

"Could you be any taller?" Lucia scoffed.

"Ask that to my ego," Resin retorted with a grin.

Lucia rolled her eyes. "God, you're almost as bad as Thorn and Lock."

They approached the door with the still unconscious Del in their arms.

"The keyword is *almost*." Resin reached for his badge to scan the door and held the door open with his foot as they shuffled Del inside.

"Is it on the first or second floor?" Lucia looked across the sleeping student to Resin.

"Shit."

"Are you kidding me right now?" Lucia cast him an even angrier glance. "We have to carry this student up these stairs? Can't you just wolf—"

"Come on!" Resin shifted his weight and the group moved up the stairs.

A few moments later, they had shuffled, huffed, and pulled themselves up the stairs. There was a brief moment when Resin had to cling to the stairs for dear life when Lucia missed a step and almost sent the whole group tumbling down.

When they reached the upper landing, Resin called out to Base with his free hand to figure out which room Del resided in.

Barb came back with the answer. "It *seems* that they're in room number 203, Unit 13!"

"Copy," Resin said.

"Coooooopy! Base clear at…"

"They do that *every* time?" Lucia grunted.

"Every. Single. Time." Resin reached with his free hand for the keys on his belt. "This should be the key for 203."

The pair stood outside the door as Resin used his free hand to open it. The key turned in the lock, and the door swung open with a loud creak.

The room looked ordinary as far as college dorms were concerned: Various pictures of bands and celebrities on the wall. Clothes strewn on the bed. A mini fridge more than likely stocked with alcohol and ketchup packets from takeout the day prior. A dead man feasting on the body of a deceased student, a desk where their papers were written.

"OH SHIT!" Resin called out.

Del slumped to the floor with a sickening thud as Lucia drew her wand.

The ghoul left its meal behind and charged Resin.

Resin felt his arms shift into their familiar forms: muscular and hairy, with sharp, vicious, ancient claws.

The ghoul dove forward, thirsting for Resin's flesh.

Resin backhanded it, sending the monster flying into the wall.

It disappeared through the wall.

Lucia stepped into the room and looked at the floor. "Resin, that's a dead student."

"Yup." Resin's arms shrank back down to their normal size. "Looks like we're going to have to give them the Viking funeral over the cliff."

Lucia threw up her hands in frustration. "THIS. *This* is exactly why I didn't want to get involved. We started off helping and now we're cleaning up after some fucking ghoul's mess."

Moving in tandem, Resin and Lucia picked up the body of the deceased student.

They grabbed a blanket and threw it over Del's deceased roommate, shuffling out of the room and back into the hallway.

Resin looked at Lucia sheepishly.

"Now, what?" Lucia sighed.

"Could you clean up the room?" An embarrassed grin rolled out across his face. "It'll look weird if everything is disheveled."

Lucia's jaw was locked tight as she raised her right hand and flicked her wrist.

In a swift movement, the blood was peeled off the floor. It roiled in the air before tumbling and dissipating. The books, blankets, clothes, and personal belongings all flew to their appropriate positions in the room. Closet doors snapped open and shut to conceal their citizens. Desk drawers received marching pens and pencils, while computer cords wound themselves perfectly and fell neatly on the desk.

Del, who was still on the floor outside their room, was picked up and carried gently to the bed. The covers pulled themselves back and wrapped the student, carefully tucked under their feet and sides.

"Sorry." Resin scanned the hallway. "I'm just trying to make sure we cover our tracks now than have you be even more pissed at me when you're pulled from your apartment to do damage control." *Plus,* Resin thought, *you said you'd help defend these kids when we first started teaming up and formed the Artificers together. We move throughout this world in a perpetual state of trickery. We cannot be who we really are. It's our task to make sure we're containing what we can when we can.*

"I get that, Resin, but you perpetuate my lack of sleep, what little I get. I don't sleep. Therefore, I'm grumpy."

"I understand wholeheartedly."

The pair shuffled back down the stairs and out into the night.

"Where are your coworkers?" Lucia looked at Resin. "Shouldn't they be patrolling around?"

If they weren't lazy, Resin thought. "Dunno. Probably walking through a building somewhere."

"You're really defenders of the youth, you know that?"

He caught a bit of a smirk on the corner of Lucia's mouth. "I just work here, okay? Not all of us could get full rides to a prestigious school." Resin took the lead, placing the student's corpse on the back of the golf cart. He used a tarp from the back storage compartment to carefully tie up the student.

"Thank god for the cameras not working, am I right?" Lucia took the passenger seat.

"Very lucky, indeed." Resin hopped into the driver's seat and turned the key over. *We'd be fucked if they did work. Can't imagine my wolf form would be a warm welcome.*

He pushed his foot forward, and the cart jolted to life.

Lucia drew her wand and turned back over her shoulder. She muttered in the guttural Nexian language the word for *conceal.* She took the extra step, which Resin appreciated. To the outside, the cart appeared to be rolling along without anyone or anything on the rear-facing seat. Resin was particularly grateful for Lucia's discretion, and that was why she was directly under him in the chain of command.

I trust her, he thought to himself. *If something happens to me, I know Lucia would help lead the Artificers and maintain the campus in my stead as best she could.*

He thought about the Artificers, the group he and Lucia had assembled after an uptick in Nexian activity the year prior. Thorn Gisalt, Locklear Stormswell, and Lauren Kreider, the other members of the Artificers, each had their own powers. Lauren's powers came on early, during her youth. Her parents sought after a witch to complete the Rendering and Sundering for their daughter before she was a teenager. Endowing Lauren with their own vampiric powers, the Kreiders paid a hefty monetary sum to send their daughter into the metaphorical hellfire.

Emerging on the other side of the ritual, Lauren Kreider rose as a vampire and a skilled assassin.

Thorn and Lock were buddies from an early age. They decided to play football for the Gristholme Geese before the end of their senior year of high school. After signing a contract, the pair came to Gristholme in their first year of college but sat on the bench. Summer conditioning came and went. That fall, they encountered Beta House. Their senior (and only) frat member, Colin Rallowaithe, disappeared after they were initiated into Beta. The pair contacted Resin, who seemed to be less uptight than the other security officers. Through secret communication and meetings, Resin eventually introduced the pair to Lucia, who detected their lineage. A few weeks later, the pair were Rendered and Sundered at Lucia's hand. Lauren joined up with the group shortly after. Thus, the Artificers were born.

That was almost a year ago, Resin recalled. *Weird how times flies.*

He and Lucia arrived at the edge of the cliffside.

They maneuvered the student's body so that their feet were dangling off the edge.

"I hate this part," Resin admitted. "It's pretty fucked up."

"It covers tracks, though." Lucia drew her wand from the arm holster under her sleeve. "Who looks after the evidence is destroyed?"

"Literally every single investigative agency or department," Resin sighed.

"Well, they haven't found us yet." She stood back from the cliffside, wand trained on the student. "I make sure of that."

Resin threw up his hands and stepped a few paces back. "Do what you gotta do, Luce."

Lucia began to mutter in the Nexian tongue.

The body, lying on the soft grass of the plateau, began to shake rapidly. It rose from the ground and floated beyond the comfort of the Great

Net. From this point, if the body were to fall toward the water, it would crash into the depths below.

Lucia's tone switched from somber to menacing as she continued her Nexian spell.

Resin watched a flicker of flame catch at the clothing of the dead student. Over the water, it looked as if an ancient beacon was lit.

Lucia made an undercut motion with her wand, grunted in anger, and finished the spell.

Resin watched as the body became engulfed in flames.

The body of the student was propelled with great force out into the far depths of the water. Gravity took hold of the body and dragged it down to a watery grave.

Resin and Lucia watched the body fizzle in the depths of the ocean.

Resin swore he saw movement under the water but didn't want to entertain such notions.

"Do you ever think that the reason so many people in the area report UAPs is due to the fact that we're launching burning bodies out over the ocean?"

"Sometimes, if I'm being completely honest." Lucia grinned a wicked smile. "Skywatchers will do anything to catch the tiniest bit of proof."

She turned to head back to her apartment.

"Lucia," Resin started. "When were you going to tell me about the injured student? Was it going to be a day later, a week later, or at all?"

Lucia stopped in her tracks, not turning back to Resin.

"If the injuries weren't serious, then I would have handled it on my own." Lucia's voice held something that Resin couldn't quite put a finger on. *Was it malice?* He thought to himself. *Trickery? Deceit? I don't like how indirect she is about this.*

"Do you not trust me?" Resin took a leap of faith. "Am I not a good enough leader for you?"

Lucia turned back over her shoulder, betraying no emotion whatsoever. "I think you are a more than capable leader, but do you believe it? Do *you* think you are a capable leader?"

Resin took a deep breath before he answered. "I do, but I haven't needed to question it before. Not bringing possible Nexian activity to my attention concerns me." *What the fuck is your game here, Luce?* Resin thought. *This is a little weird, even for you.*

"Until you eradicate your own self-doubt, then you will always question it." Lucia faced her attention back toward the Moon's Loft and set off into the night.

Resin leaned against his golf cart, growing increasingly concerned about Lucia's statements. He watched the ocean and sighed.

Why wouldn't she just tell me? His thoughts kept repeating. She told him things in the past, so why was this any different? Did it even matter that she considered not telling him?

It's about the students' safety, Resin reflected, letting his worries manifest in his mind. *That's why we do this. Yes, sometimes they die, and we must dispose of the evidence, but we try to mitigate it as best we can.* Resin was concerned at Lucia's concealment of the activity at all. Back when the pair started working together, he and Lucia communicated quite frequently. Now, it seemed as if she was withdrawing.

He turned from the ocean and got into his golf cart, continuing to play devil's advocate with himself. *Do we do a good enough job?* he pondered. *Are the services of the Artificers enough to keep these students and the world safe?*

He headed to his first south-campus academic building to begin the unlock process that he had completed several hours prior.

———— ♦ ————

He finished unlocking his last building right next to Route 13 as the student populace began to stir. It had been quite a night for him, and the questions hit him harder than earlier. He still felt uneasy about his interaction with Lucia.

His toothy maw opened wide with a yawn.

When he crossed Route 13, he looked up to the Moon's Loft and noted the closed sign.

He walked across the Boardwalk and waved at the individuals heading to their 7:00 a.m. classes.

He envied them in some ways. In others Resin was thankful to not have to deal with classes anymore.

Tom hailed him as he walked to his car. Kasey was waiting by hers as Resin trudged up the road. She was probably already clocked out.

"Have a good nap! See ya in a few hours." She smiled at him.

"Yeah! Take it easy, have a good nap." Resin waved.

Kasey got in her car and took off as he opened the office door.

Holly was sitting at the desk. She smiled and hit the buzzer, allowing Resin to pass through the locked office door with a simple push.

He entered and made his way to his locker.

A kitchenette with stove, coffee pot, dishwasher, cabinets, and fridge was well-kept. The cabinets were a cherry color, filled with all types of cooking utensils and cookware to provide a second home to the guards. Fresh coffee sat in the pot and smelled like it was brewed from freshly ground beans from the Moon's Loft. Offices ran the length of the hallway that extended from the kitchenette. Robert Horn's office was directly across from the security guard lockers and key-ring holder. The overall feel of the office was cozy but business casual. There was always a low hum of energy from the staff jumping to campus calls or exchanging updates from the night prior.

When Resin rounded the corner, T.J. was sitting at his desk with his feet propped up on the table. "'Sup, homie?" He was playing a game like Tetris on his phone, of which Resin didn't know the name.

"Hey bub, I'm beat today. Just had a long night."

"Yeah, your report from the other night was, uh…pretty blank there, shooter."

"Fuck." Resin looked at his watch and then sat down at a computer.

"You're welcome, by the way. Big Boss Tommy Boy got that one for you about 0655 hours this morning."

Resin sighed and leaned back into the swivel chair, clocking out.

He bounced out of the chair and started to undo his nightly routine by placing his keys in the lockbox and his equipment in his locker.

"So, uh, big plans today? Sleeping?" T.J. looked at him earnestly.

"Basically." He reached for his rucksack in the corner of the room and shouldered it.

T.J. laughed. "I'm just saying! Yo, Billy! Whatcha up to, my man?"

Billy Turner, a pepper-haired man of medium height, walked in and popped off his sunglasses.

"Not much, man. 'Sup dude?" He nodded at Resin.

"Hey Billy, not much, man."

"You going to get chow, or do you gotta go see the inside of your eyelids?"

"Sleep, dude." Resin released an exhausted sigh.

"The party rolls on, my dude." He and Resin exchanged a fist bump, followed by T.J.'s fist bump. It was the routine. Every. Single. Morning.

"Say, Resin," T.J. called.

"Yeah?" Resin turned back in the doorframe.

"Hang in there, okay?"

Resin turned back to T.J., caught off guard. "I always do, man."

"Okay, bud! Just making sure. You have a habit of burning the candle at both ends."

"It's my nature." Resin shifted a little bit. "I can't help it too much."

"I know, buddy. Have a good sleep!"

Resin pushed past the morning shift personnel and made his way to his Jeep parked on a little side street outside the Hall of Campus Safety. He unlocked the door and hopped in.

He immediately grabbed his old iPod Classic and began to scroll through the tunes until he found something that stuck. He sighed as he passed up Redbone's "Come and Get Your Love," but it was the album *Vessel* by Twenty One Pilots that called to him that day. The familiar glockenspiel sound in "Guns for Hands" took him back to his college days. He smiled and shifted the Jeep into drive.

Gristholme fell behind Resin as he drove down Route 13. Into the violently bright morning went the red Wrangler. Following the winding Route 13, Resin could see the town of Newton Falls perfectly.

Newton Falls was the quintessential New England town. The roads were small, and the distance between the people was even smaller. Everybody in the town knew each other. Route 13 bisected Route 63. Main Street, as it was more commonly called, was the cultural hub of the town. It seemed endless, but Main Street/Route 63 eventually made its way to larger highways. This was important to the town's commerce. Among such motes of commerce was Suzy's Diner, the meeting ground for everyone, that ran twenty-four-seven. Labels didn't matter, for Suzy Shulls was like the town grandmother. She would prick up her ears to the conversations but wouldn't tell the sources, usually. Suzy slept in the little loft in the attic so she could be close by in case something went wrong.

Mac's Barbershop and Freda's Grocery were to the left and right of Suzy's. On the opposite side were a few other miscellaneous shops, such as the hardware store, a coffee shop, a game store, and a few other municipal buildings. Further north was the access road to the power plant, water plant, and the greater forest protectorate. A safe distance away from the power plant, continuing north out of town, was a swimming pool and the old-time church. The church creeped Resin out beyond belief. It looked like a child's breath could knock it over. However, it had an attendance every Sunday that rivaled Suzy's.

Resin kept driving until he left the city limits and drove into the woods surrounding Route 63 North. This is where the citizens lived, peppered around the woods of Newton Falls and Billings. Resin's parents lived to the south of the town of Billings, where Resin had gone to university.

It took him no more than fifteen minutes to get home on any given day. Rolling into the driveway, he took stock of his home. The Cape Cod was painted a nice shade of grey with red shutters. The tall pines surrounded his little abode, creating nice cover from the wind and storms of the seasons. The picket fence around the side of his house was his dogs' playground. And a little shed with some tools and a lawnmower was nestled in the back of the yard within the picket fence.

He hoped that the sun wouldn't be so bright today.

Resin walked to the front door and flipped his keys. He began to unlock the door. As it creaked open, he couldn't help but note the air of the home. The house was almost too quiet. Resin went over and flipped on the TV. He had a weird habit of picking anything *but* American news channels. It was the BBC that always caught his attention. Plus, he loved their voices.

"A heightening in storm activity around the world has been noted by meteorologists today. A concentration seems to be amassing over the Northeastern United States…" He got bored and flipped off the TV.

"Well, shit," Resin said. "It's gonna be one of those mornings, eh?" He walked to the kitchen and grabbed a big bowl out of the cabinet. A combination of wheat cereal and almond milk hit the porcelain bowl, followed by a spoon. Resin stirred slowly and looked out into the yard from the kitchen window. He sighed happily and watched squirrels take off for the trees. Looking at all the work he had to do around the yard, he realized that this was nothing new. It was the status quo.

After he tucked into breakfast, he climbed the stairs wearily.

Lucia, what the fuck are you thinking, friend? Resin's thoughts returned to his friend's ominous parting comments. *Why do you have to be cryptic about it?*

He doffed his clothes and fell into the comfort of his bed. He curled the blankets around him, which caused him to drift slowly into a deep sleep.

This was the routine. The simple, humble, normal routine. It was this routine that Resin would miss in the days and weeks to come.

Darius

DARIUS CROSBANE WOKE UP suddenly as his dreams took a sharp left turn into a nightmare.

He went to reach for his phone on his nightstand to check the time when he realized something terrifying.

His arm wouldn't move. Darius was shocked when he came to the realization that his entire body was paralyzed. A hot band of fear tightened in his chest as he unsuccessfully attempted to get his body to respond.

He flailed inside of his mind like a rabid, trapped animal, but the flesh refused to move from its position. Panic consumed his body as his eyes looked around his dark room. He scanned the ceiling, feeling that he wasn't alone. His eyes darted to the far-right corner of his wall. Nothing was there.

He looked to the far-left corner and noticed that the light he always left on in the stairway seemed a little bit dimmer than before.

He focused on the light and realized that a wispy, slender hand was cast over the light in his hallway.

His eyes traveled the length of the shadowy arm back to the torso it was attached to.

He felt fearsome power flowing from the shadow that sat before him.

Sitting at the foot of his bed, looking away from him, was a figure in a tattered black robe. The figure rose, darkness seeming to emanate from it. There was a cracking sound, like a fire on an autumn night, as the creature's head slowly pivoted on its neck. Darius felt as if he could hear the sound of bones cracking in his own neck, the sound so violent and disturbing.

Its face met the young man's gaze in the darkness of the House of IT.

The entity had a skull for a face, with large empty eye sockets that looked as if they were crafted from some void. The mouth moved without the aid of any muscles. The robe sat loosely around the frame. The bony arms ended in bony hands that clacked together as they opened and closed.

Darius noticed that the left and right arms of the creature were reversed, with the arms dislocated in their sockets. Further vicious snaps ricocheted through his body as the entity snapped its limbs back into position. With each snap, Darius witnessed the semblance of flesh being stitched together across the bones. The sinews formed with other tissues, turning a vibrant cold hue as if someone who had been lying in a casket were bringing themselves back to their previous living form. The creature shook its head as the empty eye sockets began to materialize small white orbs that formed its eyeballs. The eyes were absorbed into a red void, which remained inside the deep-set eye sockets. The ravenous mouth with vicious points for teeth were in a wide, toothy shamble. Its skin tone was an ashen grey, with tinges of black scattered throughout.

He heard the bedsheets crumple and felt a pressure on both of his legs as the creature crawled its way toward him.

"Frey, Frey, FREY!" it howled.

Darius was trembling so badly that the creature stopped and scanned him up and down.

"Frey fear?" Its tongue shot out like a frog and sliced Darius' temple open. Blood descended his face.

Darius fought against the paralysis with every fiber of his being, feeling the desperation seeping out of him in beads of sweat.

The creature placed both hands on Darius's chest, mouth open, ready to descend upon him.

Darius smelled the rotting breath, like garbage left out in the hot sun for too long.

The creature dove for Darius's throat.

Darius closed his eyes to brace for his death.

The creature screamed.

Darius opened his eyes instinctively, but a dream-like vision crossed in front of him.

The fringes of his vision came into view first, as if waking up the next morning from a hard night of drinking. As his vision cleared, Darius saw what lay before him: a battlefield. Shields, swords, bodies of humans and of creatures that resembled the one in his room littered the field. In the distance, fires erupted around the towns. The monsters were chasing after the remaining humans with their long, pincerlike fingers, severing heads while bathing in bloody human viscera. A few humans resisted, raising guns and swords alike. They were felled by the creatures, who consumed portions of the remains to bolster their strength. The sky was an ashen white, as if a snowstorm were moving in. It was not cold by way of temperature but cold in the callousness of war.

Darius realized that he was sitting on the ground at the base of a knoll that overlooked the battlefield below.

He wiped his eyes and saw the ashes, blood, and sweat on the back of his hand.

Where am I? he wondered. *Am I to blame for this catastrophe?*

He winced as he put weight on his legs, slowly rising to his feet.

He looked back up the hill to where a lone figure was standing clad in the same ashen grey as the creatures around him.

Darius took a few steps forward, hand outstretched toward the creature.

Suddenly, the creature turned around to look at Darius.

Darius saw, against the backdrop of battle, his own face. His double's left eye was blistered with singed skin. The eye was completely white. The cause of which Darius couldn't tell, but he assumed it was from the power that radiated around the being. It appeared to be his head spliced onto one of the creatures that lay around him. The face was distorted in all-encompassing rage, his mouth sneering.

Darius squared up to the monster with fists raised.

"That's fucking CUTE!" his double screamed down. "You actually think that you can take me on?" It stretched its arms out wide, with the face contorting to violence. "DO IT!"

Darius recoiled at the shout. "This is only a dream and I'm not afraid of you!"

The monster laughed. "Oh, little Darius. If only you knew."

"Knew what?" Darius took a few steps up the hill.

"If only you knew the power that you sat on." The monster held its hand high, and a bolt of sizzling energy flew past Darius. The bolt connected with some smoldering bodies in the background, sending them several feet into the air. The piles of flesh and bone, monster and human alike, disintegrated as the energy coursed over them. "You haven't even met the witch yet, have you, weakling?"

"The witch? Witches aren't real, dude." Darius moved even closer. *This is one fucked up dream,* he thought. *I didn't have* THAT *much to drink last night, from what I recall.*

"Oh, they're real. Just like magic is real." The monster held its hand overhead. The same sizzling energy was amassing in his hand but growing larger and larger by the second.

He wants to kill me, but it's only a dream, Darius thought. *Maybe if I tackled him over the edge?*

"Magic is real? Pray tell." Darius took a few more steps toward the monster, placing himself within ten feet of the violent creature. "I'd love to learn more."

The creature's energy grew to the point that his hand shook. The energy ball was the diameter of a tractor tire. "Speak to Frey the witch, and all will be revealed." Its white eye burned.

The creature brought its arm down and released the bolt of energy with a scream that would rip out any person's vocal cords.

Darius dodged to his right as the energy launched past him like a fire hose on full blast.

He closed the gap and tackled the creature, sending the pair tumbling off the edge of the cliff.

The monster howled in anguish as they fell toward the jagged outcropping down below.

Darius noticed two things as they fell: The first was the sense that this entity *was* himself. He didn't know how it could possibly be, but he knew within himself that it was true. The second was that he didn't take into consideration how desolate and deadly the ground below would be.

The rocky crags ascended to meet them rapidly.

The anti-Darius dug its claws into Darius repetitively. Darius could feel warm blood seeping from his sides as the creature continued to wallop him.

"Fuck YOU!" the monster called out. "You don't deserve the power that we hold!"

Shit, so this really is me. He grimaced as the monster grabbed an internal organ.

"DIE!" The monster gave one final yell before they collided with the rocks.

Darius shot up in his bed, feeling the places where his double had stabbed him searing with pain.

What the fuck was that? He felt paranoia creep in around him as he scanned his room. Nothing to be seen within his space. The term *suffocation* came to Darius's mind. He got up from his bed in a fury and rushed to the mirror.

Darius scanned his face in the reflection.

He was the same as he had always been— Latino, middle twenties, not entirely lanky, but not burly.

He checked his phone for the time.

"Fuck, it's so early." He rubbed his face and looked again at himself.

That's when, in a split-second, his face distorted.

Where his eye should have been, there was a white abyss.

As soon as he tried to focus on it, however, it was just his normal face.

He rubbed his face. *I'm too tired. I need to go back to bed. I was just having a bad dream.* He clutched his side again. *At least, I think I was.*

He made his way back to bed and assembled the covers around himself. His head hit the pillow, and he drifted back into an uneasy slumber.

———— ♦ ————

He jumped awake as the sunlight crossed his face.

It was midmorning, judging by the sounds that echoed from outside. Birds were calling out to one another, and the wind gently passed through the trees. Darius could see the pines rustling as they were caught red-handed by the sun in their dance on his blinds, which were slightly ajar.

He sat with himself for a second and reflected on his weird night.

"Lucia Frey is a witch?" Darius said it out loud to make sure that it wasn't a trick of the mind. "She's magical? To think that magic exists, just like Harry P—"

His alarm sounded off, like a drill sergeant when fresh recruits stepped off the bus.

He swatted at it until it resumed its state of contentedness.

"So, I guess now it's off to see Lucia Frey."

He began to search for a sweater to fight the early autumn cold.

He found his Gristholme Geese sweater in a pile of dirty clothes. He threw it over his naked torso. Pulling up the hood, he grabbed a pair of dark-blue sweatpants he got from the campus bookstore and slowly put them on. He found a pair of trainers, slipped into them, and made his way downstairs.

Darius pushed through his door into the autumn weather that had begun to overtake the summer's brutal heat waves. The leaves looked heavy up in the trees while the pines remained as vigilant as soldiers.

His abode was the House of IT, and he was the sole occupant. It was located on the north side of campus, a hop away from the ominous Nightshade Hall. On this side of campus, there were dorms for upper-level students. There were a few classrooms in the north, but nothing like the south. He got lucky and lived in the House of IT because the school employed Darius as the student assistant to the IT department. He was in the fall of his second year and enjoyed being a student, despite its challenges and drawbacks.

Darius turned in the midmorning light, rubbing his eyes some more. He saw students milling in and out of dorms. Couples held hands as they walked up and down the Boardwalk. The birds chirped, summoning their last bits of energy before migrating. Flora and fauna were so vibrant on this side of campus, and for that Darius was thankful.

Before he knew it, he was halfway to his destination. The Boardwalk guided him in his sleep hangover to the familiar coffee shop on the south side of campus.

He reached for the door and gave it a hearty tug.

The coffee shop was oddly barren for an early weekend morning. Behind the counter stood Fernando, with whom Darius was familiar. In a booth across from him, with her back to the door, sat a woman with reddish-brown hair that came down to the middle of her back, straight as an arrow. She was furiously writing in a notebook as he made his way to the counter.

"What can I get you, hermano?" Fernando looked Darius up and down.

"Just an iced mocha, please." Darius reached for his phone to bring up his tap-to-pay.

Fernando nodded and finished the transaction. He turned to his machines and began making Darius's coffee.

Well, here it goes. Darius turned to find a seat within the coffee shop, noticing that one side of Lucia's booth was still empty.

He beelined it for Lucia and sat down across from the witch.

"You better have a damn good fucking reason to be sitting across from me right now during one of the few moments of peace I get in this life." Lucia continued to scribble in a battered notebook.

"I do. I was told to come here and tell you magic was real in the dream I had." He grimaced at how stupid that sounded after the fact.

Fernando shook his head and let out a sigh of contempt as he placed the coffee cup down on the table in front of Darius.

Lucia looked up from her notebook and closed it slowly. "Who told you to do this?"

"I'm not sure, but the dream told me you're a witch and that I was supposed to ask you about magic."

Lucia looked from Darius to Fernando, who stood behind Darius.

Darius looked behind him and saw no one. Fernando had disappeared into thin air.

"Shit," Darius exhaled nervously. He slowly turned back to Lucia.

Her eyes were trained on him with almost the same intensity as the monster from his dream the night prior.

"I don't know who you are or what your plan is here, but you're royally fucked if your intent is to harm me."

"I can assure you, it's not." Darius raised his hands in innocence. "I have no weapons or powers like a witch. I'm just a human."

Lucia extended her hand out rapidly. The blinds in the coffee shop all closed in succession, shrouding the room in semi-darkness. Enough light peeked through the closed blinds for the pair to still see.

Lucia reached from under the desk and extended what Darius believed to be a wand. It was equipped with a handle for comfortable holding and dyed a dark color for maximum concealment. Darius believed it to be some kind of oak, from what he could tell.

The wand was pointed at his throat.

"Tell me who sent you, now, or your throat gets blown out." Lucia was cold and calculating, with a blatant disregard for the cleanup the blood of a mid-height man would require.

"I just had a dream, and I came to you. There was a doppelganger-like version of myself, and it told me to go to you to learn about magic. It seemed logical to me because it specifically mentioned you. I had a night terror of a creature that had a skull for a head that—"

Lucia unleashed her spell, sending blue whisps of energy around Darius.

The whisps flooded his senses with hints of lavender and chamomile, which made him feel like he was drifting into a very fast and deep sleep.

Darius blinked heavily and looked up to Lucia. "It's real?" He shook his head violently to try and stay awake. "You're actually a witch?"

Lucia stared at him coldly as he fell into a deep sleep.

The Artificers

"WAKE HIM UP." The disembodied voice came from behind his head.

Darius felt his mental awareness slowly retrieve itself from the ether. He didn't know how long he had been out. Internally, it felt like hours—as if he had taken a nap on a summer afternoon. The sensation of sleep met with the sinking feeling of a wasted day.

The second thought that came to him was that he didn't recognize the voice.

"Fix his nose," the voice said.

It's a man, Darius thought to himself.

Two hands placed themselves on the bridge of his nose.

POP! The sound of cartilage rendered back into place. These hands felt feminine.

Darius yelled out in pain.

He tried to stand up.

Tried was the ultimate word. He blinked awake slowly to see his legs restrained with ropes to an old wooden chair. His hands were bound behind his back.

He lifted his head slowly to see a room full of people. Blinking more, he looked from face to face.

Five people had weapons drawn, eyes fixated on him. The first was a burly red-haired man with a sickle drawn, eyes vibrantly blue, dressed in athletic attire. The second man, with black hair and sea-foam eyes, had fists raised. Darius recognized Lucia, with her wand held high, wearing the same clothes as when he met her in her coffee shop, except she looked a little wearier. The man to her left was over six feet tall. He wore a security guard outfit and had a five o'clock shadow. He had a medium faded haircut with brown hair. His features were handsome, but he appeared to be haunted. This was a face, Darius realized, that had seen a thing or two. The security guard looked fit but a little burly. The bags under his eyes suggested he hadn't slept in days. His face was solemn with responsibility, and Darius believed this to be the leader of the group.

Feeling the fear bubble in his chest with all these people staring at him, he felt the presence of the final individual. She wore her light-blond hair in a ponytail, which was in stark contrast to Lucia's long, reddish-brown hair. She was dressed in a leather jacket and leather pants, like a morbid clash between a valley girl and a punk rocker. The extension of her arm was a long, curved blade that rested its tip diligently against the base of his neck.

The panic forced Darius to attempt to speak.

"Don't try." Resin stepped forward. "There are many ways to kill you in an instant. Lauren's itching for a new kill."

Lauren pressed the blade more threateningly into his throat.

Resin took a step forward. "Are you a rogue mage?"

Darius shook his head, knowing that the attempt to speak would end his existence.

"Are you a part of a society on campus?"

He shook his head once more.

"What actually prompted you to ask about magic?" Lucia spoke before Resin.

Darius swallowed.

"Speak. NOW!" Resin yelled.

Darius quivered. "I…I…I was visited by a skeleton man. It attacked me before I had a vision-like dream. He told me that I needed to seek out Lucia to learn about magic and that she was a witch."

Lauren took a step forward, which caused their prisoner to drivel. Tears began to fall down his frightened face. His bottom lip moved rapidly as the panic began to set in.

Resin exchanged looks with Lucia, the burly men, and Lauren. "You can drop your blade, Lauren."

Everyone in the room relaxed, while Darius curled inward, taut against the restraints. Darius felt like he was starting to have a panic attack. "Please can you just let me—"

"Go?" The red-haired man stepped forward, crouching down with the sickle pressed up underneath Darius's throat. "No can do, Mr. Intruder."

He rose and proceeded to lumber his way through the room.

The black-haired man came around Darius and eyed him from over his left shoulder. He made his way to a table that Darius had not previously noticed but now recognized.

Darius suddenly realized that he was in the Hall of Ancients. Except this wasn't the way that the Hall of Ancients was laid out. The table was longer with less chairs around it. The wood coloring wasn't this dark. The hall felt more expanded in real life than in his memory.

The room was large with an ornate fireplace situated behind Resin's place at the table. The light from the fire outlined his figure in the darkness. The rest of the group gathered at the table, sharing nods before training their mistrust onto Darius.

"You've been visited by a skull-headed man, you say." Resin leaned into the table. "Instructing you to just—go after Lucia?"

"Not 'go after' per se." Darius swallowed hard and trembled. "More or less to find her, inquiring about magic to learn more."

"Look, sir." Resin pushed himself up from the table, walked behind Lauren, and drove a pointed finger into Darius's breastbone. "You've put us in an awkward position. We can't just have people going around spouting that Lucia's a witch, do you understand?" Resin stepped away from the captive man and shook his head. "This isn't just some foray into your local crystals shop. Magic is real. People just don't approach magic users and say, 'I'd like to know more about magic.' That's why you're tied up to a chair right now. If this information were to get out, the world would spiral out of control."

Darius nodded through his tears. "Please just let me go."

"Afraid we can't do that, Darius." Lauren spoke up this time. "You know our faces and that magic is real now."

Resin stepped toward his captive and yelled. "WHO IS YOUR ALLEGIANCE TO?"

"I DON'T KNOW ANYTHING!" Darius yelled back at Resin. "I know NOTHING. I don't have any allegiance to anyone! I was sleeping. Woke up. Had this THING come into my room. I had a dream and saw myself with a glowing white eye and speaking about Lucia. I DON'T KNOW ANYTHING!" He felt the hoarseness in his voice as it cracked. "If anyone deserves any answers…IT'S ME!" His chest rose and fell. He felt the weight of the finality his words brought to the room. His head fell forward as he sobbed into his chest.

"Thorn." The red-haired man shot up from his seat, where he listened intently. "Would you be so kind as to cut our guest free?" Resin slowly returned to the head of the table.

Darius looked up as Thorn got up from the table.

He twirled his sickle in the air, swung twice.

The captive recoiled and winced at the sounds of the blade making its way through the air. He slowly opened his eyes to see his bonds cut, splayed haphazardly on the floor.

Thorn didn't turn his back to Darius but returned to his seat, laying his sickle on the table. *I don't like this one bit,* Thorn thought. *What little he knows is way too much for my liking.*

The silence became dense, and Darius didn't know what to do. If he got up to try and run, he felt that he would be cut down. If he listened in on what was going on, he felt like he stood the best chance, but wouldn't they kill him anyway? He wanted the whole scenario to end.

"I'm sorry we've treated you this way, Darius." Resin broke the silence. "You see, we are highly secretive. As I'm sure you gathered from your… *encounter* with the entity in your dream, this is something that most people do not get to experience." He gestured to the room. "Welcome to our home. We brought you here against your will because, should you prove to be malicious, we will kill you."

"I'm sorry…" Darius wept.

"I know," Resin sighed. "However, Darius, you've piqued our interest. We discussed it while you slept and figured that it would be best to explain what has happened to you. Jury's still out on whether we want to kill you. If we were to kill you, you might as well leave Earth knowing what you've encountered."

Resin got up once more and stood at the mantelpiece.

"The natural world around us is imbued with what humankind has called 'Magicka.' This magic comes from a fixed point in the universe called the Nexus. Think of it like a well or natural spring, flowing freely from this fixed point in the distant universe. In order to have access to the magic, there are people who are naturally born with all of their power, like Lucia. Others, like Lauren, Lock, and Thorn here, need to have someone like Lucia open their spirits and bodies to receive the Nexian energy. This is what's called the Rendering, in which one's soul is open to receiving the energy, like the cap of a bottle being removed and water being poured into the bottle. This part of the process leaves people in a somewhat volatile state as their bodies and cells get accustomed to this energy. The Nexus is being crammed into the human being at the very cellular level."

Darius watched Resin move around the room, attempting to absorb as much as he could.

"Then, there's the Sundering, in which the lid of the water bottle is returned to the human's soul. The energy is now locked inside the body and accessible to the person. It comes at a cost, though. Each time a spell is cast, or the magic-user draws on a deeper set of powers, their reserve of energy is drained a little bit. This can be recharged with a simple rest or distance between uses of magic. It can, however, be deadly should one push themselves too far.

Resin reached Darius's side at this point.

"I'm a little bit different, since my powers were transferred to me by my dad. I am a descendant of the Fenris Wolf, the same one who caused the Ragnarök, basically the end of the world, to happen hundreds of years ago. I can transform into a large wolf and launch some Nexian energy here or there if I want to."

Resin crouched down next to the captive man.

Darius looked at Resin in earnest through his tears, while snot ran out his nose.

"We go by the Artificers collectively. We take our combined skills and try to keep the regular humans safe from the magic, because it can and does bleed over from time to time. It may appear as a ghost or a poltergeist, but it could be something else entirely. Lucia makes sure that the humans can't see the Nexian entities by microdosing the water through a spell she created. Pretty brilliant stuff." He nodded at Lucia with a half-smile. "It allows us the ability to go unseen if we are in our Nexian forms or casting magic. Sometimes, Nexian entities will break through Lucia's concealment magic of their own sheer will. On rare occasions, a student hasn't consumed any water from the campus taps, therefore circumventing the microdoses. It can cause casualties from time to time. If it does, we clean it up and handle it under the table to conceal that it was Nexian magic that caused the death of a student or two. As I'm sure you're aware, Gristholme has a steady acceptance and disappearance rate. Well, now you know."

Darius let out an exasperated sigh. *Am I to become one of these numbers, some random student that wandered over the edge of the cliffside and didn't get caught in the net?*

"Regarding your predicament specifically, you sought Lucia out to learn about Nexian magic. One way we can figure out if you're a regular human or possibly Nexian is by placing your hands on this table." Resin tapped it lightly. "It uses Nexian magic to search your past to see if there's anything that could showcase your powers, if you've got the potential for powers at all.

Darius looked around the room and noticed how on edge everyone was.

Lucia's wand was drawn and focused on Darius at his knee. The raven-haired football player, whom Darius assumed to be Lock, had a few beads of sweat trickle down his face. Thorn looked like he could pounce at Darius at any moment should the wrong move be made, appearing very defensive and pressed. Lauren had a throwing knife resting gently in her right hand, with her torso cocked toward Darius right next to her. Her feet were kicked up on the table, creating a fictitious relaxed air. Resin himself had his fists balled up and looked like a caged animal. Darius couldn't tell if Resin's fists had grown hairier since he first looked at him, but upon further inspection, he saw that the fists of the man had almost doubled in size and muscular density.

"It's your choice," Resin said with finality. "However, if you wanna learn about magic, your best bet is to trust us. Okay?"

Darius shook as he looked into the eyes of Resin. *How can I trust you if you're all so on edge? Do you think my powers are going to kill you?*

Darius trembled as he placed his hands on the table.

The Artificers

LUCIA GREW WORRIED as Darius stared blankly at the wall, his eyes glowing with a soft amber light. Darius's state was not something they had witnessed before. Every Artificer had some side effects to the magic initially entering their bodies, but nothing like this. *It's almost like his body was reset,* Lucia noted with intrigue. *I've never seen anything like this before.*

When Darius placed his hands on the table, he had snapped to an almost militaristic form of attention. His body went rigid, and his eyes and mouth began to glow with an amber light.

Thorn and Lock went to get pizza from the kitchen while Lauren remained in the same spot. Lucia tapped her fingers several times and grew annoyed. She finally went behind Darius and pulled out her wand. She pointed the wand at the back of his head and focused intensely. Darius's eyes continued to glow as his head began to shake. His mouth began to open in a primal fashion.

The scream that came out was not human.

Lauren pushed her chair back, and her teeth sharpened to vicious points. Her eyes widened and turned black. Thorn ran into the room as blue lightning coursed through his veins. Sparks snapped between his fingertips. Lock summoned yellow energy to sharpen his hands into spikes. Lucia stood back, wand at the ready, and continued her spell.

"Break, damn you!" She yelled and threw up her hands in frustration. "That should have worked."

"He's fucked," Lauren said. "I've never seen the table act like this."

Me either, Resin thought to himself, leaning up against the mantelpiece. *Either this guy is a powerful potential vessel or he's already imbued with Nexian energy.*

Resin approached the man's left side. He leaned over and looked into the glowing eyes. The light illuminated upon his face like an old slide projector.

Resin looked back up to the rest of the Artificers, a look of concern across his face.

Lock and Thorn both held the same neutral gaze, searching internally for something that could help in this instance.

Lauren shook her head and crossed her arms in her seat. *This is just great,* she thought. *We have an intruder who is asking too many damned questions. Why not just ice him now? With the way that the table is acting, isn't this enough of an omen to terminate him?*

She gestured to Darius and addressed the room. "Do you guys honestly think this is worth our time? If he's this fucked and he hasn't even been Rendered yet, what use is he to us?"

Lucia felt the realization dawn inside her. *Could it be?* she thought. *Has he already been Rendered and Sundered?*

Lucia took her wand and focused on Darius again, shifting her spell to focus on the essence of Darius's spirit and mind.

She was thrown violently against the wall as Darius snapped out of his trance.

Lucia wiped the blood off her lip from the impact and coughed.

Dazed, Darius looked up, his eyes no longer glowing.

Resin laughed and shouted, "Got 'em!"

Darius shook his head and felt as if he had run a marathon. The exhaustion came from the severe migraine he began to feel. It was partly due to the onslaught of mind-rendering revelations he had learned from this group, the Artificers. The other was having his soul searched like a filing cabinet.

He felt disconnected, like his spirit and consciousness were separated and in a deep sleep.

He rubbed his face in his hands and pinched the bridge of his bleeding nose.

Lauren's fangs receded into her jawline. She looked downright annoyed with the way things turned out. *It doesn't seem like Resin or Lucia know exactly what we're dealing with here, and I don't like that at all*, she thought.

Lucia spoke, breaking the silence. "We now know that our new friend here has the potential for a Nexian ability. The table wouldn't have reacted that way without it."

Resin nodded. "Unfortunately, we didn't get to see what you saw, Darius. Anything pop up in your mind while you were unconscious?"

"Not that I know of," Darius said, exasperated.

Lauren let out an airy gasp as she caught notice of the young man's arm.

What was once bare skin held the imprinted image of a demonic-looking woman with a face in a half-decayed state. Her hands receded into bones, and a dark robe covered her figure.

"Darius." Resin looked at the bewildered man. "Does any of this mean anything to you?"

"No…" He looked at the tattoo in awe. "I have no idea what any of this means."

Lucia piped up. "I think I do. Darius, it takes a Maester of Magicka to help individuals like the ones in this room manifest their powers. Just like Resin described, Rendering is like opening the bottle and pouring the water in. The water, in this case, is the Nexian energy or magic, in simpler terms. Well, what if someone already Rendered you, Darius? Do you remember anything about your upbringing that would give cause to already being Rendered? Lauren had something similar happen when she was younger. Her parents had her Rendered and Sundered at a young age. Dangerous, but it can be done. Did this happen to you?"

"Not that I'm aware of," Darius said, concerned. "I mean, my dad left when I was really young. My mom raised me. That's it that I can recall."

"Hrm." Thorn took a few bites of pizza and kept his thoughts to himself. *I don't like this guy at all. He seems too passive. How can someone not remember their cells being ripped from their body? At least, that's what it felt like for me and Lock,* he pondered as he munched on his pizza.

Lock continued to eat pizza, content and partially oblivious to the goings-on of the table. The threat had been neutralized in his eyes. The reward of pizza consumed his mind.

Darius looked up at Resin. "Does this mean I'm one of the Artificers?"

"Technically, I guess it does." Resin sighed. "I will say though, if you fuck us over, we'll kill you."

"I have no doubt." Darius let the heaviness of the statement linger in the air. "Does this mean I need to be Sundered?"

"No. Not yet anyway." Lucia shouldered her satchel and looked around at those present. "We might be able to see if that could happen. Let's meet again in a few weeks to figure out when we can do that. Is that okay, Resin?"

"Sounds good, my friend." Resin nodded.

Darius got up shakily, rubbing his head. "Resin? Would you like to take down my phone number? Since I'm part of the group now, I figure that I should—"

"Yeah. I will." Resin pulled out his phone and took down Darius's phone number. "Okay everyone, we will see you in a few weeks. I'm going to text y'all when we are getting together next. Stay vigilant, cover each other's backs. And Darius?"

Darius stopped in the doorway as Lauren, Thorn, and Lock made their way past him.

"Keep a low profile."

The new Artificer nodded as he headed out into the night.

Resin checked his phone notifications. He felt the rise of anxiety in his stomach.

"Ah shit," he said to Lucia, the last one left with him in the Hall of Ancients. "I'm gonna be late."

"The Hall of Campus Safety is about a five-minute walk from here," Lucia scoffed. "You're the Fenris Wolf, and you don't think you'll be able to walk that far in that amount of time?"

"You know I like to keep a low profile." The wolf-man made his way to the door. "See you in a few weeks, Luce."

"See ya, Resin." She waved after him.

Now alone in the Hall of Ancients, Lucia wondered if Darius was the right fit for an Artificer.

She ran her fingers through her hair, feeling a sudden sense of frustration, exhaustion, and dread. Holding a glass of bourbon poured from a decanter in the kitchen, she swished the amber liquid around before taking a hardy sip. Her hair felt matted, and she caught herself wondering how long it had been since she showered. Judging by the way her hair was and the feeling of her skin's oiliness, it had been days.

She couldn't tell if her thoughts were mad ramblings or valid concerns.

When she was inside of his mind, during her spell, she felt that there was something deeper than what he stated on the surface. The description of his doppelganger and the visitor in the night almost made him sound like a Grimfaern.

He can't be an escaped Grimfaern, she thought. *We've kept definite tabs on the Grimfaern that came through when we summoned them from the Nexus.*

The question remained: Where did Darius Crosbane come from?

Who Rendered him? Lucia stared into the fire, feeling the question burning in her like the embers in the brazier. *Who is responsible for Darius Crosbane? It certainly isn't me, that's for damn sure.* He also had no memory of his own Rendering, which is typically a traumatic experience.

Her phone buzzed, disrupting her contemplations. Reading the text, she got up and jogged toward the door. "Fuck, I'm late." Lucia said as she quickened her pace.

She looked back to see Resin take off in a golf cart, heading in the opposite direction on the Boardwalk. She saw him from a side profile looking up at the lights and smiling, content in the moment, though making his way to work. Lucia sighed, knowing that what she was about to do would hurt Resin deeply.

Lucia Frey turned her back on her friend and made her way to the Gredalia Council meeting.

Her hands were clammy as she headed up to Nightshade Hall. She was a Maester of Magicka, someone who shouldn't fear the night, but this night felt a lot different. She ran as quickly as she could to Nightshade Hall so as not be late to the Council meeting.

A few minutes later, Lucia exhaled nervously and rapped on the door.

Minutes passed without a sound.

Eventually, footsteps came across the hall as a slender figure moved in the moonlight.

The door opened slowly.

A young woman with hooped rose-gold earrings, sandy-blond hair, heels, red pants, and a black-and-white striped top nodded to Lucia.

"'Sup, bitch?" Olivia popped her chewing gum.

"Hi, Olivia." Lucia said. "Who's all with us tonight?"

"Follow me. Brent showed up. Rob is here too. I'd say you're late but you're clearly aware, looking like that."

Lucia composed herself as she entered the building.

The roof of Nightshade Hall was comprised of glass panes for the plants that used to thrive inside. Lucia's ancestors had used this as a greenhouse in the past. Now, it was a classroom. Surprisingly it still worked, despite it being an almost-defunct building. The ceiling had holes in it, with sections of the decor peeling off or in disarray. Some doors sagged off their hinges. Desks were pushed into the corners of the marbled floor. A projector hung from the ceiling. Wi-Fi pods blinked in the darkness above. The wings of the hall held classrooms.

As Lucia looked up, she noticed a figure slowly gliding in the shadows on the stairwell leading up to the additional rooms. Lucia turned her head to listen, and she heard the figure weep softly.

"I fucking hate those things," Olivia said point blank. "It's bad enough Rob lets them stay in here. Let alone the fact that they creep around here all night."

Lucia continued to watch as they made their way to a bookcase in the main hall.

Olivia fumbled with the books on the bookcase. "I forget which book it is every time. I'm such a loser." The figure moved into the moonlight. A hand extended on the banister, skeletal. The eyes glowed icy blue as the fingers tightened on the railing, splintering the wood. A bloody bride, throat cut, looked over the banister. The mouth quivered. Lucia normally wouldn't shiver, but it sent a chill through her bones that night.

"Got it!" Olivia called back to Lucia. "Come on, we've been waiting for an hour."

Oliva pulled the book back. A section of books swung open on a hinge, revealing a hidden door that stood guard to a concealed staircase leading into darkness.

She smiled at the novelty of such a secret, the impending Council being hidden by something so cartoonish.

The pair began to walk down the stairs.

Lucia put her hand on her wand, tucked safely inside her left sleeve.

"So, uh, how's grad school?" Lucia broke the silence.

"It's not so bad. I honestly think this semester's seminar is my favorite. I hate having to drive in from Billings every day. I'm tempted to ask for a job here with Rob. Maybe get an apartment or something in Newton Falls. They're always looking for people."

"Yeah. Yeah, I get you," Lucia said, her voice trailed.

"What about you? I miss having classes with you. Can't believe I'm in grad school now."

"Uh, yeah. My journalism classes are cool. I drop off pieces to Dylan Derringer, and he reads them over the air."

"Really?! That's so cool! I'll have to tune in sometime. He fades out in Billings. It's like they've got a holy energy over there."

"Ugh. Gross."

"Right? It's too pure for me…"

The tunnels twisted and wound around, and dirt and stone slowly gave way to sturdy cavern rock.

A few minutes later, the pair entered a large cavernous space illuminated by fluorescent stalagmites and stalactites. In the ceiling were ominous dark shapes curled up like bats. They varied in color from midnight black to heather grey. Lucia saw that various holes were carved into the cavern walls, with metal bars to house something inside. Lucia couldn't tell who or what they were, but they were curled up in a ball, akin to their ceiling-dwelling counterparts. She knew the ones above were Grimfaern, but she didn't know about the ones in the cages. They were a new addition since she had last been in Nightshade.

The air was thick with cigar smoke. As Lucia coughed and pushed through it, she could see a few figures gathered around the stone altar.

"Ah, Sister Frey, so glad that you could join us, finally." The man had a slight drawl to his voice.

"My apologies, Rob," Lucia called back. Her voice came across as older than she intended. The others turned to look at Lucia, now walking up the steps to the altar. "What do we have, Council?"

"The implementation of Operation Twilight." Rob puffed on his cigar, and the smoke dissipated into the night. Rob sneered at Olivia and Brent Compton. "If we don't fuck this up, Gredalia will become a household name. Among the likes of other terror cells in the world."

Leaning forward away from the smoke, Brent released a deep cough. His low voice rumbled in his chest. "Think you could put that out? There's barely any air in here as it is."

Lucia whipped out her wand and waved it in the air. The smoke dissipated into the ceiling.

As the smoke rose, the figures hanging up in the ceiling twitched and writhed.

Brent, stocky and stubborn, was typically not amused. He was shorter than Lucia, with a less-than-athletic build and a slight beer gut. Brent was a student that had been a member of Beta House with Thorn and Lock before leaving the frat entirely once Olivia had convinced him to join Gredalia. For the sake of privacy, he lived in one of the upperclassmen apartments alone. Rob saw to it that all of the members of his operation lived alone to make sure their movements were not tracked, even though Olivia lived in Billings. When Olivia joined Rob and Lucia, she had moved out of the grad-school apartments in downtown Billings to a small private apartment that Rob personally funded.

Lucia would often walk through the Willow Apartments, returning from searches for components, where she would see Brent sitting on the steps of his apartment. She would wave to him casually as her burlap sack of mushrooms and miscellaneous findings swayed in the breeze. Brent would nod, his hand wrapped around his scotch glass, reclined in a wicker chair. He often looked like he hadn't slept in days. Brent's Nexian power turned out to be lycanthropy, or human-wolf hybridism, following the Rendering and Sundering at Lucia's hand.

Lucia nestled herself in between Rob and Olivia.

"Care to elaborate for our friends here?" Lucia looked up at Rob, knowing that he enjoyed elaboration and sitting in the driver's seat of the conversation.

Rob puffed again on his cigar. "Yeah. So, you're all probably wondering why there are those masses quivering up in the ceiling. Those are

Grimfaern. Lucia knows who they are. They've been around for a long time in the Nexus but are few and far between on Earth." He looked up at the shrouds nestled in the ceiling. "They're gonna be our ticket to getting what we want."

Brent rubbed his hands together in excitement.

Olivia smiled, and Lucia kept a stone face.

Rob took a drag of his cigar and continued: "We use the Grimfaern to achieve our world domination."

"Why would we want to do that?" Olivia asked.

Rob ground his teeth at being cut off. "*Because,* Olivia…" he seethed. "We're going to use the Grimfaern to mimic some of the students, sending them home over winter break."

Brent nodded and rested his chin in his palm, lost in thought.

Lucia nodded. "So, the Grimfaern act as a time bomb, and we launch their detonation."

Rob's eyes lit up in the ambient glow of the rocks. "When they get home to their families, they'll paint our symbol on the wall. Once that is done, on Lucia's magic command, they'll attack their families and convert them into Grimfaern. Once we amass enough Grimfaern, we will launch them upon the world powers, bending them to our will. We'll leave enough humans to do our bidding, but we will walk like gods among the Earth."

"What about the actual students?" Lucia said, egging Rob on. "They're still going to be alive, right?"

Rob smiled menacingly. "Brent, would you care to show us what happens to the students after their Grimfaern walks free?"

Brent dropped down from the steps and jogged over to the sides of the cave walls. He went to the closest one and looked into the bars, confirming something was inside.

Brent pushed a jutted rock above one of them, and the bars dropped.

He reached in and grabbed someone by the wrist. She wailed as he pulled her forward against her will.

"Please sir! I'm just a first year. I don't wanna die!" she wailed as Brent threw her into the dirt of the chamber.

"Shut up!" Brent said as he kicked the student in the stomach.

She cried out in pain.

Brent nodded to Rob.

Rob snuffed out his cigar on the stone altar and looked up. He opened his arms to the ceiling. A deep guttural roar came from his chest.

Lucia's mouth opened in horror as the rest of the Council stood vigilant.

One of the Grimfaern fell from the ceiling and slammed into the floor with a squelch like a wet noodle. Upon collision, it began to writhe.

It got to its feet, and Lucia saw a creature like the one she had propelled over the ocean.

What sat on all fours was a lanky and menacing entity. Its spinal column protruded against the taut black-grey skin. The nimble limbs carried long bony toes and fingers that seemed to sense movement in the ground but could come together to form dangerous spikes.

The Grimfaern looked from one individual to the next as it shifted to each person's movement.

The face was what haunted Lucia the most: the receding caverns for eyes that ended in wild, sanguine irises that flitted around, looking for the next kill.

The mouth opened in a hiss as Rob stepped toward the creature.

"Time to eat." Rob patted it on the back.

The lithe creature bounded toward the student, who got up and ran.

She circled around the altar's floor and saw the ascending steps to her safety.

The student took off for the stairs, panting nervously as her breath caught in her chest.

The creature took several bounds and launched itself into the air.

It collided with the student and knocked her to the floor.

She screamed in horror as the sickening *crunch* ended her life. The Grimfaern's jaw unhinged, revealing ominous rows of sharp teeth. It began to consume the student head first with slurping sounds. The grim noises echoed through the cavern. Contrary to her expectation, Lucia noticed that the Grimfaern's body pulsated and started to shrink with each bite instead of swelling up due to the consumption of the student.

As the creature continued to devour the student, hair started to grow from the top of its head. It matched the red of the dead student. The tufts started to take shape, turning into the spring of curls that the student had possessed.

A few moments passed, and the Grimfaern now looked like the student it had just devoured.

"Jesus," Lucia said.

Rob smiled and motioned to Olivia. "Go ahead, ask it some questions."

Olivia looked over to it and cocked her head. "What's your name?"

The Grimfaern looked up innocently at the Council with its false face. "Kamilla Thompson."

The council members exchanged looks of excitement when it spoke again.

"I'm a first-year student."

"What's your mission?" Brent called from his new position next to Rob.

"To await the Gredalia Council's orders." The Grimfaern looked back and forth between the members.

Rob grinned viciously as he relit his cigar. "Most excellent, my child. I have a favor to ask of you."

The student looked back at Rob. "Yes, Your Grace?"

Rob descended the steps of the altar and walked to where the Grimfaern stood. He puffed the cigar, leaned forward, and put his hand on its shoulder.

"You know where the chapel is on the south side of campus?"

It looked up at the ceiling as it searched the memories of the dead student.

It bit its lip and nodded innocently.

"Go start a fire."

The Grimfaern's mouth grinned the most unholy grin that Lucia had ever seen on a living creature, human or inhuman.

"I aim to please, Your Grace." The Grimfaern hissed as it bent over backwards, where every vertebra cracked in its back.

It touched its hands to the ground, sprung up, and sprinted out of the room.

Rob smiled as his bastard child ran. "We're gonna terrorize the world."

Resin

RESIN TURNED AWAY from the north. Worried about his friend Lucia, he continued to the south toward the House of Campus Safety.

His phone vibrated. He pulled it out and squinted into the neon pixels.

Tom (Gristholme Security): Resin, come in a little early tonight if you can. We need to talk about your leave and schedule.

Kasey (Gristholme Security): You coming in tonight? I wanted to make sure you're okay after that student the other night.

"Jesus, guys, come on," Resin sighed.

Within the fading autumnal sunlight, he saw dusk envelop the college. Students milled about in their crewneck sweaters and scarves. Coffee cups from the Moon's Loft were in nimble hands or stacked in trash cans. A chirping sound from the students came from the Boardwalk as youth collided with the siphon of time. Memories for the first-years, final moments for the seniors, and adventures stacked amongst the rest for the sophomores and juniors. Frivolity, encapsulated in the waning light of summer, pulled the strings of the students as they went about their way.

Resin caught himself as he stared at the students. He wanted to join them in such a mystical moment.

He sighed and, against his desires, turned southeast toward the House of Campus Safety. Resin shoved his hands into his pockets and carried on.

When he entered, Barb looked up through her reading glasses and waved a gloved hand at the young man. "Well, *hell-o,* Rezzy! Ah-HA ha ha." Her lungs forced out a hearty, raspy voice. "Good ta see ya! How ya doing now?" She coughed.

"I'm good, Barb." Resin said flatly through the glass window.

He walked to the door and tried to get in.

He slammed face first into the secured door as she coughed into her fist.

She looked up at the irritated security guard and jumped. "Oh! You need to get in! Lemme get that for ya!" She smiled wide at him as he heard the familiar buzz of the door.

He kicked it with his heel and bounced into the room. He headed back to the locker room. His home away from home, as his supervisor Jeff Volrund called it, was big enough for the essentials: his tactical vest, gloves, cuffs, extra pair of boots, scarf, overcoat, hat, and a few other smaller items. It was adorned with his unit number, 13, and a picture of his recent visit to Bar Harbor a year earlier with his parents and younger brother, Jake. The photo of Bar Harbor made him yearn for his wanderlust, for Resin's true home was the road. Whether it was on his motorbike or in a vehicle, Resin loved going to new places and meeting new people.

Suiting up was his favorite moment of work. Getting ready to rock for the night at large. Resin grabbed his keys, utility belt, and flashlight and threw on his windbreaker with the script Gristholme *G* and outstretched goose on the left breast.

As Resin turned away from the wall, he startled at seeing Trevor Klein siting with his legs crossed on the table. "Are we having fun yet, Mr. Rezzy?"

"Fuck off, Trev!" Resin cut back. He hated it when Trevor played this game.

He heard the words in his head before they even left Trevor's mouth.

"Oh, Mr. Rezzy! Please come over for dinner tonight."

Resin rolled his eyes at Trevor as Kasey walked in.

Kasey looked up at Resin with a look of slight frustration and annoyance. "You never texted back," said the woman, deadpan.

Resin looked back at Trevor, who shrugged with a you're-fucked look.

"I was trying to get some work done…"

"At the Hall of Ancients? Sure." She grabbed her keys and walked out of the room.

Trevor made a snarling cat noise.

Resin, in a fit of irritability, grabbed a pen and chucked it at Trevor.

"Oh, Mr. Rezzy! That tickles."

Resin took the keys and went to the kitchenette, awaiting the nightly brief from the officer in charge.

Kasey began her nightly process of making coffee.

Barb told her relief what needed to be done for the night.

Trevor threw on his suspenders and overcoat.

When Trevor began to speak, Kasey looked up from her coffee. "Talk and I'll fucking kill you."

Trevor raised his hands in defense and sat down at the table.

Jeff Volrund came down the stairs that led to the kitchenette and looked around at his staff. His deep gruff voice permeated the room. "Well, I guess everyone's, uh, chipper tonight?"

"Yeah," Resin sighed, "Yeah, I guess we are."

"Good! Good!" Jeff chuckled nervously as he made his way to the coffeepot. "Glad to hear it!"

Jeff was a former pilot who had served in the air force during Desert Storm. His beard was well trimmed. His flat-top haircut was beginning to be peppered with grey.

He poured a cup of coffee and turned to face everybody. "Well, time for the nightly brief! Resin, you and Trev are gonna split south campus. Kasey, take north and the vehicle. I'm going to be in the office doing some paperwork from an incident that happened today. A student seemed kinda feral in their apartment. We responded to it earlier, and the student appeared to be having a seizure of some kind. It was almost like something out of a horror movie. She couldn't remember specific details that her roommate asked her about. The amnesia part of it concerned us, so Trev and I ended up calling the squad and transferred her to Billings. Super weird, but it happened before Resin and Kasey arrived. Any questions?"

No one said a word.

Jeff waited back as Trevor and Kasey moved on. He knew that both Kasey and Trevor were going to sync up in a matter of minutes and pal around together for the rest of the night anyway.

"Hey, Resin…you got a second?" Jeff said timidly.

"Yeah man, what's up?"

Jeff sighed before he began. "I gotta ask, have you seen anything weird lately?"

"Huh? Um, no man. I haven't seen anything weird. Why would you ask?" Resin tried to skirt the issue.

"Right, right. This student seizure business kinda rattled me a little bit." He chuckled again. "I've seen some things, but it's creepy when the patient or student loses control of themselves, be it a medical condition, drugs, or alcohol. You were in the army, though. You're made of sterner stuff." Jeff turned and began his ascent to the stairs. "Anyway, don't get into too much trouble tonight."

"I won't!" Resin called back. He headed to the front door and stepped out into another moonlit night at Gristholme.

———— ◆ ————

As another shift ended, Resin felt the overwhelming sense of exhaustion that came with working third shift. But it was one step closer to payday and one step closer to his weekend.

When he finally exited the building, he hopped into his Jeep and headed west toward his home. The familiar sites and haunts carried him back to his driveway in the span of fifteen minutes.

The pine trees welcomed him in their somber watch.

He got out of his car and sighed. He felt the relief of being off work and looked forward to the rest his bed would provide.

He reached for the door.

The wind rustled through the trees as Resin scanned the wood line. It was then that something moved.

Crouched on all fours, it meandered through the trees. It was a canine-like figure.

Resin stepped into the yard.

He shifted his feet in the earth and inhaled slowly. At this the creature stopped and turned to the Kirkbride house.

What Resin saw could only be described as morbid.

It looked as if someone had taken the body of a pit bull and sutured a human head atop the neck. The face was a dreary, bleached-white dome with a languished look. It had a permanently stretched grin, almost suture like, with cracking teeth and purple gums adorning the face. The eyes looked as if they were screaming or had seen something startling. The skin was taught, like someone stretching a piece of gum to the point of tearing.

Resin watched it like a hawk.

The creature now noticed Resin and his stance. It turned to square up to him. "*THRAK. THRAK.*" It challenged Resin, as far as he could tell. He didn't speak whatever language it was spewing at him.

"I don't know what the fuck you are," Resin snarled, "but these are my woods. So, you best well fuck off."

The creature cocked its head and snarled at the man.

"Gods know I didn't send you an invite," Resin retorted. "I've got enough problems as it is without staring at that ugly mug of yours."

"*THRAK. THRAK.*"

It cocked its head the other way and positioned to strike.

Resin sighed and felt he had wasted his dig on the creature. "Well, it was worth a shot anyway."

The creature took off and began to charge Resin. It frothed at the mouth as it jumped over the gate and barreled for Resin.

"Come on, creep!" Resin cried as his nails grew. "Let's see whatcha got!"

The vicious white teeth were clicking while the monster made its way on all fours.

The fight had begun.

Resin lashed out at the beast with his claws, only to be knocked to the side. The monster appeared to be stronger than him.

Resin did not often encounter beings stronger than himself.

It pounced on top of him and used its endlessly smiling teeth to bite clean through his skin, sending blood trickling down his arm. Resin felt the weight of the creature, like a grown man sitting on his chest.

He kneed the monster in the back, hoping to hit a vital organ.

The creature slacked just enough for Resin to shove with all his might, sending it tumbling over backward across his backyard.

He leaned onto his back in a half-moon shape and propelled himself back onto his feet.

Resin drew from the Nexian energy deep in his cells. It felt like a runner's high coursing through him, but amplified tenfold. The Nexian energy unlocked, and Resin's powers started to unleash.

His body began to take the shape of a large half-man, half-wolf. His shirt ripped, and his muscles grew into lean, rippling sinews. His senses heightened, and he picked up the scent of the creature, now ten feet away from him.

Like a sprinter taking off from the starting block, his claws dug into the earth as he launched himself forward toward the creature.

Resin did a summersault and swung at the face of the beast.

The monster deflected Resin's blow.

Resin threw another punch, and the monster knocked away the blow.

They attacked at the same time and locked hands, each attempting to knock their opponent off balance.

"Gree…" The toothy maw hissed. "Greda…Gredalia."

Resin growled deeply and snapped, "Gredalia? What the fuck is a Gredalia?"

"C…Cou…Counc…Council." The voice sounded as if it had smoked a million cigarettes at the same time, with whisps of paper for lungs rattled by coarse warm air.

"Listen up," Resin belted. "I don't care what the fuck you are. I don't even care what the fuck you're doing on my property. You're attacking my home. You need to leave and take this fucking *Gredalia Council* with you."

It exhaled in a wheeze. "Gredalia Council…is…here," it responded, swallowing deeply and maintaining its hideous smile. "Gredalia is… Gristholme's elite."

Resin let up his assault. "Why are you telling me this?!" He yelled at the Smiling Man.

"Because it is TOO LATE FOR YOU!" The Smiling Man pushed him back with a force that knocked him to the ground. Resin's blood splattered across the lawn from a deep gash in his side.

The Smiling Man bounded forward with hopes of capitalizing on his opponent's vulnerable position.

Resin felt pain in his left flank as he grabbed the Smiling Man by the face.

He pushed his foe back with a quick shove, then punched him square in the face.

Blood spewed from the canine-like nose as Resin's enemy recoiled.

It wiped its nose before it got down on all fours.

It sprinted toward Resin once more.

Resin stood to full wolfen height. He took a deep breath as the Smiling Man drew closer and closer to him.

The Fenris Wolf's power harkened back to Ragnarök, when the Norse gods fought to keep the universe in existence. The Fenris Wolf was incorrectly designated to be the World Ender in Viking lore. In actuality, the Fenris Wolf was designed to keep the world together as the Peacemaker while the gods fought. The Wolf harnessed great power during the gods' war. Once the fight ended and peace was restored, the wolf hid away in the form of a human on Midgard, or Earth. The power was passed down from designated human to designated human. Through Resin's ancestors, the power of the Peacemaker descended unto him.

His father described the powers to Resin and taught him secrets about the powers that had been passed down for generations. Among them was a hidden power that, during times of extreme duress, could nullify an enemy.

For Resin, that time was now.

He took one more deep breath before feeling his energy begin to build. Resin took the seconds between himself and the Smiling Man to channel his Nexian energy into the tips of his fingers.

The Smiling Man launched itself in the air toward Resin, front paws outstretched and primed for the kill.

Resin extended his fingertips, releasing the stored energy from his body.

A ravenous bolt of green energy launched itself from within the wolf and collided with the Smiling Man. It cried out in pain as the energy rendered the Smiling Man's cells back to the Nexus. It disappeared into the wind.

The wolf began to feel himself render back into the normal form of a human.

His muscles bristled in the autumn air, feeling the inevitable cold of winter seeping its way into the wind and trees. He looked at his wound and stumbled his way into the house.

He held his side and grabbed a towel from the stove. He applied direct pressure to the wound and made his way to the stairwell. He climbed gingerly, leaving a trail of blood behind him.

As the entrance to the primary bathroom gave way, the young security guard lurched forward and grabbed the sink. His arms shivered as he pushed himself up. Looking around, Resin saw that the tub was empty. The beckoning of the clean, white porcelain made him chuckle. He reached for the knobs and turned them on. A deep breath ensued. Looking down at the cuts and gashes in his body, Resin decided it was time for a little assistance. He clenched his fists and closed his eyes. He inhaled deeply and tensed his muscles. His body began to shake.

In a primal fashion, Resin grunted and strained. His flesh slowly stitched itself back together. His body, with help from the Nexus, would create new cells and heal the wounds he sustained from battle. In a matter of minutes, all that was left of his fight was the dirt and dried blood. In the time it took him to heal, the bathwater rose to an adequate height.

He got into the tub and stared at the ceiling. His thoughts dissipated into the water in which he sat. As Resin closed his eyes, the fight replayed in his mind.

Resin snapped himself awake in the bathroom. He nodded off in that short amount of time. The room around him was unholy with the cold temperature.

"Shit," he said. "I guess I forgot to put on the wood furnace." Resin gingerly got out of the tub and grabbed his towel. Out of the corner of his eye, he noticed movement in the mirror.

White arms.

White arms flailing wildly.

Resin jumped to his pants on the floor. "Fuck, fuck, fuck, *fuck*, fuck, fuck…" He struggled with one pant leg as the left arm grabbed a hold of the wall.

"Jesus Christ, come on!" He threw his other leg into the pants and yanked them up. The belt threw itself together when the right arm grabbed a piece of wall. The sinews tensed as the porcelain-skinned face pushed itself through the veil. The wheezing, rasping voice was more succinct this time as it spoke from the mirror.

"Listen, you little *fuck*." The monster hissed through its clenched, cracking teeth. "You think you're just gonna get away that easily, well *fuck you*." It pulled its torso through the mirror at this point.

"Get the fuck outta my house!" Resin said as he launched a bar of soap at the monstrosity. It hit the beast dead on and caused it to flinch.

"You're gonna get *destroyed* by Gredalia. They're pissed. They're pissed that you little *shits* have been fucking with their enterprises. That's why they summoned me to this plane of existence." Its body now tumbled onto the floor. "The Smiling Man is gonna finish his meal!"

The maw opened again to reveal a barbed tongue. It flew like a loose arrow and wrapped itself around Resin's arm. Resin smirked and used the tongue as rope-like leverage against the monster. The Smiling Man's tongue retracted like a winch, and Resin's body slid across the floor with heels dug into the ground. Resin allowed the monster to think it had the advantage as he wound his foot back, to the Smiling Man's sudden horror.

Resin's years of high-school soccer experience coursed through his right leg as he squared up to the beast and punted as hard as he could. The impact of the side of his foot caused the tongue to loosen. The creature slid into the bathroom door and smacked its head.

"You think a little punching practice is gonna dissolve me?" It hissed and crouched. "THINK AGAIN!" The Smiling Man unleashed a torrent of dark energy from its mouth.

Resin dodged out of the way and lunged toward the creature.

"Fucking Nexian creep." Resin flexed his hands as his claws came to the forefront. "Didn't know you guys could climb through mirrors now."

The Smiling Man titled its head and clicked its teeth. "Fool," the Smiling Man said. "It was Gredalia who sent me through the seeing stone."

"I've never heard of this *fucking* Gredalia," Resin said as his hands clasped the throat of the Smiling Man. "Hell," he said as he moved to the mirror, "I don't even know if I wanna hear it from their *minion*." The Smiling Man began to writhe and grasp at the hands that held him. "All I want is for you to get the *fuck* out of my house!" He threw the creature at the mirror.

Resin extended his hand and felt the Nexian energy leave his body. He commanded the energy to become a one-way portal so that the Smiling Man could only leave and not come back.

The Smiling Man screamed in pain as the mirror absorbed him.

Resin, in exhaustion, collapsed to the tile floor and noticed the saliva and blood around the room.

"Fuck," he exhaled.

Lauren

LAUREN THREW HER LIGHT-BLOND hair back as she made her way toward her car. She got in and turned the key over. She backed out and headed toward Newton Falls.

Lauren turned on the radio and found her favorite country music station, thankful to drown out Dylan Derringer's early morning broadcast as it vied for the frequency space. It was reported by the students that Dylan's frequency would hinder external radio stations from coming through on campus.

She finally had a moment to herself to reflect on and assess the Darius Crosbane business.

Lauren Kreider drove through Newton Falls, following the signs for Billings. The town sat in between forests of tall pines that stood vigil on either side. Newton Falls was asleep except for Suzy's Diner, which was open 24/7. Lauren never understood how Suzy did it. She wasn't a Nexian magic user, from what Lauren could tell. She just enjoyed people.

"Gross," Lauren said aloud with disdain in her voice.

She had about thirty minutes to kill before she met her contact.

Lauren grew up with Nexian magic users for parents. Both were Rendered and Sundered in the vampiric tradition many years before Lauren was born. This entailed a séance, a lot of blood, and a sacrificial human free of any impurities. The vampire-to-be would drink the human completely dry of all blood and then begin the Rendering. A group of vampires would chant in Nexian, summoning the Nexian creature to bestow vampirism upon the non-Nexian initiate.

When it came time for Lauren to be Rendered and Sundered, she slipped into a dream state in which she spoke to a veiled figure with long tendrils for fingers. It extended its hands forward, and the tendrils shot into Lauren's eyes, mouth, nose, and ears.

She awoke on the floor of her parents' living room, coughing. She was only ten years old.

Nexian vampirism was unlike anything she thought possible. It wasn't the twinkling vampires or the ones that get roasted in the sun. It was, in fact, the complete opposite. The sun actually *strengthened* her. The Kreiders could move in and out of sunlight like predatory cats stalking wild animals. Same basic benefits, but without the need for SPF 50 and copious amounts of blood.

"Any blood will do, really," her mother said. "Just so long as there's heme iron in the blood somewhere. You don't need to drain humans *all* the time—only the bad ones." She winked at Lauren.

When she inquired about the origins of vampires hating the sun, her dad stated that a story he heard at a family reunion years back indicated that a small village discovered that one of the Kreiders had magical powers. This resulted in Lauren's ancestors being burnt alive at the stake.

Call it fiefdom, call it the Dark Ages, but the legend that vampires hated the sun was a loose translation of "being hog-tied and lit up like a Christmas tree."

They lost more than a few family members this way.

Lauren also asked if there was any truth to a Van-Helsing-like string of Nexian hunters that roamed the earth to extinction.

Her father rolled his eyes and tsked. "No, sweet child, there are no Van Helsings. There's a Fenris Wolf, but that's different."

It was that day that Lauren learned of the Fenris Wolf, an ancient Nexian entity that was foretold to bring the end of the world at the appropriate time. In the here and now, it moved from host to host. The new host would act as ambassador between humanity and the Nexians who lived on the planet. Her father told her that Marcus Kirkbride had been the Fenris Wolf during his stay at Gristholme.

"He was a good steward," her father, Ambrose, reflected. "Never failed to see who was a Nexian and how best to clean up after us. Really begs the question of whether we *should* exist with humanity."

Lauren asked her dad how to tell whether someone was a Nexian.

Her father considered the question with a sigh and a concentrated face. "It takes a certain skill and amount of time among fellow Nexians, but they typically act different than other humans. They're fixated on something out of the ordinary and can notice things that humans can't. You'll see what I mean when you spend more time amongst our kind."

Lauren took a hard left turn onto the state route and saw the sign for Billings University in the distance.

"Gag me with a stake." She floored it past the university.

She felt an odd presence, as if a beam of sunlight slapped her in the face after taking the recommended amount of vitamin D, radiating from the college.

"Gods," Lauren swore. "Can it get any happier?"

She felt sick to her stomach.

She exited the state route and turned onto the boulevard, which led her to a ritzy hotel.

"He really must have laid it on thick." Lauren pulled up to a compact car and investigated. No one was home.

"Perfect." She smiled wickedly to herself.

She spun her car around and turned down the radio, parking under the shade of a tree several rows behind the compact.

Lauren sat in her car and ran a hand through her hair. *I know that this won't be the easiest, but it's best,* she told herself.

She looked up at herself in the mirror to check her hair and makeup.

Anyone looking in would see a beautiful, stylish woman.

Lauren searched her spirit, looking for the wellspring of Nexian energy.

She summoned it from within.

Looking back into the mirror, her eyes burst into a hue of dandelion yellow with deep-purple slits for pupils.

The human skin had retreated, pulling taut against the bone. Her skin grew ashen, with a hue that showed the heart under it wasn't beating. Her fingers grew bonier, and her nails darkened. Her face was also taut, with the cheekbones protruding so sharply they could cut a cold steak. If she couldn't use her cheekbones, she would use her teeth—needlepoint-sharp rows smiled back at her in the mirror.

Lauren looked around to see if there was anyone in the parking lot as the sun began to go to sleep for the day. Her vampire eyes did not pick up any signs of movement or heat signatures out in the open air.

Good, she thought. *No one to be seen.*

Lauren was risking exposure by trying something she'd been practicing for a few days.

Now was the perfect time.

Okay, here we go, Lauren thought.

She knew that teleportation was a risky business. You had to be *focused.* If not, you could end up above the waters of Madagascar or Tasmania. She heard from her mother that a distant cousin had once teleported her face into the queen's private chambers and her ass into a local tavern.

"Someone was excited, I can guarantee you that," Her mother had stated. "My bets are, it *wasn't* the queen or your cousin."

Lauren felt her body radiate with energy, like after having too much coffee. She knew she had to be *fast* to make this work. She let go of the steering wheel and rose up through the roof of her car using Nexian energy. She ran as fast as she could for her target's car. She leapt off the ground to close the distance.

Lauren felt the wind in her hair as she glided through the air.

The energy felt unsteady inside her body, like a queasy stomach about to retch.

She soared through the roof and landed in the passenger seat without setting any alarms off.

Lauren breathed a sigh of relief, letting her head rest against the seat.

She was poised, ready for the arrival of her target.

Lauren let her eyes close. She wiped her nose, saw the blood, and noticed the amount of energy she had expended during her flight.

However, Lauren discovered through her risky experiment that she could walk through solid materials.

———— ◆ ————

"She's kinda tacky."

Darius jumped and smacked his head on the ceiling of the car. He leaned forward as the headache radiated in his consciousness. Lauren had watched the whole goodbye transaction from Darius's back seat. He appeared to be shaking while the mysterious lady gave him a kiss and hug. *For two people staying in a hotel the night prior, I guess that's a success,* Lauren thought.

"Her name is Carolína," Darius seethed. "Lauren, how…the *fuck*… did you get into my—"

Lauren popped up, hugging the passenger seat as she spoke. "Darius, you're brand new to the Artificers. You really think we're gonna show you our base of operations and then let you wander off into the world on your own?"

Darius's eyes widened. "Wait, did you see me…*naked* with her too?"

Lauren bugged her eyes out at him. "Ew, gross. No, I let you have your throes of passion. I slept in your car last night."

He shook his head and rubbed his eyes. He wasn't entirely sure he believed that. "Lauren. How the hell did you get into my car? Did you use your powers?"

Lauren smiled and looked up. "Now, that's more like it." She grabbed Darius's arm. "Let's go back to Gristholme. We can try and figure out *your* powers together!"

"Don't you think it's weird that you didn't just text me and schedule a time to hang out?"

"No! Besides, this is way more fun." She smiled wide at him, hiding what she was thinking. *I'm still not entirely sure that you're NOT a threat, Darry boy. It's nothing personal. I don't believe Resin has ruled it out, either.*

"Y…yeah. Yeah, let's go back to Gristholme."

Lauren smiled and patted his shoulder. "See you there." She made her way back to her car, content in her mission's success: scare the piss out of the newbie.

———— ♦ ————

Twenty minutes later, Lauren began to drive up the hill toward campus. The midmorning sun was shining through the pines, creating a natural equivalent to stained glass. She followed Darius's car while singing Dolly Parton's "9 to 5" at the top of her lungs.

The pair made their way back to Darius's house.

His little Honda rolled to a stop.

Lauren pulled up beside him, windows down, and continued to sing loudly.

"Is there any way you could, like, not scream and yell?"

"It's Dolly Parton, Darry. You need to be enlightened about the Queen." She turned down the music and adopted a more serious tone. "So, I followed you, we already have this established. Resin wanted me to keep track of you after what he saw at his house this weekend."

Darius got out of his car; hesitation sprayed across his face. "What did he see, Lauren?"

Lauren shifted in her seat. "It's a Grimfaern. They're like these… mythical creatures created from the Nexus that magic comes from. Resin believes some of them might be on campus."

Darius's voice became elevated. "They're on campus?! What about the students, Lauren? Are they safe? Do we—"

"We. Do. Nothing." Lauren flipped her hair back and opened her car door. "At least, not right away. We must gather intel first and assess what the hell the Grimfaern are doing out here. Resin is concerned about their presence on the campus. The Grimfaern alluded to the fact that they're being controlled by a group of people. It mentioned this *council* of sorts, though we don't know much more than that. Which is why we"—she got out of the car and shouldered her designer bag—"are going to train you. Can I use your bathroom? I need to change."

"Absolutely," Darius said. He went up the steps and fiddled with his key chain. He turned the keys in the lock and allowed Lauren inside, motioning the way to the bathroom.

She made her way in and toward the way he'd pointed.

"Change into something you don't mind getting dirty!" she called through the wall. "We're going to get a little rough!"

Darius groaned as he made his way up the stairs, missing Carolína that much more.

———— ◆ ————

The pair had been walking north of the Willow Apartments when Darius finally called up to her. "Are we there yet?"

She felt the power in her legs as she kept walking. "Darius, you poor baby. It's like five more minutes." Another disheartened groan came back from over her shoulder.

"Jesus Christ, Lauren," Darius huffed.

She knew just where she was going. In fact, she was sure her heart carried her more than anything. She and Thorn had snuck up to this very field to watch the stars during their first year. It started as light hand-holding, as it always does, and progressed to the pair collapsing into each other's arms later in the evening.

Lauren was sure she could see her innocence running off into the tree line.

"This is where we're going to teach you how to fight," she said, turning back to Darius. "We all know you've got some shit, based on the table, but what do you actually have?"

"I guess we'll see, Lauren." He looked nervous.

Lauren bent down to tie her shoe. She pressed her boot hard into the ground to release a little throwing knife.

She snapped her wrist and yelled, "THINK FAST!"

Time seemed to slow as the knife flew through the air.

In fear, Darius raised his hands up to defend against the attack.

Then Lauren saw something arise from the ether—a hand-and-a-half sword with a long black blade. It leaked purplish necrotic energy from the hilt. The blade looked razor sharp.

She heard metal clashing against metal as her knife hit the ground.

Darius managed to summon a sword from the Nexus without even thinking about it.

Lauren knew he was powerful, but this confirmed it. Cat-like reflexes that summoned vicious swords yielded a powerful Nexian user.

He's not even Sundered yet, Lauren thought as a chill ran up her spine. *Wait 'til Resin hears this.*

"Oh, shit!" Lauren said in excitement.

"This thing is actually kinda cool." He gripped it tighter and looked up at Lauren, mirroring her excitement. "How did this happen?"

Lauren pulled her daggers from their back holsters and stood upright. "Darius, you sought to defend yourself. You pulled power from the Nexus, and it gave you a sword. That's how you manifest your power. It's just as easy as willing it into existence. In this case, your brain did so at lightning speed. Be careful though, if you use too much Nexian energy, it'll hurt ya. Might come up as extra-sore muscles or a bloody nose, but it happens."

Darius shifted his feet and positioned himself into a stance, seemingly unfazed by the new information. "Let's spar!"

Lauren smirked and disappeared from where she stood.

Darius flinched, looking around the field. He couldn't see Lauren anywhere.

He rested his sword on his shoulder and listened to the birds in the trees. He took a few steps forward, feeling a shift in energy.

He felt a breath on his ear as Lauren whispered, "Boo."

Darius grasped the sword with both hands and swung as hard as he could, sending a blast of blue energy spiraling through the air.

Lauren appeared again and sent a swift kick to the back of his leg. Darius collapsed to his knees, cried out in pain, and dropped his sword. Lauren flipped midair, hissed, and drove her daggers down at Darius's back. Darius rolled out of the way and kicked his sword up to his hands. Lauren vanished again, reappearing to his right. Darius blocked a few dagger attacks with his sword.

This continued for several minutes.

Darius kicked at Lauren. Lauren jumped out of the way. Darius took the sword and brought it down toward Lauren. Lauren blocked it with both daggers and disappeared again. Darius dropped his guard long enough for Lauren to appear behind him, daggers to his throat.

She blew the hair out of her face and smiled.

"Kneel, bitch." She pressed her chest into Darius's back.

Darius dropped to his knees.

She released her daggers from his throat and smiled. "That was a lot of fun! Let's call it for tonight."

Darius looked up at her and smiled. "You gotta admit, I had you for a minute."

She laughed as the pair walked out of the field. "Nah, baby boy. That was me at fifty percent."

Resin

IT HAD BEEN A FEW WEEKS since the Artificers' initial meeting with Darius, and already things were going to shit.

Resin was sprinting toward the chapel since its fire alarm went off during Campus Safety's shift-change meeting. It was Campus Safety's responsibility to show up first, to see if there was a legitimate fire or if it was a fault in the alarm system. Some of the fire alarms were faulty due to age.

He radioed into base that he was arriving. They responded that he was clear.

Seeing the chapel not ablaze, he proceeded slowly to the doors.

The air was still.

He opened the fire panel and reset the alarm. It appeared to have been pulled as a prank.

The giant wooden doors creaked as Resin pushed them open. The echo vibrated around the sanctuary. The pews were at attention as the security guard made his way down the main aisle.

The floor groaned in pain as Resin looked up. Adorning the ceiling was a beautiful array of paintings. Some of the Christ, some of earlier Bible stories. Resin himself was in awe of the ornate nature of the building. The time it took someone in years past to build and paint such a display was something of utter fascination.

Descending from the rotunda were beautiful stained-glass windows. Each window held its own Biblical figure. The central figure, naturally, was the crucified Christ. Resin began to walk again, toward the center of the building. Beneath the rotunda, there was an altar with a few steps that ascended to a stage and a pulpit where the rector of the church spoke on Sundays.

Resin studied the Christ image and the intricate glass.

The blood that flowed from His side was vibrant. It caught Resin's attention. He noticed the way the blood popped against the cream color of skin.

As Resin stood in his thoughts, he noticed the blood wasn't just stained glass.

It was real.

Resin turned around on his heels as he heard a voice shout at him. "HELP ME, MISTER SECURITY GUARD!"

Resin descended the stairs and put his hand on his mic. "Are you hurt? Where are you?" He scanned the ceiling and made his way down the walls until he spotted the pale girl in a pew several feet behind him.

She grinned a savage grin.

"Ah, fuck." Resin put one hand on his handcuffs and kept the other one on his mic. "Are you hurt?"

"Yes," she whispered quietly. Her eyes, vibrantly green, slowly began to roll into the back of her head.

Resin took a few steps back, feeling his mouth drop open in horror.

Her body writhed and twitched unnaturally.

Her bones splintered out of her appendages as she thrashed around. Resin put more distance between himself and the girl. Once she finished thrashing, she smiled as the blood poured out of her body.

"Mr. Security Guard?" she said in the most childlike voice possible. "HELP ME, I'M BLEEEEDING." Her voice dropped to something from the bottom pits of Hell itself. Deep, menacing breaths exhaled from her lungs. Her teeth sharpened into vicious points. "AND HUNGRY." Her jaws unhinged and went slack.

The white eyes looked through Resin.

As he turned around, he noticed the light switch by the church entrance was twitching.

Resin grabbed his flashlight and sharpened his claws. The switch flipped down, sending the room into darkness. He heard the little feet run up the aisle toward him.

"DIE, KILLER, DIE!" the Grimfaern bellowed, and it leapt at Resin.

Resin flipped on his flashlight and saw her soaring through the air.

The girl latched onto his arm, teeth sinking into his soft flesh.

Resin yelled in pain and started to swing the flashlight at the body. Solid thumps landed upon the torso as it wailed.

Flashes of light caught the young woman, and Resin could see things he hadn't before: the vicious grin, the black-blue veins running through the pale skin, talon-like hands and feet, and blackened gums.

The pair fell to the ground. Resin dropped the flashlight in the struggle and accidentally smacked it away from them as they wrestled. The Grimfaern took a lunge for Resin's throat, mouth open. Resin took two fingers and jabbed them into the Grimfaern's eyes.

The Grimfaern wailed, letting Resin go.

Falling on its back, blood shooting out of the now forlorn eyes, it spoke like a child again.

"Mr. Security Guard, I'm gonna tell the student council that you're beating kids. You're gonna lose your job." The crackling sound of its bones while it moved echoed through the sanctuary. "Then you're gonna lose your house." A trail of blood followed the foot it dragged on the floor. "And your loved ones." Its smile broke out again as it yelled, "AND YOUR FUCKING LIFE TOO."

It charged Resin again, tongue flailing in the air.

Resin ran up the steps and grabbed a candlestick. "Not today, little bitch." He swung at the face, hearing a squelching sound as he connected with the skull. The vibration reverberated into his body as the creature dropped to the floor.

She began to cry and pull herself back to the main aisle. Blood leaked into the red carpet.

Resin dropped the candlestick and walked down the aisle. The crying continued from the small body on the floor.

"GET BACK!" it yelled pathetically. "I'LL FUCK YOU UP, YOU BIG PIECE OF SH—"

Resin picked up the demonic girl by the throat. "Who the *fuck* is this goddamn Gredalia Council?"

She smiled through the pain. "They're here. They're…mean." She winced, and blood shot out through her teeth. "They're gonna make you a pelt on the wall."

Resin tightened his grasp around the small throat. "I'm *not* in the mood to play fucking games! Spill or die."

She gasped and clawed at his hands, writhing against the grip. "Fuck you, Cujo."

"You're a fucking Grimfaern, how do you know what Cujo is?"

She smiled the vicious smile and quivered. "Why don't you go and find out?" With a few last tremors, the body stopped moving.

It didn't initially occur to Resin that he was gripping the body of what appeared to be a first-year, dripping blood onto a relatively noticeable carpet. Nor did it occur to Resin that he was just standing there like a fool, with a dead body. Finally, he realized he needed to get rid of it somehow. All this swirled in his mind when the radio called out into the chapel.

He knew that anyone walking in wouldn't see this, but he couldn't afford to take any chances. *It's the principle of the thing, though,* he thought.

"Base to thirteen, checkup."

"Ah, fuck." Resin looked around as the blood began to drip down his arms. He grimaced as he reached for his radio. "Thirteen to base, I'm fine. Just a rodent in the ducts."

"Coooopy. Base clear at…"

Resin began searching the room to find something to put the body in.

He walked through one of the wings and found a trash can. He sighed, looked down at his hands, then back at the garbage can.

He lifted the body over the can and let go. The small body fell limply into the trash can. Resin picked up the lid and placed it on top.

He reached down for his phone, placing a hasty phone call.

Thorn and Lock came into the chapel and exchanged looks like disciplined school children as Resin stood next to the trash can.

"If anyone asks, say you were looking for a dumpster." Resin coughed. "It doesn't smell good."

"What is it?" Thorn's gruff voice echoed in the sanctuary.

"More importantly, what happens if someone discovers it?" Lock followed.

Resin pinched the bridge of his nose in frustration. "For the love of God, please just get it the fuck out of here. Dispose of it over the side of the cliff. When we can get everyone together, we will figure out what to do next. This is something tied to a bigger threat than we've ever faced before. This thing isn't your run-in-the-mill student. This is a Grimfaern."

The two students exchanged a look and returned it to Resin. "Our dads fought these in the past," Lock said. "I don't know anything about them though."

"Exactly. They were sealed off by our dads when they were here. The question is, why are they back now?" Resin looked down at the trash can. "I need you guys to be on high vigilance. See if something in the student population is causing this. I made sure Lauren knew, since she was taking Darius out, but these things are vicious."

"Like a bad witch?" Lock asked.

"Or maybe an alien of some type?" Thorn added.

"Just…something out of the ordinary." Resin looked at them both, concerned. "Y'all, Grimfaern are nothing to mess with. They're…" He looked up in shock.

"What!?" the other two cried out.

"Changelings," Resin finished. "Shit, we gotta call a meeting tomorrow."

"We have class, bro." Thorn threw his arms up in the air. "And practice for football."

"Sometime, then." Resin walked away, looking up into the chapel.

"There's blood on the floor!" Lock exclaimed.

"I radioed in that it's just a rodent of some kind. Normal humans can't see the blood on the floor, the Grimfaern, or us when we use our powers. It's all about the water, remember? Lucia sees to it. However, once the Grimfaern have gone into a human form, I'm not entirely sure that they can't be seen by humans. It's Nexian, though, so I'll have to ask Lucia about it."

Thorn shook his head. "I hope you're right, man. Come on, Lock." The pair heaved the trash can and began to walk out the doors. "Resin?" Thorn called to the security guard who was inspecting the blood.

"Yeah, man?"

Thorn looked slightly concerned. "Will we be okay? Do you think this is related to Darius coming into the fold?"

Resin looked back down to the ground. "I think we'll be okay. I don't think it's based on Darius showing up. Darius has been here for a while. Could be, but I don't know, guys."

They nodded. Lock chipped in, "Hang in there, Resin. We need you, man."

Resin felt weary. "Thanks, bro. I appreciate you guys!" They smiled and nodded, carrying the trash can out the door. "We need each other right now more than anything."

Resin walked around the chapel. He wanted to see if any possible clues could be found for his report in the Artificers' journal.

Everything else looked straightforward. The pews were lined up as they usually were. There were kiosks in the paneling of the wall for candles, candlesticks, et cetera. Resin opened and closed several of these. He inspected them inside. Nothing too out of the ordinary, he thought. Just normal church things in an otherwise normal church.

The stained-glass windows caught his attention for a minute. Each one, as he previously noticed, contained a different depiction of the Christ. What caught his gaze was the one stained-glass depiction of Christ pointing down to the floor.

Resin stopped and looked at the floor as well.

He noticed the stairwell that descended to the basement tucked back by the entrance.

He swore under his breath and searched for the flashlight.

His footsteps echoed down the wooden staircase as he hit the final undercroft step. He had to duck on his way down to avoid hitting his head on the floor of the church, which served as the ceiling for the undercroft.

In the undercroft, the church stored a few miscellaneous things—chairs and a bench or two. There was a children's classroom adjacent to the stairs and a small library. Resin gripped his flashlight tighter and scanned the room. It wasn't until he did a double take at the bookshelf that he saw it.

Tucked behind the shelf was a spray-painted marking of a fiddlehead fern.

Resin gently pushed the shelf out of the way and stared at the marking in depth. "The fuck?" He pulled out his phone and took a few pictures.

He pushed the shelf back in place with a loud grunt.

As he headed up the stairs, Resin pocketed his phone. He needed to have a talk with everyone as soon as possible.

Resin stepped outside of the chapel, feeling dismayed by the happenings.

The Gristholme night, which began to herald the end of summer, captured Resin's mind for a brief second. He could hear a party brewing in a distant south-campus dorm. The sounds of frivolous youth capsized the stillness of the night and held it hostage. The steady thumps of bass caught the breeze and reverberated his way. He prayed silently that nothing would come of such a loud event, though he knew in moments he would be called.

Peace doesn't last forever, Resin thought.

True to Murphy's Law, the call rang out into the night.

"Base to unit thirteen," Barb called.

"Go for thirteen," Resin responded.

"I have a student calling in that they're trying to sleep before their midterm tomorrow, and their neighbor is blaring music loudly. Could you respond?"

"Copy," Resin said as he moved through the coniferous trees and into the night toward south campus.

Thorn and Lock

THORN AND LOCK WOKE UP from a very uneasy night a few days after they disposed of the Grimfaern over the side of the cliff. Thorn had drank a fifth of whiskey straight out of the bottle. Lock had had just about as much. He had passed out on the couch before he could ask for the last dregs to call it a fifth.

Thorn got up off the floor and stretched toward the ceiling. He noticed he had lost his shirt at some point in the evening. He looked down at Lock and scratched his crotch.

"Eh, Lock?" Thorn kicked half-empty beer cans across the room. "Lock!"

Lock's eyes shot open. He sat up abruptly. More beer cans and food crumbs launched themselves into the wilderness of the football players' frat.

"Lock, the fuck happened?" Thorn swayed. He placed his hand on the edge of the couch.

"Well," Lock said in a gruff voice, "you remember the Zetas?"

Thorn felt the heat swell to his face in embarrassment. "We didn't, did we?" He continued to scratch.

"Well," Lock huffed, "there were about fifteen of them…"

"FIFTEEN?!" Thorn grabbed his forehead with his other hand.

"Yeah," Lock said. "Does it itch?"

Thorn blinked at him a few times, noticing what his hand was cupping. "No, not yet. I don't think that happens that quickly."

Lock smiled up at him. Lock had known Thorn ever since they were babies. They had grown up with their moms in Billings. Lock remembered riding bikes through the cul-de-sac together, going to the pool, and the ceremony. The ceremony took place right after their first season of football last fall. Lock remembered Lucia leading the ceremony. Lucia was crucial to it. Lock recalled in that moment just how scared they were. They both lay in the circle Lucia—acting way beyond her years—had drawn, and then she had begun the incantation.

Thorn looked down at his friend, wondering what was going through his mind. He recalled the day that his friend had made the same face when they went through the Rendering and Sundering ceremony. The ceremony granted them their powers. Although they both jokingly called Thor and Loki their dads, it wasn't the case. They just emulated their powers, and Norse paganism was the closest thing they had as a frame of reference.

Lucia's job was to provide the incantation and the elements so that the two young men could become arcane powerhouses. In the time since, there had been nothing but an intense brotherhood between the pair. Thorn looked out for Lock in every way he could and vice versa—if Lock didn't fuck it up too badly.

Thorn stretched again and sat down on the couch once more. "Are we going to class today?" He couldn't remember what day it was.

"Tomorrow, buddy," Lock said as he covered his eyes with his hand.

"What do you want to do today, then?" The red-haired man asked.

Lock looked around the room, taking in the disaster around them. He vaguely recalled the feminine underwear that were precariously draped on the mantel of the fireplace. He had thrown them. Hadn't he thrown them? He wasn't too sure. "We could try and clean this place up. See if we can find anything out from the other fraternities."

Thorn looked over at Lock and smacked his arm. "Bro! I think that's the smartest thing I've ever heard you say."

Lock nodded, "Yeah, you said the same thing last night when you got two girls to give you head one right after the other."

Thorn's face fell to something like concern. "Oh yeah?"

Lock nodded quickly. "Yeah. I got with Sarah, too." Thorn now looked disgruntled.

"Sarah! I've been trying to get with Sarah for the past two years."

Lock sheepishly twiddled his thumbs. "Yeah. I know. She was really drunk and thought I was you."

Thorn stared at the floor in disbelief.

Lock leaned in to try to see what was going on in his friend's mind. Thorn's hair fell into his face. "You know how much I love you, man. I'm sorry I—"

The words were stunted as Thorn punched Lock square in the jaw. Thorn stood up, and his eyes rippled with magic, turning multiple shades of blue.

"I can't believe you *fucked* the girl I've wanted to be with!"

Lock coughed blood onto the floor. He felt his hands turn into green spikes.

"I was also drunk, Thorn. But she was good. Really good." He sent Nexian spikes through the air, which hit Thorn dead in the center of the chest like ice shards against concrete.

Lock jumped across the coffee table and began to wallop on Thorn with his newly formed spikes.

Thorn shot a streak of lightning that hit Lock in the shoulder, and the smell of smoldering flesh echoed through the room.

Thorn charged Lock and cracked him in the jaw. Lightning shot from his hands and singed Lock's hair.

Lock formed his fist into a boulder and slammed it into the back of Thorn's head.

Blood shot out of Thorn's mouth and sprayed onto the couch.

He wiped his mouth and shifted his weight. "What the fuck? When did you get so strong?"

"Do you even lift? It's called a weight room, bro." Lock charged his friend.

Thorn dug his feet into the floor and clenched his fists.

Lock leapt over the couch and dove for his friend with righteous anger.

Thorn wound up.

The look on Lock's face transitioned from confident to concerned when Thorn threw his entire strength behind the fist. A crack of thunder echoed through the house as Lock smashed into the couch.

Thorn stood over his friend and panted. "The game is done." He cracked his knuckles, then his neck, and extended his hand to Lock.

Lock smiled and grabbed the hand. He was lifted to his feet by his old friend. "I didn't fuck her, bro. I was just in the mood for a good brawl."

———— ◆ ————

The weekend passed, and classes resumed on Monday morning. Thorn and Lock got up early and went to lift, per their football program's usual requirements. The boys trekked south along the Boardwalk and took in the sight. Resin was going through his usual morning unlock schedule, making his way through the academic buildings before the sun crested the sea.

The boys waved at Resin, who waved back at them. This was their routine.

"I wish that he'd get out more, you know?" Lock, with gym bag shouldered, mused.

"Why do you say that, bub?"

"Does he have like, a love interest or anything? We're out here trying to get laid and pass our classes enough to get degrees, maybe get picked up by a national football team. He just walks around and hopefully, you know, makes enough money to survive and live through the next week.

Then, he likely goes into debt to live a basic, semi-normal life, being a veteran and all. He may or may not have a social life, considering we are it. Is this what happens when we graduate college? Are we just pawns slated into a greater mysticism known as capitalism? Or are we something more? Are we just little suburbanite drones that hop into our cars for our frequented routes to nine-to-five jobs? When Resin waltzes through the night, making sure everyone is safe, is he a servant of safety or a servant to rigidity?"

"Lock, you really need to *stop* doing the readings for Philosophy 202."

"It's nice to fall asleep to, I can't help it."

They crossed Route 13 and saw other faces emerge from the dorms of south campus, all headed to their personal mecca: the athletic facility. It was just south of the Pearson DFAC and overlooked the sea on the southeast side of campus. Large vibrant windows showed various bits and bobs of exercise equipment. Like pilgrims hearing the clarion call of the church bell, the various athletes were moving through the morning fog to stake their claim on the various benches and machines. This building was a little bit older than the science quad but was still turn-of-the-century. The fluorescent lights shone like beacons in the early morning through the front entrance of the high glass doors. Inside, a miniature DFAC food court was available to grab a snack from. The bottom floor held the weight room, some various gyms for basketball and volleyball, and a small lap pool.

The boys pulled open the heavy doors of the athletic facility and made their way downstairs. They smelled bagels and coffee drifting in from the café. Lock cast a glance at the café and saw a young woman with a crop top and form-fitting jeans preparing a brew for an athlete. She looked up and smiled at Lock before returning to the customer. Her strawberry blonde hair was tucked behind her ear. Lock started to deviate from the path as Thorn smacked his arm.

"Dude, we gotta stay in the zone."

"Sorry…" He cast one more glance at the woman, who met his gaze once more. "I think that, uh, girl really likes me."

"Hrm?" Thorn looked up and saw the woman. "Oh dude, that's Cadi Reich. She's a babe."

"I'm gonna get her number once we're done."

"Do you, man."

The wide stairs carried them down to the bottom floor where the puzzle-piece foam mats interlocked on the weight room's floor. The smell of stale BO mixed with watered-down disinfectant assaulted the nostrils. The sound of metal crashing into metal echoed around the room. People were giving silent nods to each other with their headphones on or earbuds in.

Thorn and Lock wanted to bench press. Throwing their gym bags into cubbies that lined the weight room, they laid claim to the only bench available in the room.

That's when Thorn saw her.

Olivia Golanzo was conversing with cheerleaders on the treadmills. She was wearing a crop top, leggings, and running shoes. Her hair was a sandy-blond color cut in an under fade, her bob pulled back into a small ponytail. From what Thorn remembered, she was in either the Zetas, the Taus, or the Sigmas, but he couldn't remember which society she belonged to.

Lock followed his eyes and he let out a gasp. "Dude! She's smokin'!"

Thorn sighed in annoyance. "Don't ogle at the gym, bro. You don't want to come across as pervy. Hit the bench."

Lock lay back on the bench. His tank top showed tattoos, chest hair, and some sweat that was beginning to form. His black sweatpants were crisp, despite living in a condemnable building with Thorn. He set the plates to three hundred and started his bench press.

Thorn kept his head on a swivel as the pair continued their workout.

———— ♦ ————

About an hour later, both boys emerged from the gym to see that sunlight had drenched the pines of the Gristholme campus. Students were milling about at this point, carrying stuffed backpacks and satchels to their classes. Lock checked his watch and held his hand out for a handshake and a half-hug, the bro way.

Thorn sized up Lock and obliged. The pair laughed as Thorn shouldered his pack.

"We'll see ya after my 9:30!" Lock called as he made his way to class.

"You got it, bub!" Thorn called back.

Thorn doubled back toward Pearson to grab breakfast before his longest day of classes. He decided to take the Boardwalk headed north then hang a right down a path that led to the large wooden doors of the DFAC. He pulled out his student ID and scanned himself into the building.

Thorn stopped, shaking his head in annoyance. His thoughts strayed to Cadi and how he had forgotten to ask for her phone number.

From this main entryway, one could ascend the stairs to a few classrooms and WGSO radio hosted by Dylan Derringer. Dylan played 24/7, which didn't make any sense to Lock, considering that he'd have to pull all-nighters and be on the air through sleep cycles, but stranger things had happened.

Thorn smelled the scent of waffles drifting to him through the entryway, which brought his attention back to breakfast. This entryway had another staircase that led to more dining below, with glass ceilings that cast natural light inside. Various posters about proper nutrition and student productions lined the walls.

He intrinsically followed the smell of the waffles and smiled to himself as he scanned his student ID to get his meal for the day.

The cafeteria was modern, with large ovens for cafeteria workers to cook for the students of Gristholme. Café workers milled about, rushing here and there to keep up with the ravenous students. Various assortments of cereal, oats, and fresh fruits were laid out for all to see, as well as sausage, pancakes, waffles, and various types of coffee and tea. A central bar rotated these items in and out to create a postmodern buffet-style experience. Thorn snagged a coffee and a tray, picking up a lot of fresh fruit and waffles from the main bar. He said hey to a couple of football players and grabbed plates without looking.

He made his way to a bench in the main dining hall.

Adjacent to the kitchen and buffet, the DFAC opened into a hall that would rival any in Asgard. Long tables divided by school year held the students of Gristholme. Lock didn't really adhere to these standards, because he didn't care much, and picked a table near some third-year girls.

They eyed him with annoyance and immediately got up to leave.

Thorn shrugged and began to chow down. It took him longer than he would have liked to realize that he was eating blood pudding. At first, he thought it was just a joke with food coloring, until he saw the blood clot.

"Fuck me, man." He dropped his spoon and went back to get some more food.

———— ♦ ————

He finished his breakfast about fifteen minutes later and looked up to see Olivia tucked into a corner with some of her friends. He watched her for a second or two, considering making an advance. He checked his phone and jolted as he realized how late he was about to be.

He grabbed his rucksack and fast-walked to the exit.

South campus was something of an enigma. It was smaller than the north side of campus but held more buildings. Two large halls, McKinley and Watson, housed everything from the social arts to hard sciences. The two buildings mirrored each other on campus, tucked between the library and the DFAC. Each building was three floors high, with multiple access-card entrances on either side of the building. As Thorn's luck would have it, his literature class was in McKinley, which was the closest to Pearson DFAC.

He eyed his phone again as he scanned into the building.

Various bulletin boards with accoutrements heralding cross-country and international semester-break trips and campus extracurriculars lined the walls on either side. Thorn put his hand on the railing and took the steps two at a time. He was heading to the third floor.

He jogged down the hall to his classroom and opened the door.

Professor Calgary looked up at him with annoyance. "Just in time, Mr. Gisalt. Take your seat, please." He was a five-foot-ten man wearing horn-rimmed spectacles, with a hawkish face and sleeked, combed-over hair. A neutral-colored cardigan draped his spindly frame, almost concealing the trousers that matched.

"My apologies, professor." The class giggled and spoke in hushed whispers.

"Be quiet!" Calgary mean-eyed the throng of students. They immediately silenced themselves. "This isn't a time for locker-room gossip. This is a time to study the *great* poet, Edgar Allen Poe…"

Thorn saw an empty desk in the back of the classroom and beelined for it. He lifted his rucksack around the students, making sure he didn't crack someone in the head. The classroom was organized in neat columns with thirty desk chairs. Windows lined the room, showcasing students walking on the Boardwalk or playing a game when they should be studying. Since Literature 101 was one of the few general education classes everyone on the campus needed to take, it was always full.

He slumped into his seat, taking out his book on dark romantic-era literature, and tried to stay awake.

"This is, of course, *after* Poe went to…" Calgary droned on.

Thorn took his phone out of his pocket to put it on silent when he noticed a text message: *Step outside.*

Thorn looked up to the classroom door and saw Olivia's face in the window.

He scanned the classroom, wondering how in the hell the students didn't see her whole face staring in at them.

They didn't.

Thorn had half a mind to ignore it when he did a double take.

Olivia's mouth was contorting into a vicious, mocking grin. Teeth pointed into sharp pricks of bone, with the edges of her mouth peeling back toward her ears. Her eyes changed from warm brown to savagely necrotic, with ichor rushing out of her ears, nose, and mouth.

Calgary seemed to not notice whatsoever, nor did the class.

It's gotta be the water, Thorn thought to himself.

"And once Mr. Poe drafted 'The Raven,' well, the rest they say…"

Thorn shot up and made his way to the front of the class.

"MR. GISALT!" Calgary shouted.

"Urgent. Bathroom." Thorn doubled over, feeling the heat of shame cross his face. The class rightly broke out in laughter.

"SILENCE!" Calgary hissed. "I will not be affronted by you, Mr. Gisalt. Take your things and leave at once."

Thorn glanced at the door, seeing Olivia licking the glass and tapping.

Thorn rushed back to his seat, grabbed his rucksack and notebook, and ran to the door.

He threw it open wildly, ready to grab the entity by the throat and start the fight.

The hall was empty.

Not a single sign of a Nexian entity in the entire hallway. There was only calm, as the morning block of classes were all safely in their rooms.

Thorn heaved a sigh of annoyance and made his way to the west exit of the building.

He stepped out into the brisk fall morning with his rucksack shouldered. He pulled out his phone and sent a text to Lock. A few seconds went by, and Lock responded: *Fucking-A dude! That's crazy!*

Thorn sent back instructions to Lock. He decided he was going to see a witch about a brew.

He looked over to Watson Hall before turning back north toward the Moon's Loft. He passed students on their way to classes on the Boardwalk. Each student echoed their companion or their phone, laughter and quiet contemplation clashing for supremacy. Thorn hit Route 13 and crossed the street to the coffee shop.

Fernado looked up and smiled. The shop was empty save for himself and Thorn.

"Gizz! What brings you in today, mi amor?"

"Don't call me Gizz," Thorn huffed. "That's like seven years of bullying I want to repress. Is Lucia in?"

Ferdi looked around and up at the ceiling in contemplation. "I think she's at her Monday-Wednesday-Friday class? I can call her if you want me to."

"Nah, it's okay, Ferdi." Thorn looked around the Loft. "I'll just take a Cold Witch's Brew, if that's okay!"

The ghost nodded while Thorn scanned his student ID to pay for the java. As Ferdi got to work, Thorn couldn't help but feel unease at the perversion of Olivia's visage. *That had to have been her, right?* He was grateful no one else saw the monster, which told him that everyone was still drinking the water.

He leaned up against the wall and looked outside, studying the scene. *This Artificers shit is a lot to deal with*, he mused. It wasn't like before when they would go on missions to Billings to keep a rogue vampire or Nexian entity in check. This seemed more present, more threatening, and it was in their backyard.

Ferdi slid the coffee across the counter to Thorn and smiled, saying, "Thank you, boo. Have a good day!"

Thorn grabbed the coffee and looked up. Ferdi had disappeared on the spot.

"Off to see the boyfriend, I guess." He sipped the cold coffee and exited the shop.

Checking his phone, Thorn noticed a text from Lock, saying that they'd catch up for dinner as Lock needed to take care of a paper before his next class.

Thorn decided to spend the rest of his day walking around campus, taking in the autumnal season and the smell of the dense pines. He wound up back at Beta House a few hours before he and Lock were supposed to get dinner.

———— ◆ ————

The pair made their way to Pearson for the evening meal. With rucksacks shouldered, they kept an eye out for anything out of the ordinary. Lucia was behind the bar as they passed the Moon's Loft on the Boardwalk.

She waved, as did Ferdi.

"Isn't it weird that he's a dead-ass ghost but his boyfriend's not?" Lock said aimlessly.

"I just wonder how the sex life works," Thorn said. "It's not my business though. They're happy, right?"

"Yeah, man," Lock said. "So, Resin wants us to look out for suspicious people?"

"Yeah. I don't know how he wants us to keep an eye out for people when the only thing we can go off of is the fact that there are these Grimfaern somewhere on campus." The pair scanned their school IDs to get into the dining building and then scanned their cards once more for their evening meal swipe.

In the atrium, a large statue of a goose taking flight ascended over the students.

"I hate our mascot," Thorn deadpanned.

"It could be worse," Lock said.

Thorn's laugh boomed into the echoing hall.

Several students jumped and swore as their food hit the floor.

"Sorry!" Thorn called out. The pair walked into the buffet area and grabbed some vittles for their evening meal.

They made their way to the third-year's table and grabbed a seat. They tucked into their food as a pair of cheerleaders walked by.

Thorn and Lock looked sideways as the voice called to them.

"Hi, boys," the voice penetrated through the chatter. Olivia placed her hands on the table and leaned in. "I'm glad to see you."

"What do you want, Olivia?" Lock said brusquely. Thorn was on guard, considering his run-in with her earlier.

"Don't be so *mean*, Locky boy," Olivia chided. "I come on simple terms."

"Terms?" Thorn scoffed. "Who said we were in a talking mood?"

Olivia leaned back and crossed her arms; her hair concealed her face from the sides. "Listen. I need you Beta fucks to pay attention, okay? There's a meeting for all Greek-life houses and societies tonight. We need you two to show up, considering you're the only ones in Beta House."

"We've never gone to something like this before," Lock started.

"Or been invited," Thorn finished. "What's it about?"

Olivia smiled. "We're doing another mixer this year. With everybody. Also, I don't know why you're even still a frat. Your numbers are too low."

Thorn spoke through clenched teeth, "We *had* three last year, before you convinced Brent to go to Sigma Beta."

"He didn't *like* you fucks, anyways." Olivia rolled her eyes. "So yeah, show up tonight per student council and ResLife."

"Where? You haven't given us a fucking location, dipshit." Lock said.

"Nightshade." Olivia said matter-of-factly.

Thorn and Lock exchanged looks. The Champion of Loki spoke: "Seems a little off the grid for a Greek-life meeting."

Olivia scoffed and walked away. She called over her shoulder, curtly, "See you there, *bitches*."

The boys both sat in silence for the remainder of their meal. Thorn wondered what Resin would say, while Lock thought about why Olivia was so hot.

———— ◆ ————

The boys finished their dinner and began to head back to Beta House when Lauren caught Thorn's arm.

"Hey!" She smiled up at Thorn. "Do you by chance wanna get dinner at Suzy's sometime this week?"

"Um…" Thorn stalled, nervous by his ex's excitement to see him. "Sure? Why so?"

"Cuz I miss you." She smiled up at him, a hand on his arm.

"I miss you too."

Lauren touched his red beard. "It's getting a little long. It looks good!"

"Thanks, sunshine," Thorn said as he reached up and ran a hand through his facial hair.

"No problem!" Lauren tucked her hair behind her ear. "I need to go talk to Lucia before class, but I wanted to tell you Darius's training is going well."

Thorn nodded. "Any idea what his powers are yet?"

Lauren shook her head and looked at the ground. "He's…getting there. We think it has something to do with his mom, but nothing's manifested yet."

He stole a glance as she looked down. Her form fitted the dress she was wearing perfectly. The way that he remembered her during their time together was just as she looked here. Sadly, however, they were on opposite sides of the path. They had called things off for good, or so he thought. She was also heading toward the dining facility while he was headed back to Beta House.

He longed for her with a sharp pang in his chest.

Lauren looked up and smiled again.

"I'm sure I'll see you later." Lauren put her finger on Thorn's chest, tapped it lovingly, and turned toward the DFAC. She felt his gaze follow her as she walked away.

Thorn shook his head and quietly screamed to the sky.

She was too good for his own good.

Lock had politely removed himself from the star-crossed lovers out of respect when he felt a buzz in his pocket. He pull out his phone to see who texted him.

As he checked his messages, he saw one from Resin with a time stamp of two hours prior.

Hall of Ancients, tomorrow, 1930. Matters to discuss. Be on high alert for the next few days.

"Fuck," Lock said. When he looked around, he noticed Thorn walking toward him.

"Miss her yet?" He asked Thorn, a grin breaking across his face.

"Shut up," Thorn replied, lost in his thoughts. "Anyways, we've got to deal with this society meeting tonight. Let's head back to Beta."

The pair made their way up the path back to their frat house.

At Beta House, Lock dropped his rucksack and went to the fridge for a drink while Thorn jogged up the stairs.

Lock lingered in the fridge for a second, scoping out any snacks, gagging at the old, rotten food they had neglected inside.

Lock closed the fridge as Thorn came down the stairs in a pair of basketball shorts and a cutoff shirt.

"Thorn," Lock said. "This is probably going to be a rather formal event."

"Fuck 'em," Thorn said, as he grabbed a bag of crisps and his sunglasses. "Let's go, baby boy."

————— ◆ —————

Later that day, the pair made their way to Nightshade Hall in the fading light. They meandered through the woods, hoping to not attract any attention. The windy night around them sent leaves flying down from their trees. Lock shouldered his rucksack and looked over at Thorn.

"Are you sure you want me to bring this? It's really heavy, and I'm not sure this is what you think it is."

"We need it," Thorn said.

"Okay, man," Lock hefted the rucksack higher onto his back.

The Betas got to the door and stopped. Thorn looked between the doorknob and Lock. "You gonna get that, man?"

"Seriously, Thorn?!" Lock wailed. "I've got this rucksack filled with fucking—"

Thorn put a hand to Lock's mouth. "Fine. We'll take the 'cookies' inside, and I'll get the door." He reached out and turned the knob. It turned slowly with the resistance of age. Thorn put a shoulder into the door and crossed the threshold.

Walking into an empty room was the first trigger. The second was the string Thorn accidentally pulled with his foot, sending the crossbow bolt infused with silver flying into the air.

Thorn wailed as the arrow burned his muscles and skin. He yanked it out of his shoulder and felt the blood squirt into the night.

"LOCK, NOW!"

Thorn fell out of the way as Lock heaved the rucksack into the center of the room. He barely avoided another loose bolt that soared through the air.

"Come out, Olivia!" Lock called into the hall. The voice's echo dissipated through the structure. A minute passed. Two minutes. Five minutes. Nothing came and no sign of Olivia anywhere.

Thorn called out to the girl once more. No words came back. Lock nodded to Thorn and then motioned to the scuttling noise that came from the upper balcony.

It scuttled for a few seconds and then stopped. A large sniff echoed into the room, followed by more scuttling.

Lock and Thorn slowly crept to a side room and waited. The high ceilings of Nightshade Hall were topped with skylights for the greenhouse-turned-classroom. A simple staircase led to the second floor.

Lock looked back to make sure nothing would sneak up on them through the rear door. Thorn watched carefully as he saw a white hand appear at the top of the staircase.

What he saw next looked uncannily like the previous entity he and Lock had stuffed in the trash can at the chapel.

A Grimfaern, breathing and crawling on all fours like a feral animal, patrolled down the stairs. It sniffed the air and noticed the rucksack in the center of the floor. It cocked its head, with strands of hair falling into its face. The vigilant eyes focused on the pair of intruders.

Thorn motioned for Lock without taking his eyes off the creature. That was when he saw the Grimfaern's physique shift.

Its bones crackled and shifted as it transformed from a spindly under-ling to a feminine figure with long slender legs and full bust. It slowly made its way to the rucksack. Thorn's mouth dropped open as Lock ogled at the naked form of a woman sitting on his rucksack.

"Come play, you annoying fucks," Olivia called out.

Thorn pulled out his sickle, sending a bolt of energy into the newly formed Olivia. Lock followed suit, casting a yellow column of energy, trapping Olivia against the far wall. The yellow column rendered itself into chains that bound themselves to the walls, holding their target a few inches off the ground.

She struggled against the chains. "LET ME GO! LET ME GO, YOU SICK BASTARDS!"

Thorn and Lock made their way to the center of the room and tuned out the cursing woman. It was then that they heard the tumblers in the bookshelf shift. The pair looked up and saw the shelf slowly swinging forward.

The Smiling Man appeared and looked up at them with blood streaking out of its gums. Its teeth looked cracked from the constant strain of the smile.

"Hello boys. It looks like you've tied up my girl."

Both boys' mouths fell open in surprise.

The Smiling Man sat back on its hind legs and cocked its head. "You're about to be *fucked*." He laughed as the bookshelf flew open.

Grimfaern of all shapes and sizes came spilling out of the entryway.

They ran in all directions to surround Thorn and Lock.

Thorn looked back over his shoulder, grabbing Lock, who was gawking at the monsters. Thorn headed for the front door.

Lock crossed the threshold and regained himself with just enough time to slam the door shut with Thorn's assistance.

Grimfaern slammed into the door. The wood began to splinter around the edges of the door. Shards of wood sent pain up their arms as they struggled to keep the main door closed.

Thorn and Lock strained for a moment. Hideous screeches broke through the thick wood.

Finally, Thorn had had enough. He shot Lock a glance before he made his decision.

"GO!" Thorn called out. They both took off for the woods as the moon began its watch over the sleeping college. Their only goal at this point was to get to safety at the Hall of Ancients.

The Artificers

DARIUS WALKED INTO THE Hall of Ancients feeling depleted as hell. Between meetings, late-night trainings, classes, and secret rendezvous, he was having a difficult time maintaining appearances since he became an Artificer a few weeks ago. This meeting Resin had called was scheduled for 7:30 p.m., and all he wanted was to get some extra sleep.

Gods, I hope this isn't longer than an hour. Darius sighed.

Lauren had her usual spot, with her feet kicked up on the chair adjacent to her. She twirled her hair while she intently stared at Thorn with a huge smile.

Thorn was staring at the table, lost in thought.

Lock whistled in the kitchen to himself as Darius walked in.

"Hey there, bud! Got some vittles for ya." Lock raised up a skillet of eggs.

"Thanks, man," Darius said bluntly.

"No probs, hombre." Lock continued to cook and carry his tune.

Darius descended the stairs as Lucia walked out of an adjacent room. Her face was concealed by her hair, but Darius noticed something had changed about her. He couldn't put his finger on it, but she seemed tired herself.

"Hey Luce," Darius started, feeling like he was walking on thin ice for using a nickname.

She looked up and said weakly with a smile, "Hi, buddy."

"You okay, witchy girl?" Darius smiled a little. He felt weird that he was only hanging out with Lauren for training purposes. *Just trying to fit in here,* he thought.

Lucia returned the smile weakly as Resin walked into the room.

"Good evening, everyone." Resin nodded to all. "I'd like to begin tonight's meeting with a concerning topic. Thorn, Lock, and I have been attacked by Grimfaern, with myself being attacked twice. Lauren and Darius, I know you haven't come in contact yet, but they're essentially changelings. We think that there's a likely chance someone is controlling them, but we're not sure who.

"I originally thought, when I was attacked, that mine was the only one," Resin continued. "However, Thorn and Lock have reported many of them in Nightshade Hall, where they barely escaped.

"The one that attacked me is called the Smiling Man. It was last seen by Thorn and Lock inside of Nightshade. It came out of the basement with a swarm of them descending upon our friends. Lucia and I have discussed what this could mean, or if it was an illusion." Lucia nodded, looking at the table. "We think it's highly likely that these were real, and that they're camped inside Nightshade Hall."

Lucia looked up and began to speak. "Resin's plan is to keep gathering intel on these things and maybe make some kind of assault once winter break hits." She shook her head. "I disagree. I think we need to strike them now. Fast and hard to the point that they go away forever. Resin was assaulted by this Smiling Man, doing some rough damage to him. If they get to the students…" Lucia grimaced. "It's going to be a rough ass time for everyone."

At least for you lot, Lucia thought to herself.

Lauren sat up in her chair and looked down the table at Resin. "We're just gonna sit here and wait while we know where they are? Let's smoke them out and fight them."

"That's not how this works, Lauren," Resin said. "This Smiling Man can come back and attack us the minute we turn our backs. Recon and intel are still ways of being vigilant. If they attack a student, we move."

Lauren's chest rose and fell in annoyance. "I getcha." She sat back down and crossed her arms.

Thorn stole a glance and smiled to himself. Lauren looked beautiful tonight. He debated about making a move again.

"Does anyone have anything for the good of the team?" Resin looked from member to member.

"Yeah. I got something." All eyes turned to Darius, who stared into the table. "How fucking *dare* you, Resin. The lot of you."

Resin looked at the rest of his squad and returned the look back to Darius. "Come again?"

"You're just gonna brush these students off? You're gonna let them sit there, helpless students, and get picked off slowly to the point where questions will be raised?"

Resin moved over and sat next to Darius. His face held genuine concern.

"Well, Darius, you see, we kinda protect them with our powers. It's our role to make sure nothing happens to the populace here at Gristholme and the world abroad. Sometime back when Lucia's family and the Norse first arrived in these parts, there was a moment when they knew the land was inhabited by something bigger than what they had known in the past. The gods had touched this place, they believed, but we all recognize that as the Nexus. It was a marker for the events of humankind to unfold, as far as we can tell. If there was no Gristholme, there would have been no Plymouth expedition. No westward expansion. No British invasion. No anything. It was here that they set the markers for the beginning of destiny.

People have fought against these kinds of monsters for centuries. Some are more vocal about it, but around the time our parents came to school here was when they took a vow of silence about the whole matter. They fought the demons and ghosts that walked through this plane of existence. My dad specifically was a champion of Fenris Wolf, the one who brings Ragnarök—the end times." Resin looked up sadly, sighing. "This was supposed to happen in the eighties if not for the events that unfolded.

My dad, Thorn's dad, and Lock's dad, along with Lucia's grandma, attacked an underground group on campus that was supposed to bring the fighting to an end. The underground group called themselves the Variant.

"My dad told me just how terrifying they were. They would string the kids alive up in the trees, deep in the woods where no one could find them. They'd relish the screams and tears of these students to the point where the pain would drive the barely living souls to insanity. It was then that they would kill them.

"No funerals were had for these students. No one cared. At least, that's what they thought anyway. The Variant were crafting a summons to invoke monsters of the Nexus to come on through. We thought it wouldn't matter, or that there would be more time between the next attacks. My dad and I were wrong, so it seems." Resin rubbed the palms of his hands against his eyes, revealing how tired he was to the rest of the group. "How fucking dare us, Darius? How fucking dare *you* for assuming that we don't give a shit about people dying left and right."

For fuck's sake. Lucia bit her bottom lip to refrain from laughing out loud. *I don't give a damn if they die. He's being a little* too *theatrical.*

The room sat with an awkward air. No one spoke.

"Resin," Lauren spoke, "your team just wants a direct action or order to combat the encroaching darkness."

The rest of the group uttered their agreement.

I feel fucking cornered, Resin thought. *Why can't they just accept waiting? We can't go charging into this thing without knowing who we're fighting, even with our minimal contact.*

"So, what's your great plan?" Darius said, undertones of anger coming through.

Resin caught it and sighed.

"We have to wait." Resin said. "You need to be Sundered, Darius. We need all the power we can get if we're going to fight these things. We need to at least wait until you're Sundered."

"Let's do it now, then," Darius said adamantly. "Right here, right now. We can then take this to them and fight."

"Darius, I appreciate your initiative, but it takes time for me to gather all the components and get rest. It drains me. I basically open y'all up to the Nexus and close you back up, like liquid in a jar, but it takes a lot out of me."

Darius huffed. "Time. Time. TIME! These kids don't have that, from what you're saying." He pointed toward south campus. "Y'all are supposed to defend humans? Give me a break! You can't even decide on what to do next!"

Resin clenched his fist, resisting the urge to fight the newcomer. "Darius, I get why you're angry, okay? We have these powers, we're concealed, but who is going to save the humans if we're dead? Thorn and Lock said that Olivia Golanzo is compromised. They're already a step ahead of us. Would you, in your infinite wisdom, recommend diving headlong into a crock of shit and fuckery without planning or making sure your team is good to go and that casualties will be at a minimum?"

Darius was shaking from frustration. *Fuck you, Resin. You didn't have to humiliate me.* "No," Darius responded, reserved. "I guess not."

"Then mind your tongue." Resin unclenched his fist and scanned the room. "Anyone else have anything for the good of the group?"

Lucia looked annoyed at the whole conversation. Lauren looked indifferent, even bored. Lock looked worried, with his dark-black hair a mess. Thorn was looking at Darius but met Resin's gaze with the confirmation of a soldier trusting his senior leader. Resin looked at Darius, who met his gaze as well.

Resin swore he saw a flame in Darius's eyes.

"Resin, I've got something."

Resin turned to Lauren, worry crossing his face. "By all means, Lauren, the floor is yours."

Lauren put her elbows on the table and feet on the floor. "Thanks, Resin. I think we're all a little concerned about the hesitation on our group's part. If they're as serious as it sounds, why aren't we stalking Olivia? Why aren't we trapping her and ending this thing, here and now? Why aren't you gung ho about our strength and tactics? It feels like you don't have faith in us." Thorn and Lock nodded in agreement. "We need your faith if this is as dangerous as you're saying it is."

Clever, Lucia thought smugly. *Tell the wolf how you all really feel. Watch him squirm and feel incompetent.*

"Well, I'm sorry if I made any of y'all feel like I don't believe in you," Resin said, looking to each member once more. "I wouldn't have you in this room if I didn't trust you."

Well, that's awkward. Lucia played with a pen that was on the table.

"In fact," Resin continued, "I wouldn't have you in this room if I wasn't willing to die for y'all in the line of combat. That's why I care about this and want us to take our time. One bumble-fuck and we've pissed away the secrecy we cherish so much. Yeah, they can't see us because of the water when we are using Nexian magic, but that's what makes this situation so dangerous: They could change into something or someone. Whoever is controlling them is *here,* somewhere.

"How would you feel if you were a non-Nexian studying for finals and a magic user came into your room and tried to bash your room-mate's skull in? Your roommate sees you disappear into thin air to fight this intruder because the water masks you when you're using magic. The intruder *also* disappears because the intruder is also a Nexian magic user. Now your roommate is questioning their sanity as the now-vanished entity severs the roommate's head. Said roommate then falls to the floor, head gone, blood squirting everywhere, dead. Scenarios like this are avoided by taking extreme caution. Who knows whether our pressure wouldn't cause our enemy to retaliate by causing an uptick in student deaths?

"Not to mention, you *all* have recognizable faces. Even if you were to disappear to fight the Grimfaern, you don't think that the poor bastard who saw you disappear from the spot wouldn't rush out of their dorm, fly through the night to Campus Safety, and tell them all of this? They wouldn't grab a drink of water on the way out and forget about it, would they? That's a pretty big risk to take."

Resin, exhausted, got up and looked at Lauren. "I've thought a lot about this, which is why I believe the best bet is to wait until winter. I really appreciate your concern, all of you. It means a lot that you care this deeply. I don't like it either, Lauren. I do want to be proactive and keep Grimfaern from using harmful Nexian energy on the population. I don't think this is just an isolated incident. I think this is part of something bigger."

Eh, close enough, thought Lucia. *You got the larger points. Sad to think that you'll still be blindsided by Gredalia.*

"Luce, you got anything?" Resin's hesitation came through his voice.

"Not really, no. I think that waiting until winter is a good plan. It's as good as any right now unless someone else has a better idea?" Lucia gestured to the room. When she saw no one wanted to speak up, she sighed contentedly. "I think that about sums up my thoughts about the issue. Also, just keep an extra eye out for Olivia. We don't want to stalk her. That would spook her and alert her to our situation, if the Smiling Man hasn't told her already." *Olivia would kill me if I told them that,* Lucia thought. *However, I have to keep up appearances here.*

Resin nodded. "Next steps, keep training Darius, keep a lookout for unusual activity, and monitor Olivia from a distance. Darius, what do you think about Sundering? Are you okay with it?"

"I think I wanna do this," Darius said after a few moments of silence. "At least try to complete it anyway. Are there any major limitations to this power? Is there an infinite pool to draw from, you know, to use these powers?"

The room went silent.

Lauren was the next to speak. "It kinda depends on how strong your powers are. How they build over time can affect the stamina you have to cast, shift, or use your spells. Given a dangerous enough situation, even

Lucia could be worn out. Her body could essentially collapse and die. We took such a huge interest in you because your powers are strong, and you haven't had them as long as all of us. *That's* something worth noting. We're concerned your Sundering will be something that will ruin you if we don't taken the correct steps. That being said, we have the best spellcaster in the world, Lucia Frey. If she thinks that you're ready, then I say you're ready. I'm sure everyone else wouldn't be too far off."

Lucia piped up from her spot across from Lock. "I agree, but only if you're ready."

"I am," Darius said with finality. "I want to be of some help, more than I already am."

Resin nodded; a smile crossed his face. "Okay then. Lucia, you and Darius line up a time where you can complete the Sundering. Everyone else, keep vigilant. Sound good? I'll reach out with our next meeting time. See you soon!"

The murmurs throughout the group were met with random notes of nervous laughter, from what Resin could tell, due to the intense exchange between himself and Darius.

Darius was halfway to the door when Resin called out to him.

"Darius," Resin said.

Darius turned on his heels. "Yeah, boss?"

Still seems to be a little guarded, Resin noted. "Darius, I'm sorry for the way I spoke to you tonight. I care a lot about someone new coming on, and I don't want you to think I don't care about what we do here or how our actions effect the students."

"It just seems odd, you know?" Darius was keeping his emotions in check. "There's all this talk, planning, whatever, and no follow-through."

"Be careful what you wish for, friend." Resin sighed worriedly. "Danger comes when you least expect it."

Darius nodded in agreement with pursed lips. "Yeah. See you once I'm Sundered, Resin."

"See ya."

Darius continued his path to the door.

Resin waited for Darius to leave.

He looked through the windows, making sure no one was lingering, and went to an unmarked door on the other side of the room.

He whispered an old word in Nexian, stepping inside.

He descended the stairs to an old room. It was such an old room that it held something that few had ever witnessed, including Lucia. She didn't know the word to get in, and thanks to Resin's diligence, she never would.

This was a cabinet of curiosities. The whole building was made into one from around the time that his dad came to school here. The building hid and housed various rooms that extended into deep caverns or housed weapons. One particular section housed an infinite cupboard and pantry that kept the house well-stocked with vittles. His dad gave him special instructions on how to take care of its denizen. The denizen gave life to the building, keeping its magic up as an anchor for the Nexian energy. Should the denizen fail, the Hall of Ancients would absorb into itself and disappear forever.

He rounded the corner and smiled as the light hit his face. Nestled into the ancient mortar of the basement, resilient as ever, was the World Tree.

Resin pulled out sage and a lighter from his pocket. Igniting the plant, he set it into a bowl on a table next to him.

Next, he pulled a bottle of liquor from his pocket and poured it into the bowl. Following that, using a knife on the table, he cut his hand. He dripped the blood into the bowl as well.

Setting the bowl in front of the World Tree, he got down on his knees. He looked up into the tree and put his bloodied hand upon it. The handprint dissipated into the flesh of the tree.

As this happened, Resin heard it reach out to his mind in a deep, primeval voice.

"Son of Fenris Wolf, Seeker of Knowledge, Wolf-Walker, Denizen of the World Tree, what is the purpose of your visit today?"

"I need to know about the Grimfaern, Your Idyllic Grace," Resin said, head bowed.

The tree's leaves rustled, despite the lack of wind in the place. "Ah yes, *Grimaulnus Faernus. Goothruk,* in Nexian." The World Tree sighed, and the leaves rustled more. "A descendant of the Grimfrost, a descendant of the Frost Giants, these offspring are the only thing that could transcend the original Ragnarök into this plane of existence." The tree's voice echoed in the wolf's mind. "I remember once that they tried to cut me down." It smiled through its words. "Your father stopped them just in time."

Resin's eyes were forced to look down at the base of the tree in reverence.

"Nasty things, these Grimfaern. Who brought them here?"

"I do not know, Your Wise Grace," Resin said softly. "I'm worried that they're going to do something heinous against the population here on this campus."

"Why does this strike you so?" it said calmly.

"Your Grace, it feels this way because they're attacking *us.* One called the Smiling Man is leading them."

This caught the tree's attention. Resin saw in his mind various visions of what appeared to be a man, similar looking to Lock. In the vision, the man used arcane energy to slowly create an entity that appeared to be the Smiling Man. The man left, while the Smiling Man awoke and walked the planes of existence. The tree heaved and the vision faded.

"Young Kirkbride," it panged. "Such visions are growing fewer and fewer."

"I know, Dear Tree," Resin said.

"One of your Order must do the Sundering. It's the only way I can continue to survive."

"I know, Dear Tree." Resin sighed. "I believe that we've found someone."

"Can you rely on them?"

"Soon," Resin said.

The Artificers

LUCIA RAISED HER GLASS as Semisonic's "Closing Time" came on over the speakers. Looking up through her drunken haze, she saw a man with an open-collared shirt grab the microphone and instruct everyone about cleaning up and leaving.

She saw in the mill of the crowd Thorn, who was dancing with Lauren. Lock was trying to win over some girl from the Zetas, with little to no luck at all. The girl was as interested in him as a child was in getting medical shots: not at all, and the result was painful. Darius looked over from his conversation with a man from Delta Kappa who wore blue jeans and a DK shirt. When Darius noticed Lucia looking at him, the Delt touched Darius's arm affectionately before leaving the party.

A collective groan rang out through the crowd as the students of Gristholme ended their Friday-night booze fest at Alpha Society. Lucia was amazed that Alpha Society and the OmiTaus were the only major fraternities to intermingle with the rest of the student population.

Back when the college was first formed, Lucia's grandmother Althea proposed that the Nexian users intermingle with the student population. The biggest concern, argued the Nexians, was being *seen*. This manifested in different ways. For Nexians like Resin, their human visage would change into a true Nexian form when their powers were activated. Other Nexians who were permanently in their Nexian form needed to engage in a ritual by Maester Althea, who would shroud their Nexian form so that they would appear human. It was like a mirror reflecting back a human visage to other humans, except behind the mirror was an otherworldly entity.

Lucia didn't quite understand the physics of it herself. Every time she asked her grandmother about it, Althea would attribute it to being a Nexian wonder.

"I can't tell you exactly how I knew what to do," Althea told her granddaughter. "I just kind of *willed* it to be, and the tainted water would allow Nexians to move around the campus. It *should* hide them, since Nexian magic is being performed, but I guess I slipped a little clause in there somewhere." She winked at Lucia. "That being said, don't muck up my Nexian spell. The wording must be said *exactly* to protect both sides of this equation, okay?"

Lucia had agreed, still concerned that her grandma didn't elaborate more and left it to just *magic being magic*. Even though she was a witch, Lucia learned to suspend disbelief where it was warranted.

There were several Nexian Greek houses that still existed among the student population. Those houses were Omicron Tau vampires (shortened to OmiTaus), Zeta Tau sirens (shortened to Zetas), Delta Kappa Shinigami (shortened to Delts), Beta Deltas (shortened to Betas, consisting of Thorn and Lock and formerly Brent before he dropped out of Greek life), and Alpha Society (shortened to Alpha), who were a hodge-podge of Nexians that Lucia couldn't keep track of.

What this implant was for, she still wasn't entirely sure. Lucia attempted to remove it once, but it caused her vision to go blurry, as if the implant had attached to the very cellular fiber of her being. She was convinced that Rob would have some genuine solution once she finished her servitude. He seemed to have experienced something similar in the past, which he kept closely guarded to his chest, to keep Lucia nearby. She thought she caught Rob saying the word *aliens* to describe them, but she wasn't sure if this was a thing or his way of rationalizing it. From her interactions with them, they seemed more like dryads or sylvans in demeanor than beings who wanted to invade your planet from their saucer.

The Alphas and OmiTaus frequently hosted parties with a select guest list. The Alphas wanted to showcase their oddity in its full glory, which attracted various artsy and hipster types. The OmiTaus were a little more nefarious in their doings, however. Several events happened where Resin and Lucia had to pull students out of the OmiTau frat, both alive and dead. Certain sections of the campus (be it the cliffside and the Great Net or the OmiTau's fraternity house) held a certain sway and pull that compelled humans to do things against their will, should they be caught off guard.

As always, Lucia was *extremely* grateful for her grandmother's water concealment spell.

Lucia wanted to make sure students weren't being held against their will with the Alphas.

She had received her invite for Alpha's "pledge drive," where the society threw a rave in the basement of their house to the south of campus.

She decided to invite the others out, including Darius, to be a safeguard against any fuckery. Going to the place she had been bugged made her *extremely* nervous. Though she'd never admit it to the rest of the Artificers, she wanted them there as an extra set of eyes.

Even a Rendered person is better than nothing, Lucia thought.

Darius made his way over to Lucia with a half-smile on his face.

Lucia shot another glance back at Lock and saw the Zeta slap him across the face so hard that blood shot out of his mouth. She stormed off, her hips swaying in her tight dress as she retired for the night. She opened a door to the upstairs dorms and disappeared into the night.

Darius recoiled in surprise, his half-smile leaving his face.

Lock sat down against the wall, head in his hands.

Thorn, Darius, and Lauren descended upon him.

"ARE YOU OKAY?!" Lauren yelled in a laughing manner right in Lock's ear.

He recoiled before answering, "Yeah. Yeah, I'm good."

Thorn helped him off the ground. "Strike out?"

Lucia made her way over to the Artificers.

"Didn't even get to bat, man." Lock wiped his nose and swore. "She said I wasn't her type."

"And what's her type, then?" Lucia threw her drink into the waste bin, which was piled high with beer cans and a few condom wrappers.

"Anything but me, apparently." Lock mimicked the girl who broke his face and heart.

"Sounds like I'd have a shot then," Lucia said, laughing.

The Alphas were now ushering people out of their space. Several of the pale, silverish, and sylvan members of the Society were directing people toward the exits. Lucia saw several students who did not look of age, who either snuck in or were brought in as pledges for Alpha. These students quickly vacated, hoping to not be seen by Campus Safety.

The Artificers exited into the chilly autumn night. Lauren looked around at the pale exterior of Alpha Society's house and asked the rest of the group, "Do you think that one of the other Nexian Greek houses is having a party?"

They all exchanged glances in nervous anticipation. The night was young, and with everything that was happening, they all deserved a night off to get shit-faced if they chose. As students were milling around the campus, the sounds of drums and bass music was coming from the north side. Thorn and Lock looked up and smiled to themselves.

Lauren nodded at Lucia, who was staring off to the south at the sea. "Do you have to go? We never really get to party together, and it'd be fun to have you along." She smiled at the witch.

Lucia turned back to her friend and took a pause. *How can I party with them while I'm helping their enemy? How long can I keep this up?*

If you don't go with them, she heard in her conscience, *they'll get suspicious and figure it out sooner rather than later.*

"Absolutely!" Lucia smiled back at Lauren.

Darius shot a glance to where Lucia had been looking. He saw a flash of a red jacket disappear into the trees.

I hope they're okay, Darius thought to himself. *I'd hate to see someone pass out or be injured. Might as well go check on 'em.*

"Hey, y'all, I'm going to meet up with you wherever you head to next. Just text me." Darius took off for the tree line, hands in his pockets.

"Oh, uh…okay, man," Lock called after Darius.

"He should be fine," Lauren said. "Probably just trying to help a drunk student."

Lucia smiled a knowing smile.

"Cool. Well, while Darius is off fucking about, I'm gonna call this boy." Lauren giggled.

Thorn's head snapped up with an eyebrow raised. "Boy? Do I need to worry about this boy?"

"Are we together?" Lauren eyed him up and down, phone in hand.

The group's eyes turned onto Thorn.

"I mean…no…"

"Then why you jelly, Thorny boy? We're platonic. Unless you wanna change that, then don't worry about it." Lauren put her phone to her ear.

"Hi? Is this Tevin? Hi! This is Lauren…"

Lucia groaned in annoyance.

"What's up?" Lock said.

"I fucking hate Tevin," Lucia said.

Across the state route, up the Boardwalk, and hidden in the pines was the fraternity house of Omicron Tau. The exterior was neo-Gothic style with gargoyles and grim statues of death and life. One statue was a new mother holding up a barely swaddled baby, while its opposite statue showed the famous scene from *Julius Caesar* of Brutus's betrayal.

Lucia's hesitancy with the Omicron Tau ran deep. OmiTaus were notorious for being flirts and then draining their one-night stands. This was problematic for the Artificers, as they were trying to keep the existence of the Nexian entities under wraps. Pre-Artificers, Lucia and Resin had to fake the deaths of several students to convince some very concerned administrators and parents that their students slipped and fell off the cliffside. The cliffside was among the many "cursed" things at Gristholme talked about by the students. For Lucia and Resin, it served as a cover for tossing the bodies over the side of the cliff. Lucia added in a spell to make it seem like one would be compelled to jump, one night when Resin was working, to supplement the claim that the area was "bugged" with some kind of supernatural factors. From there, the legend took off. Various bullshit "reports" of the Wailing Woman walking the cliffside (mostly furnished by Dylan Derringer at Lucia's behest) served as a warning to those who invaded her space.

Lucia tried to shake off her preconceived notions and enjoy the potential rager that the OmiTaus were throwing.

The group walked through the wrought-iron gates to see a black man with a slender build open his arms welcomingly. He spoke with a southern drawl. Lauren recognized Torique from the lacrosse team. He bore deep scars on his forearms. His muscles were sinewy and taut, showcasing how rough the sport could be.

"Greetings, y'all! Party of four?"

"Yeah, believe so." Lock looked around to see no one else besides the Artificers outside the frat. He looked back to the group and mouthed, "Darius?"

The rest shrugged, not mentioning their newest member's tardiness.

"Most excellent. Please make your way inside. Tevin's abode is your abode."

Thorn whispered to Lock, "That's ominous."

Lucia nudged him in the side, annoyance on her face.

Torique bowed his head slightly, giving the facial expression that spoke, *Don't think I didn't hear you, sir.* "Be well and enjoy the solace of the night."

The group moved forward up the cobblestone path to the OmiTaus' frat house.

The brass bat knockers on the door were very well polished, despite the gaudy Gothic exterior. The doorknobs were adorned with an open mouth, an angry face, and a tongue sticking out. Everyone exchanged looks while Lucia reached for the brass tongue, held it, and turned it.

The door swung open, revealing the sound of the drums and bass music slamming into the walls.

We must have heard someone opening the door when we were down south, Lucia thought.

"Could you imagine if they had made the knocker a penis?"

Everyone turned slowly to look at Lock.

"What?" he said, unashamed. "Like could you?"

"YES WE CAN," Lucia shouted, causing everyone to startle.

"Sorry…Jesus." Lock pushed past everyone and made his way in.

The others followed shortly behind.

Vaulted ceilings with stained glass of various scenes of vampiric "heroism" spanned the entirety of the roof. Some depicted vampires slaughtering their human assailants while others crafted scenes of flagrant debauchery and an abundance of blood. The vibrant moonlight caught the glass and created a makeshift disco-ball effect in the center of the room. The room was spacious, with ancient tables and chairs lining the walls underneath artwork and books from all ages. The artwork that adorned the wall ranged from paintings dating back to somewhere in the fourteenth century to the last few years in what seemed to be a family tree. The far wall of the room had a central staircase that split into left and right stairs and took the frat members to their respective rooms via balconies that stretched half of the room.

One tapestry, hung where a typical religious cross would appear, was of the OmiTau symbology. A chalice with overflowing red liquid was the fraternity's sigil. Underneath was the official school version with *O. T.* for Omicron Tau. An aged chair that looked very much like a throne sat below the banners.

They made their way into the room. Lauren smiled and extended her arms as she approached Tevin Vaynewright. The black man with dreads descended the stairs with a grin on his face.

"Tev!" Lauren squealed as she received a hug from the captain of the football team.

"Lauren, darling." Tevin had a southern drawl as well. "Baby, it's so good to *see* you! It's been almost a semester." Tevin was about six foot two, wearing an open dress shirt revealing a dad bod. The sides of his head were shaved into a bald fade. To Lucia, he exuded a regal presence every time she had the displeasure of meeting him.

As Tevin took Lauren by the arm, Lucia couldn't help but recall the times that Tevin had inadvertently pissed her off. She had more than her fill of cleaning up after these bastards. The first time was when she and Resin had to cover for the OmiTau spring rush (and the blood bath that took place). Then there was the OmiTau fall mixer (literal human-sacrifice blood in the punch bowl of Pearson), the OmiTau–Delta Yule Duel (because who doesn't love a Shinigami/vampire brawl?), and the infamous OmiTau Eternal Ball (more students who "fell off the cliff").

"I remember I was telling Lucia at the Yule Duel that the way she can clean up blood puts even us vampires to shame. We'll get into that later." Tevin motioned for them all to make their way up the stairs.

Keep it cool, Lucia told herself, attempting to stave off her anger. *You don't need to kill anyone tonight.*

They all followed, noticing as they ascended the central stairs that the students who were dancing with the rest of the vampires were *not* vampires. They appeared to be hypnotized by the music.

"You didn't roofie them, did you?" Thorn scowled.

Tevin laughed and slapped Thorn on the arm. "What? No, you sick fuck. They're here of their own volition."

"Kinda childish to play with your food," Lucia deadpanned, discomfort sprawled across her face.

Tevin's face dropped. "Are you here to dance or critique my practices? That's Resin's job, honestly." He nodded to a student from across the room. The student stopped dancing and walked over to Tevin and the Artificers. The student was a young male about five foot ten. He got down on both knees so that he was about waist-high with Tevin. It did not look comfortable to the Artificers, as the man's knees were on the stone stairs. The man's eyes were glassed over, and a smile tugged at the corner of his lips.

"Please, Sire?"

"Look, we're not here to kink-shame you or shut you down, we're here to party." Lauren dragged Tevin away from his dinner. "You owe me one, yes?"

"Yes, I guess I *do*." Tevin looked down at her arm, and his eyes lingered there.

Thorn, who looked miffed by this exchange, emitted an air of haughty annoyance.

"So, why don't you let us party with you, and we'll just mingle without causing too much of a stir. I may even…throw in another favor for you."

Lock coughed audibly and tried to say "ass-kisser" under his breath, hoping it would be drowned out by the music.

Tevin turned and studied Lock for a second before returning to his date. "Why, certainly." His eyes flicked to the visibly flushed Thorn Gisalt. "Now or later, my dear?"

Lauren reached up and whispered something in his ear.

Lucia sighed and looked at Thorn and Lock.

Thorn was still visibly discomforted by the hypnotism of the vampire frat. Lock was looking around, sizing up the room. Lucia did the same.

There were ten vampires in total and six students. Some of the vampires decided to double up, much to Lucia's annoyance. There were three exits: two leading to the dorms of the frat and one to the main front entrance. No one seemed to be sleeping up in the vaulted ceilings.

Lucia wondered how they would 'take the night off' with the OmiTaus. Initially, she didn't think that there would be any problem, because the group had been on edge lately. With Darius's arrival and her own dealings, Lucia was feeling more threadbare with each passing day. She was hoping to have at least one last good time before the world burned down.

I just wish they weren't all so revolting, Lucia frowned, lost in her thoughts. *OmiTaus just don't know when enough is enough.*

She was starting to regret her decision to go out that night.

Suddenly, Lucia saw the door swing open, and Darius stepped into the main hall, his chest rising up and down like he had been in a brawl or completed strenuous exercise.

"Yup," Lucia said aloud, disgust in her voice, "I regret everything."

Lauren had her arms around Tevin's waist and looked back at her friends.

There was a moment of stillness in the air…

…until Darius made his way into the center of the room, shouting at the students who were dancing on the floor.

"Shit," Lock said, with panic sweeping through him.

"WAKE UP!" Darius yelled at the students, who were under the spell of the vampires. "Come on then! You gotta go! Show's over!"

"Um, what the fuck is he doing?" Tevin said, his lack of amusement directed at the Artificers. "THAT'S OUR FUCKING DINNER!"

Tevin kicked his servant in the throat so hard that the vertebrae shot out the back of his neck. The vampire's perfect teeth grew to needle points as he called to the rest of his coven.

"KEEP THE STUDENTS INSIDE! DON'T LET THEM ESCAPE." Tevin turned on the stairs to meet Thorn's boot square in the chest.

Tevin tumbled ass over elbow down the stairs, colliding into the dead body of the student at the base of the stairs.

Darius tried to corral the zombified students toward the front door.

Lucia threw open her coat and grabbed her wand, launching a zap of electricity through the air and hitting a vampire on the right balcony. Arms and legs flailed as the vampires fell with a *crunch* upon impact with the floor. Everyone who was dancing ducked from the zap, recoiling from the loud feedback from the speakers.

Lock felt the magic course through him as his skin turned to stone, resembling a stone golem he once saw on holiday with Thorn. He felt once-warm flesh harden into granite.

"I've got to get them out as quickly as possible," he said.

Lauren ran down the stairs, balled her fist, and drove it deeply into Tevin's groin.

Tevin wailed in pain as he doubled over.

"You fucking bitch!" Tevin yelled.

Lauren kicked him in the stomach. "Fuck you. You can't even get a date without hypnotizing someone." Thorn smiled as Tevin yelled out again in pain.

Lauren's eyes grew wild and vicious when she grabbed Tevin's coat and propelled herself from the steps toward a pillar, dragging Tevin with her. She slammed him into the pillar and dark sludge launched itself from Tevin's mouth. Lauren recognized it as vampire blood, coagulated with lifelessness. "Look up the word *consent* in the dictionary. Study it. Learn it."

Tevin looked to his coven and shouted, "GET THEM! GET THEM, YOU FUCKS!"

The vampires launched themselves into the air, attempting to render the Artificers useless. Thorn shot a bolt of lightning at a vampire wearing midnight blue before he could jump into the air or react. The vampire was thrown into the clock that rested in a wide perch above the main entrance. He slumped with a smoldering chest in front of the clock, defeated and unconscious.

Darius ducked out of the way of a falling vampire as he continued to usher the student cattle outside.

Lauren, afraid that Tevin would try to call more shots, brought her foot down on Tevin. She smiled in victory as her foot descended through the air toward his face.

Tevin threw his hands up and caught Lauren's foot, throwing her off balance. He laughed as he hopped up, wounded but still in the fight. Lauren tumbled down the altar steps and landed at the bottom in a heap.

Tevin, shirt flapping in the breeze, was slowly rising into the air. His coven mirrored him, rising into the air to begin their flight.

It was then that Lauren looked over her shoulder to the wall and saw a vintage radio. The knob turned itself to the right, causing the volume of the song to be louder than a banshee's scream.

"COM-PLY-UNCE!" The song's synth escalated.

"Muse?!" Thorn exclaimed, bewildered and excited.

"You've got to be fucking *kidding* me," Lucia huffed. "They've always got to be showboats. Can't just murder people in the quiet." She conjured another bolt at a vampire, which missed wide, screaming over his shoulder.

Tevin's frat launched themselves on the Artificers. They were peeling off to barrel down on Lucia, Thorn, and Lock. Fangs bared, shrill screeches, and eyes wild, the vampires leveled out with the floor of the frat and flew at their prey.

Tevin tutted as he descended closer to Lauren.

Lucia, anticipating a frontal attack, reached into her satchel and grabbed a small drawstring bag. She took a pinch from the bag, threw it into the air, and snapped her wand with a flourish. She blew at the floating powder, which her wand treated like powdered snow on a ski slope. The powder propelled itself at her five vampires.

The vampires' eyes rolled into the backs of their heads as they collapsed from the air and into the concrete floor. Lucia dove out of the way as the first vampire collided headfirst into the pews. The rest of the four vampires collided into their cohort, splintering the pews aligned along the wall. Wood and limbs stuck out in various directions.

Darius saw two vampires emerge from opposite sides of the room, one to his left and the other to his right, eyes locked onto him.

He finished getting the final student out and closed the door behind them.

He blinked and saw that his left hand was extended, with his Nexian sword radiating purple energy in his hand.

The vampires started to run toward him.

Darius felt the energy rush throughout his body, filling him up with what he could describe as power.

That powerful energy wanted out.

The first vampire swung at him with a fist.

Darius deflected it with the hilt of his sword, feeling an unnatural athleticism that felt like a fight-or-flight response surging through him. He could feel it in the air: the specific avenues and maneuvers he needed to land in order to fight.

He didn't say no.

Darius pushed the vampire back with Nexian energy and did a backflip over the second vampire, who came charging after him.

Missing Darius, the vampire took off in flight toward the central action.

Darius raised his right hand and launched a dark purple bolt of Nexian energy at the flying vampire.

He caught the flier square in the back, causing the vampire to lose consciousness and crash into a bookshelf next to the stairs.

Darius, sword held up in front of him, ran toward the stairs and the main action.

Lucia, who recovered from her dive, got up and felt weariness creep in. She had skipped her run this week and felt considerably winded. She breathed heavily as she looked at Lock and Thorn, who were engaged in close combat with the vamps.

Before Lucia had put the vampires to sleep, the boys had drawn weapons and planted their feet. Thorn's sickle radiated with electricity while Lock's hands shone with vibrant red energy, turning the massive palms into a shield and a sword filled with Nexian energy. The first vampire came at Lock, who swatted the vampire away and into Thorn, who swung with the flat end of his sickle.

The boys decided it was time to play ball.

The first vampire, caught unawares, took a hit to the face and collapsed in a heap to Thorn's right. Lock braced with his shield for the second vampire, but this vampire saw what happened to the first. The vampire pulled up to avoid being hit by the Nexian shield, ascending back into the air. Thorn conjured a bolt of electricity at the third vampire, who was sent tumbling into the wall behind the altar. The vampire was rendered unconscious by the electricity.

The fourth and fifth, who had wised up at this point, decided to extend their claws. Their human fingernails grew into gnarled, rotten spikes. The vampires dove at Thorn and Lock and latched their claws into the boys' shoulders.

Both Thorn and Lock yelled out in pain and collapsed to the floor as they wrestled with the vamps.

Thorn struggled on the ground with a vampire gnashing its teeth at his throat. Thorn charged his fist with electricity and plunged it into the throat of the OmiTau, who gasped for air and released. Thorn rolled into a half-moon shape and kicked the vampire off himself. Springing to his feet, Thorn took off after his opponent.

Lock wasn't as graceful, however. The vampire collided with Lock, who fell back onto the floor while the vampire was wailing on him. The stone held up at first. After two punches, blood rolled from his nose and mouth.

The third punch fell, and the vampire stopped.

The vampire reeled back for one more final blow when Lock looked up at his foe and spat a large loogie into his face. The vampire initially shrugged this off, until his face began to burn.

Lock spat another loogie into his enemy's chest. This caused acid burns to appear on the vampire's hands, face, and torso.

Darius came to Lock's aid, swinging his sword with two hands at the burning vampire.

The vampire crossed his arms just in time, blocking the brunt of the sword attack, but was propelled back into a bookshelf.

Darius helped the granite Lock get to his feet before turning back to the fray. He clocked Lauren, who was struggling to get up.

The wailing vampire's screams echoed through the chamber as Tevin touched down on the floor, making his way to Lauren.

"I'm glad you mean nothing to me, Kreider." He chuckled. "Nowadays, it's so easy to move on from one to the next when there's a whole campus to suck. Prime choices of meat, all to myself." He grabbed her face and picked her up off the ground. Lauren groaned in pain. The vamp was incredibly strong.

As he lifted her up, her feet dangled a foot off the floor. "You weren't prime, though. Not after all the vodka you had. You practically *begged* me." He wound up and threw Lauren with great force into the pews. The sound of splintering wood echoed through the hall.

"Beg for mercy, fuckboy." Tevin was hit in the head and knocked off his feet as Thorn threw the unconscious body of his opponent. Thorn strode forward, hair and eyes charged with electricity. Lucia blocked Tevin in from escaping. She looked up at just the right time: a vampire in the rafters wanted to make another fly by.

Lucia, annoyed and pissed, felt her spring of Nexian energy churn, wanting to be released. She pointed her wand and muttered in the Nexian language forcefully.

The vampire, writhing, flying, and wailing, disappeared into thin air.

She felt the rush of blood to her head making her dizzy, so she leaned against a pillar.

Tevin, lying on the floor, attempted to get up by shoving 250 pounds of lean muscle off himself. The boot in his chest shoved him back into the floor as Lock held his Nexian-energized foot to the lead vamp's chest. "Move and you die."

Tevins's blood-stained mouth smiled at the room. Lucia finally joined Lock, Thorn, and a limping Lauren over the body of the OmiTau.

Tevin motioned to the spot where the vampire had disappeared at Lucia's hand. "Did you banish Murdock? He's a pledge, witch bitch. He was just doing a fly by, not exactly worthy of banishment."

"I don't give a fuck, Tevin. I covered for you once, I'll do it again. However, Resin will need to know about this. You fucked up big time. I'm not sure how, but we'll figure out a way to make you realize the weight of what you've done here." She looked up at the rest of the wearied Artificers. "Murdock was just a taste."

Tevin couldn't stop smiling at the group, sputtering around the blood he was coughing up, "Like I care."

"Oh, you'll care." Thorn wound up and landed a punch into Tevin's face.

Tevin sighed in pain and passed out, unconscious.

"You okay?" Lucia asked Lauren, who was limping up to the group from where she collided into the church pews.

"It was a booty call, what can I say? Sorry, Thorn, that you had to hear that."

"I don't give a fuck." The red-haired man was almost wheezing. "Not my pasture to graze in."

Darius grimaced, looking particularly unfond of the verbiage.

"Ew." Lock looked at Lucia. "Luce, what gives? Why are we so out of breath? What's going on?"

"I'm…I'm not sure." *Lies,* Lucia said to herself. *It drains them, even though they completed the Rendering and Sundering.* "Have you guys been working out your powers? You know, growing them through training?"

Lauren was the only one who didn't look ashamed.

"It could be that." She surveyed the scene to make sure no other vampires were getting up. "Come on, I gotta call Resin to make sure he comes in here and investigates before the vamps wake up. He'll want to see this."

They all retreated to the front entrance.

As they walked, Lucia felt the tension of the lie she just told brush up to the back of her throat in nervous vomitus. She knew better than anyone the weight that these powers carried. One could only draw so much at a time. The bigger the spell, the more the Nexus wanted in return. If one didn't regularly practice with the powers, then the big fights left one feeling like a toddler squeezing a tube of toothpaste: a crumpled-up receptacle in a death grip.

Thoughts creeped into Lucia's head as she and the Artificers limped out through the large doors and into the quiet night at Gristholme College. Did she have to follow through with Gredalia's plan? Was it the logical choice to sit at the right hand of terror?

Was Rendering and Sundering the right thing to do if the human Nexian users were only to die like pawns in the Gredalia game?

She took a pause, with the group moving forward. She dug into her pocket, picked up her phone, and called the Fenris Wolf.

During her call, she took great care to study Darius, who dissipated his sword before leaving the frat. He looked completely unharmed, besides being a little winded. No major damage appeared on his body or skin. He looked like he did any other day.

I wonder what Olivia needed, Lucia thought, remembering back to the red coat in the pine trees and Darius following after Olivia.

As she continued walking, she finished her call and felt the doubt roll in like a London fog. Whatever her future choices may be, they were not only going to hurt the people she was walking with.

They were going to hurt her, too.

The Artificers

LUCIA LOOKED UP from her cup of coffee as Darius walked into the abandoned coffee shop. He had specific instructions to meet Lucia a half hour before midnight.

She noticed that he looked particularly sheepish today. *I don't recall the others looking this nervous,* Lucia thought. *They were pretty eager. Darius doesn't seem to be at all.*

She smiled at Darius when he sat down across from her.

"I thought you slit people's throats when they interrupted you?" Darius chuckled nervously.

"Well, I was expecting you to meet me here. That's the difference." Lucia rubbed her temples, trying to recall everything she needed to do for the ceremony. "Are you ready?"

Darius sighed heavily, letting the worry show across his face. "I…I guess so? I know we established that I'm already Rendered, so I don't have to go through that misery. How does the Sundering work, though?"

Lucia returned the sigh, gathering her thoughts. "Think of the Nexian magic being water, stored in a well. You're the bottle. I draw the water from the well and put it inside of you. This is Rendering: preparing your body to be a magic user. Sundering is where I put the lid on your water bottle and seal it, and that's how you retain your magic."

"Doesn't it run out? Do I *dry up*?!"

Lucia saw the worry transition into fear upon his features. "Not if you practice," she started. "Well, I shouldn't say, because it could be potentially problematic for the Artificers. What makes you so special, Darius, is that you're *already* Rendered. We don't really know why this is the case. There are assumptions, but we don't want to jump to conclusions here. It should be an easy process."

"Is it painful?" Darius was wringing his hands.

"I don't think so." Lucia shrugged, showing no emotion.

"How would you know? You haven't been Sundered."

"I've Sundered a few people, lest we forget." Lucia scooted to the edge of the booth and grabbed her coat. "No one has died yet."

"Died?!" Darius cried out. "People die during the Sundering?"

"Nexian users aren't perfect, Darius. Remember that. Sometimes we get it wrong too. Someone looks good enough to be a vessel of Nexian magic. You attempt to do so, and they disintegrate or combust. It happens, but it's pretty rare. It hasn't happened to anyone my grandma or I Sundered. You'll be fine."

He incredulously got out of his seat and followed Lucia to the door.

Lucia threw her satchel over her shoulder in the process, rooting through it to triple-check that she had all her components and her spell book. The pair made their way up the Boardwalk toward the deeper woods of the plateau.

In the silence, Darius felt uncomfortable. *I wanna ask what it's like,* he thought. *It just seems like this is supposed to be a sacred thing, like a pilgrimage.*

Lucia seemed to be whispering to herself as they passed the Hall of Ancients on their right.

Some kind of ancient magic? He scanned around to see if anyone was watching them. *A protection spell, perhaps?*

Lucia broke her whispering. "A warding spell against any nefarious Nexian entities. We should be good."

"The lack of certainty worries me." Darius kept looking around for anyone that might look suspicious.

"If you would stop flailing your head around like the French royals during the Reign of Terror, then we could probably gain more certainty." She picked up her pace, causing Darius to break into a light trot.

"Sorry," he huffed. "I'm still getting used to the magic being concealed by the water."

Lucia let out an exaggerated sigh and said, "Come on."

The pair eventually met the end of the Boardwalk at the base of a warped tree. Darius swore that there was a human face in the bark of the tree. He turned and looked to Lucia for clarity.

"Don't look at me like that," she said. "This wasn't me."

"Is that a human!?" Darius cried out.

"It will be if you don't keep it down. To be honest, I'm quite unsure if it is or isn't. We gotta go into the depths of these trees here."

"Shit. Okay, Luce." Darius followed behind her, attempting to dodge the dense brush of the woods.

The pair trekked for what seemed like an hour, with Lucia continuing to mutter while Darius pulled briars and thorns out of his clothes. They passed through a thicket of trees that formed an arch, and Darius realized that they were in a clearing.

Trees were cut down and pushed against other older trees to form a circle, with a few stumps and logs for sitting. Leaves were scattered on the ground, with pine needles sprinkled in. In the center of the clearing there was a slab of stone that stood vertically and was wide enough for a book. A ring of hand-sized stones sat in front of the slab on the ground, large enough for a human to lie down comfortably.

"My bed, I assume?" Darius pointed to the stone circle.

"Appears to be so." Lucia left Darius behind and walked to the slab. "I'll just finish setting up, and then we'll be good to go."

"Alrighty then." Darius began to look around the clearing. Where the light was coming from, he was unsure. There was a soft, amber glow coming from above the tree's canopy. Looking deeper into the forest, it seemed to go on for infinity, with darkness splashed in between older and taller trees. "You're sure we're on campus, Luce?"

Lucia looked up briefly from her spell book. "I never asked my grandma, so I can't give you a firm answer." She threw a green powder over the book and makeshift podium. "My guess is that we are, but it's possible we're in a Nexian construct similar to the Hall of Ancients."

"How does *that* work, anyway?"

She pinched the bridge of her nose in annoyance. "Can't you just let magic be magic, Darius? The water, the powers, the pocket dimensions… can't it just be mystifying?"

"Tell that to scientists," Darius paced around the circle. "It has to be solved."

"I guess so," Lucia clapped her hands together. "It appears to be ready for you now."

"It?" He pointed to the circle of stones.

"Yes," Lucia shrugged her shoulders nonchalantly. "You're ready for your transformation."

Darius stepped inside the circle gingerly. He looked at Lucia, who had her arms crossed.

"Shit!" she exclaimed.

Darius flinched, yelling out, "WHAT?!"

Lucia raised a hand, "Phone. The last thing I want is for tech to meld to you."

Darius reluctantly handed his phone to the witch.

"Now, please proceed."

He got on the ground, feeling the cold slowly seep into his bones.

"Alright, just hang tight." Lucia lifted her wand like a conductor's baton.

"Lucia, how long is this going to—"

Lucia snapped her wand down in a cutting motion, like the downbeat of a piece of music.

Darius felt his body grow rigid, his fingers locking into place below his waistline, like a soldier at attention.

Lucia began to speak in a guttural distant language.

Darius felt his senses grow dark to the world around him. His spirit receded into the depths of his mind when a vision came to him.

Back on the war-torn battlefield, Darius saw his doppelgänger with its empty white eyes staring back at him. A snarl pulled on the corner of the double's lips.

"I assume this is what you're looking for?" the creature said, raising its hand. Purple and black flames shot out of its palm and arched themselves toward the sky.

"I do believe so, yes," Darius stated hesitantly. "Though the witch said it would be painful." His gaze was focused on his double, but in the blink of an eye, he felt the searing pain of a blade piercing his torso. It wasn't just any blade, however. It was *his* blade, the blade that he summoned from the Nexus.

The double put a hand on Darius's shoulder and whispered something indecipherable to him as he started to lose consciousness. The monster patted him on the shoulder and grinned.

Darius blinked once more and closed his eyes.

He woke up screaming in the clearing, feeling as if his veins were on fire.

Lucia continued to mutter the guttural language, flinging her powder in the air and flourishing with her wand, seemingly unalarmed by the way Darius howled.

He felt his body release from its rigidity with the onset of convulsions. One arm threw itself wide with the hand curled into claws of pain. The other arm twisted itself in a way Darius was sure it wasn't supposed to. Both arms and legs continued in this pattern for what seemed to be several minutes. His torso rose and fell not with breath but as if his heart were pumping with the rise and fall.

Darius felt his blood run cold and then warm again. He grimaced with eyes closed and yelled out at the world around him. His eyes flew open, and he noticed everything was sharper than before, as if his vision had amplified itself beyond human capabilities. His back arched, and he felt the weight of his sword fall into his hand.

The added weight brought on a surge of debilitating pain, his blood changing from fire to magma.

He looked back at Lucia standing at the arcane pulpit. Lucia's face was both her own and a combination of those who came before her, with each visage fading in and out as she completed the spell. It occurred to Darius that this was the manifestation of her blood line and her power: her ancestors channeled through her, bringing the task to completion.

Lucia's voice rose, sending leaves and pine needles into the air.

Darius felt his veins explode, blood shooting out of his very pores. He cried out in agony as he looked around him. The blood floated to the sky and carried on, like a balloon let go by a small child.

"Darius!" Lucia's voice echoed in the distance.

He felt his senses return to his new body.

"*DARIUS!*" Lucia called, sounding as if she were two inches from his ear.

He opened his eyes.

"It's over, man." Lucia was sitting on a log across from him.

Darius looked around. He was lying on the ground, but the pine needles and leaves that were in the immediate area were now firmly pressed into the trunks of the trees that surrounded them. Lucia looked much the same, just more worn out than when they had started. "Are you okay?" Darius sat up.

"Yeah." She spat on the ground, wiping her mouth. "I'm fine, Darius."

"Oh, okay." He nodded. "I guess pretty powerful witches can handle powerful spells, right?"

Lucia smirked. "I guess so." She groaned in pain as she stood up. "Remember how I told you that big spells drain you? Well, that played out in this situation. You weren't the typical case of Sundering."

"Uh, why's that?" Darius stood up with a perplexed look on his face. *You're one of the most powerful magic users I've met so far. If I'm a difficult case, is something wrong with me?* His thoughts leaped to the worst-case scenario.

"I don't know." Lucia gathered her belongings from the podium. "What I *do* know is that I think we've yet to see the potency and the potential of your powers."

"Wow." Darius followed her toward the entrance of the secret Sundering place. "Basically just means more training, right?"

"Sure, Darius," Lucia said. "More and more scenarios will dictate what manifests. I can't wait to see how you do in other trainings."

He smiled a content smile and walked through the thicket with Lucia leading the way. *I guess things are going to be okay! I'm a full-fledged magic user now. Hopefully, I'll be of some use to these guys.*

After the pair made their way back onto Gristholme's grounds, Lucia decided to follow Darius back to the House of IT.

Just to keep up appearances, she thought.

Darius took a few of the steps before turning around to Lucia. "Are you sure I'm going to be okay?" He looked tense and worried. "I don't want to evaporate into the air tonight with some weird side effect."

"I believe you'll be just fine," she said. "Just take some pain pills to kill your headache. Typically, people feel a headache coming on an hour or two after their Sundering."

"Sounds good!" He waved goodbye to Lucia, who gave a half-hearted wave back. "See ya soon!"

"See ya." Lucia waited till he closed the door before taking off in a rushed walk back to her room, feeling the gravity of the lie she just told flood her bones.

Lauren

LAUREN DUCKED OUT OF Darius's window and proceeded to the training ground. She had given Darius exactly one hour to meet her there and another thirty minutes before Olivia showed up. She had sent the text message to Olivia stating it was time to ride the lightning and face the truth. Lauren had been tracking Olivia for several weeks, ever since Resin officially announced the interest. The assassin spent her days snooping on Olivia's whereabouts and how she went in and out of Nightshade Hall. She had witnessed several other figures leave, but those were not her target. Her target was the five-foot-six woman with hoop earrings, a sassy attitude, and a position on the cheerleading squad.

Lauren went to games dressed as a sports-loving "it girl" who wanted nothing more than to be with Thorn. She wanted to see him score a touchdown, and she hollered in the student section when he made the right play. *I fucking hate playing the role of the "it girl,"* she would grumble to herself in her own mind. *I don't care about spiced lattes, dances, and designer clothes. However, if it helps me blend in, it helps me blend in.*

After she cheered on her "favorite player," though, she would monitor Olivia's movements. Olivia would shoot glances over at the boys. It didn't *immediately* constitute a threat, but Lauren noticed that Olivia moved closer and closer to the boys' spots on the sidelines during the game. Thorn would later tell Lauren how Olivia had been making weird eye movements, or her face had contorted in some magical way. All of this concerned Lauren and Resin greatly.

She was pondering this as she went to the training field where she and Darius sparred. Her hopes were that Darius wouldn't botch the plan. *God, the shit I'll get if this doesn't go through,* she thought. *If I'm not dead first.*

Lauren stuck to the woods, hoping that she wouldn't be seen by Olivia before the rendezvous. Her weapons pressed into her back as she took off in a light jog. Her nerves rang up her legs and into her hands. Students passed Lauren without paying her any mind. To them, it looked like she was just out for an evening jog in typical running attire: trainers, shorts, and a baggy T-shirt. In reality she was wearing her leather assassin uniform, with her primary weapons on her back and her blades easily accessible from the utility belt slung over her left shoulder.

The leather was something she typically wore, and it fit her perfectly thanks to the magic it was enchanted with. This leather was armor that took a fair bit of the brunt of a magic attack (she had tested it with Lucia several weeks before Darius became a member). The suit could transform into whatever she wanted, as well as conceal her weapons. This only became problematic if someone directly touched her, at which point they would see one thing and feel another. Most of the time she wore the armor to classes, as she was not too much of a touchy-feely person. However, there were some days she left it in her room under lock and key to keep it away from prying eyes.

Lauren passed the Willow Apartments and watched on as some of the students (some not fully clothed after a drunken row) passed out in their yards. She knew that if she stayed around for too long, Campus Safety would roll up. She was fine seeing Resin, but she didn't want to see Kasey or any of the other security officers. The thought of the other officers kicked up a bit of distrust in her gut, and she didn't like it.

Turning back to make sure she wasn't followed, Lauren saw no one of particular interest. She found the familiar path and took to it lithely. Flora and fauna melded with her as if she were moving through water, unencumbered by the presence of the foliage. Ten minutes later, Lauren entered the outer rim of the clearing.

Looking around, no one was in sight.

Lauren skirted the edge, watching and waiting for Darius and then Olivia to show up. The moonlight was directly above the field, with the wind gently obscuring her noise. She found a perfect spot to kneel and blend in, feeling her assassin suit lightly camouflaging her. Darius had exactly thirty minutes to show. Olivia another thirty minutes. It should go as planned if Olivia followed the text correctly. If Darius followed the plan, he would make his way to this location before Olivia could sense that something was up. He wouldn't spring the trap Lauren had set the night prior, but it was important he followed the note *exactly.*

Please Darius, she thought as she scanned the field, looking for anything out of the ordinary, *please don't fuck this up. I'm banking on you wanting to* actually *test your new powers beyond some silly sparring with me.*

As the wind rustled through the trees and grass, Lauren scanned the opposite tree line. No animals or humans were present. Not even a single hoot owl pierced the wind. She rested on both knees now, taking in the surroundings and blending into the environment. Fifteen minutes passed. Another twenty went by. She did not see Darius.

Where the fuck is he? She felt the blood rush to her head.

She was just about to call it a lost cause when she felt a tap on her shoulder. Lauren reeled around, grabbing first the ankle and then the throat of whomever it was that had managed to sneak up behind her. To her chagrin, it was Darius.

"The fuck is wrong with you?" she whispered. "YOU are pushing into the time that Olivia is going to be here."

"Why did you want me and not the wolf, the *actual* witch, or the two totems of gods?!"

"Keep your voice down!" Lauren hissed. "She's going to be here any minute."

"Lauren, why did you set a trap of Nexian fire?"

Caught off guard by such a question, Lauren raised an eyebrow. "Okay, so how the fuck do you know about Nexian fire?"

He removed her hand from his throat. "*My* Nexian powers allow me to see Nexian-based traps. Since those are arcane in nature, I can see 'em."

"Ah, piss," Lauren spat.

Darius crouched down next to her, staring out at the field they sparred in.

Lauren's breath caught in her chest as an ethereal black haze engulfed Darius's right hand. A light wind carried the haze into the night, and the ominous Nexian blade was left behind.

"I'm ready." He nodded to the field, eyes alight. "She's approaching."

"Dar—" Lauren looked to her left, and the man had skirted back around to a position of flanking. Lauren felt the magic course through her armor, shifting into its true form: black and red armor with a buffer to piercing damage.

Olivia had followed the path like the text from Thorn had explained. It was quite the remote location for what had been described as a "talk."

Talk with his penis, more like it. She laughed to herself.

The wind and moon created an ominous feel. She turned to Brent, who was starting to twitch savagely. "Take the perimeter, wolfie. I don't trust this meeting. Where's Lucia? Didn't you ask her to join us to stomp out this shithead?"

Brent growled.

"Okay, fuck, sorry I asked. We'll do it without Her Witchiness then."

Brent dropped to all fours and took to the perimeter opposite from where Darius was sitting.

Darius saw the wolf figure and reminded himself that it wasn't Resin. He waited with the blade in hand. *Make your move, bitch,* he thought to himself.

Olivia, thinking that she was meeting Thorn, took a few steps out into the field. The air seemed calm, and Thorn was nowhere to be seen.

The nerves rose in her chest, and Olivia took a few steps forward, feeling the pebbles shift underneath her combat boots.

Suddenly, Olivia went airborne, flying ass over elbow through the air as a blast of fiery energy came from behind her. Lauren had placed what appeared to be rock salt on the ground in a circle, hoping the wind would not scatter it to the point of breaking integrity. "Once someone crosses through the circle," Lucia had said to Lauren, "the trap triggers."

A barrier of light-blue flame formed around the path, just as Lucia told her it would. The ethereal fire was lit, which would keep wandering students out for the duration of the fight.

Darius stood and felt invigorated as the sword pulsated Nexian energy through his body. His eyes shifted from soft green to midnight black with pulsating red veins. Brent, getting caught in the blast, was thrown into the moonlit center of the field. The fire went around the clearing and illuminated only Lauren. Lauren, having cast the spell, stepped into the ring of flames.

"Sup, bitch." Lauren stood to full height. "You fucked with my boys. Now I'm gonna fuck with you." Lauren's swords graced the night air and caught the moonlight. "You're gonna suck steel."

Olivia got up off the ground, using Brent as leverage. "Really? Think you can just fuck with *me* like that, little chickadee?" Olivia raised her hand, her brows furrowing. "Suck on this."

Lauren felt her eyes widen. She asked herself a worrying question: *Why is my hand moving toward my skull?* Looking down, she saw her hand trembling as it made its way toward her face, though her subconscious mind was resisting it. The sword turned in her palm, as Olivia tried to force Lauren to impale herself.

Darius saw that Brent was attempting to get to his companion.

It was then that he decided to act.

Standing up from the darkness, he felt the sword pulsate with energy and his body propel forward.

Lauren felt tears of fear fill her eyes, wondering if this was going to be the catalyst for her demise. In her fear, her teeth sharpened underneath the ominous eye of the moon. She struggled, she fought, but Lauren felt the sword beginning its descent toward her neck. The vampire assassin pushed back so strongly that she felt either her body or her mind would break.

As she thought she was done for, a figure launched itself from the woods and barreled into Olivia, causing her concentration to break and the spell to fade from Lauren.

Darius Crosbane looked like something out of a horror film: His eyes were a shade of violet-black, his hair spiked viciously, his teeth thin but strong. The sword that he summoned pulsated a black fire that Olivia could only assume to be from the underworld or similar hellscape. His veins popped, his muscles were tensed, and his voice seemed to be a few octaves lower than Lauren remembered. The ringing of the swords through the night noted that this would best be a conversation for later, should Lauren and Darius make it out of this alive.

Brent, now realizing there was a larger fight about to happen, popped back onto his feet. His face was now hairier, with his own set of sharpened teeth. His silvery-marigold eyes looked at both Lauren and Darius.

Darius took the reins of the conversation, sword pulsating and a deep voice ringing out. "Get the *fuck* off my grounds."

"I don't think this is going to be *your* jurisdiction on that one, demon boy," Olivia said. "This is Gredalia Council territory."

"The fuck is that?" Lauren said. "Is this your secret swingers club?"

"It sounds more like a geriatric gardening club," Darius chided.

Both he and Lauren laughed.

"Answer me this: You've got your little shit minions that tried to kill people. Why didn't you send *them* after us? They're much more expendable." Darius twirled his blade.

"None of your fucking business, hellspawn," Brent's voice gurgled.

"Steady there, Balto," Lauren retorted. "Be sure you take your preventative. Did mommy get your glands drained? Is that why you're such a moody boy? I have a bone if you need it." She licked her lips and teeth.

Olivia snarled, "Cut the bullshit. We know that you lot hang out with Thorn and Lock. We know they ran tucked-tail back to you and cried about the Grimfaern. I remember it vividly. They were so scared."

Darius tensed up on the blade and brought it in front of him.

Lauren, knowing Darius's inexperience with magical parley, decided to take point. "We know that these Grimfaern are here on our campus. Did you bring them to this plane of existence? If so, to what end are they here?"

"You think we're just gonna spill Gredalia's secrets to you? Think again," the wolf-man snarled.

"How many of you are there?" Lauren dropped her blades to her side, attempting to be cordial. "We will tell you how many there are of us."

"We can't trust you." Olivia raised her hands again. "You're full of shit."

Darius held his sword out in front of him, awaiting the next move.

Lauren smirked and drew her blades back to their original positions. "Shall we begin?"

Several moments passed between the members of Gredalia Council and the Artificers. Darius felt his power slowly building. The longer he stayed in this state, the more he felt he could do. He wanted to test it, but he waited to make sure one of the others made a move first to allow himself the time to build his energy.

Brent was crouched low with spittle dripping from his mouth, ready to spring.

Lauren, with her tight bodysuit of armor, looked like a badass in the moonlight. Her steel swords grinned like freshly cleaned teeth against the backdrop of bloodied gums.

Olivia, with shoulder-length sandy-blonde hair, wore leggings and an oversized sweater, trying to look as incognito as possible. It was quite the sight to behold, except for the tension in the air. Another few moments passed. Lauren stood back up and sighed. "Why is this the game that we must play, Olivia? Tell me why you attacked Thorn and Lock. Tell me why you are such a coward that you couldn't fight them yourse—" Lauren winced in pain as the air escaped her lungs. She dropped to her knees. Her swords would have fallen limp at her sides had she not stuck them in the ground as supports during the fall. She looked up at Olivia, who was laughing. The laugh followed Olivia's pointing finger to Lauren. It felt as if Olivia had a pair of vise grips around her lungs.

"Lauren, if you try anything, *anything at all,* I will snap your papery lungs in half. Better yet, I'll feed you to the Grimfaern feetfirst. This way, you can slowly watch your body—"

Olivia's body went reeling several feet back as Darius dropped his outstretched hand and a bolt of dark Nexian energy struck the Olivia square in the chest.

"You're done talking. I've had e-fucking-nough of you," Darius growled.

Brent, seeing his friend in pain, stood up finally and cracked his neck. A loud roll of vertebrae, almost like the sound of a snare drum roll, echoed into the silence of the field. Brent's eyes locked onto Darius. "You don't call the shots here, American Gothic."

Darius raised his hands to the air, looking at the ground. *"Come on, then! DO IT."* Olivia clutched her chest, noticing the unnerving energy seeping into her skin.

Lauren's teeth craved the blood seeping from Olivia's chest.

Brent's breathing picked up.

Darius, in the moonlight, felt the euphoria continue. He felt invincible. The night was his. He slowly lifted his eyes to meet Brent's.

Brent howled into the night and launched himself through the air.

Darius held up his blade and waited, breathing just like Lauren taught him.

Olivia gritted her teeth and stood up, motioning back at Lauren. "It's your turn to die, you bleached bitch." The air around her vibrated as Olivia launched herself at Lauren.

Lauren took a deep breath and held up her swords, mirroring Darius.

Brent hit Darius's blade with his claws and tried to rip it from his hands.

Darius braced for a blow, noting that Brent was on his toes.

As the wolf tried to rip the blade out of his hands, Darius kicked at his knees. Brent, still holding on, caught the blow to his thigh. The wolf tried to rip at the sword again, but to no avail.

Darius flicked the blade quickly and slapped Brent's wrist.

Brent let go of the blade.

On the opposite side of the field, Lauren braced herself for Olivia. Olivia, wounded, launched with as much might as she could toward the vampire. She landed off-kilter, opening herself up more than she should have. Lauren exhaled lightly and saw the opportunity she was waiting for. Time slowed. Lauren's blade sliced upward in a graceful motion, connecting with Olivia's stomach.

A squelching sound radiated throughout the field. A gasp escaped a pair of previously taut lips as Olivia clutched her stomach and her knees hit the grass.

Lauren stood over her prey. "Gods, that blood smells so good." She licked her lips. "Too bad, I'm afraid you're gonna be tainted."

As she spoke, Lauren felt her feet lift off the ground. Olivia had played possum. Her eyes glowed a faint purple-pink hue. "Fuck you!" she wailed as she threw Lauren back in an invisible pulse of energy. Lauren tumbled through the air, colliding with several trees. Her head hit the branches with a loud *thwack!*

She fell toward the earth, stunned.

Darius looked in the direction of Lauren and Olivia. Noticing only Olivia, he knew he didn't have much time. Darius spun and drove the pommel of his sword into Brent's nose. Purple eldritch energy launched from the pommel, causing Brent to lose consciousness. He slumped to the ground, cross-eyed, arms limp at his sides.

Darius took his stance over Brent. The blade pressed into the wolf's chest slightly.

"Let Lauren and I go, and I'll spare your wolf."

Olivia grinned sharply. "What makes you think I'm just gonna spare her life?" Though bloodied, she raised her hand and Lauren floated forward, also unconscious.

"Because if you don't, your buddy here is gonna be on my table for breakfast." He pushed a little deeper, causing blood to start leaking out of the chest. "I'm not fucking kidding."

Olivia raised Lauren into the air in response. She was now fourteen feet above the ground. "You think I am? I swear to God, if it wasn't for you and your troop fucking with Gredalia's plans, we'd probably be on good fucking terms. But that's not here, that's not now. You've been too close to the epicenter. You can't be allowed to fuck up something so good."

"Yeah? What's that little lady?" Darius felt emboldened, holding the tip of the necrotic blade into the chest of the wolf-man. A tiny stream of blood started to run into the dirt. "Gods, he is looking a little rough."

Olivia frowned and kept sending Lauren into the sky. "Wanna play? Cause I can keep this up for about ten more feet."

The standoff between the two seemed to last for ages. Darius stared into her eyes. "Tell me why Gredalia is making those monsters. That's what you're doing right? You're making Grimfaern, but why?"

Olivia held Lauren floating above the field. She was looking as tired as he felt. "That's telling, demon boy, and I can't tell *you*. You'll just go back and tell your leadership what we're doing. We can't have that now." She winced and put one hand over her stomach.

"You're not thinking this through correctly." He blinked his eyes. "I only get information. You still live, and your friend too. Your body right now is on the brink of death. Lauren got you good." He twisted the blade and Brent let out a groan. "Choose. Now."

Olivia smirked. "Chicken." She sent her hand flying forward and Lauren went soaring through the air. Darius's eyes rolled back in his head. He looked up to the sky with the whites of his eyes and felt eldritch molten wings sprout from his back. Kicking off the ground, Darius ascended through the air. Olivia, clutching her stomach, let her jaw go slack. Unhinging her lower jaw, she let out a sickening roar into the night sky.

As Darius flew up and caught Lauren, he flapped his wings to slow his pace and hold his position. Hearing the echo of Olivia's voice and remembering her range, he climbed higher.

There was something about Olivia's voice, though, that made Darius feel compelled to go back to her and answer her call.

As he soared over the field, he saw them.

Olivia walked over to Brent and dropped to her knees. Cradling him, she looked up at the sounds rustling through the trees. One hundred, no, two hundred Grimfaern came romping into the field at tremendous speeds. As Darius watched, Olivia raised her hand, and one of the Grimfaern scooped her up, followed by Brent. The pair was carried away into the stampede making their way deeper into the forests that surrounded Gristholme. The sounds of the monsters faded after fifteen minutes. Darius still cradled Lauren as he made his descent back into the field.

Upon landing, Darius laid Lauren on the ground.

"Hey girl, come on, you gotta wake up." He began to smack her face lightly. "Come on!" Darius looked up nervously. He reached for his phone and decided to call Resin, who was currently on shift.

The Campus Safety car pulled into the field, and Resin got out. Darius heard the click of the radio and saw the familiar form walking toward him.

Darius would have asked Resin for a drink if he weren't too intimidated to do so and if Resin wasn't his superior in the Artificers. Darius liked the way his uniform looked on him, as he was so used to the jeans and flannel that Resin often wore. As the security officer approached, Darius snapped out of his thoughts and looked up at his leader.

"So, we were in the field and—"

"Stop. We gotta get our story straight so Tom and Rob Horn don't investigate this too deeply. When you called, I was in the office checking several things over. You and Lauren were walking through the woods when you got jumped by a bear."

"Sure, a bear, yeah. Sounds good to me, man." Darius swallowed hard. "When can we talk about this?"

"Soon," Resin said in a hushed voice. "I think Tom and Kasey are here." The siren echoed into the night as a second security car pulled up. Tom approached first, while Kasey hung back. Resin turned down his mic as Kasey's voice came over his earpiece.

"Hi there. My name's Tom." He extended his hand to Darius. "What's going on here? What happened to the two of you?"

"We…got attacked by a bear," Darius said as he cradled Lauren in the crook of his arm. Lauren coughed and nodded slightly. Resin looked at the medical bag Tom brought and began bandaging the pair.

"We'll get you to a hospital." Tom walked back to the car.

Resin looked up and noticed Kasey looking on, scowling.

The Artificers

"THOSE POWERS ARE gonna kill him," Lucia said aloud as she stood in the Moon's Loft.

She rubbed her eyes and felt the weight of Darius's transformation wash over her like a riptide.

This was *not* normal. The prior Artificers had smooth transitions into their powers. Resin had been Sundered through the Fenris Wolf prior to him, which was normal for his situation. Lock and Thorn both came out of it on the other side with success. Lauren had been Sundered as a child.

Darius shouldn't be as strong as he is, Lucia thought as she poured herself a cup of coffee for the night ahead. *He's something else entirely…*

But what? her internal voice called back to her.

"I don't know," she said out loud.

Lucia carried her cup back to her favorite booth and tucked in for a night of homework, spells, and ponderings. *Gredalia would absolutely love someone of his caliber,* she thought, taking a deep sip of coffee. *It's almost too good of an opportunity to pass up.*

Lucia felt her jaw drop when she thought about Darius's interaction with Olivia the other night before the OmiTau fight.

It was then that her phone rang.

"Hello?" she answered.

"Lucia, my dear!" A comforting voice came from the other side of the call. "It's been ages, darling. When are you going to come up to the studio for a visit?"

"Dylan, it's midnight-fucking-thirty, and I don't really know if my plate can handle another story at the moment."

"Come on, Luce. Twenty bucks and a little trip to visit yours truly would be a fine enough form of payment."

"Trip?" Lucia asked.

"I have something for you, but you need to come to the studio. Be thankful, because I've never done this for anyone ever."

"Dylan, why me?"

"'Cause you're the only person I know who can keep this big of a secret a secret."

"Okay, Dylan." *Fuck*, Lucia thought. "I'll be over in twenty minutes."

"Splendid, my dear. See you in a tick."

"He sounds so much like John Mulaney it isn't even funny," the witch said.

She trotted up the stairs of the Moon's Loft to her apartment. With a quick assembly of boots, her coat, and her wand, Lucia Frey was ready to take on the world. She reached into her mini-fridge and grabbed a rabbit leg. Pulling a plate from the table, Lucia put it down in front of her plant, Gideon.

The plant extended its arms and took the leg begrudgingly.

"How dare you be ungrateful! I'm running low on funds, but that may have changed."

Lucia patted the plant and stepped into the night, using the side door in her bedroom.

The air caught her off guard, mostly because of the way it sat. It was as if someone had blown smoke in her face, yet no matter how it cleared, it still stuck around her eyes.

She descended the wooden stairs and headed toward Dylan's studio.

The pine trees swayed in the light wind—a wind that also caused the witch's hair to fly into her face. Annoyed, Lucia tugged her trench coat around her and made her way to the Boardwalk. The Boardwalk was barren, which was unusual. Students would normally be milling about, coming to and from lovers' truancies or getting kicked out of the library for studying too late by Campus Safety. Lucia usually saw a student or two on her rounds at night for the Artificers or Gredalia Council. This night was different and completely void of human contact.

Lucia's destination was Gristholme Tower, protruding up from Pearson Dining Hall. Against the backdrop of the trees, Gristholme Tower cast an amber light onto the surrounding pines. It didn't take Lucia long to reach the hall. She felt herself propelled forward, as she wanted to know what exactly was happening with Dylan and why he was being so mysterious.

Lucia used her student ID to scan herself into Pearson.

She stepped inside to witness the chandelier and the entryway.

Looking up into Gristholme Tower, the stained glass of both Biblical and historical moments took Lucia's breath away. This place really was an incredible treasure. The lights on the lawn projected onto the stained-glass windows, giving them an ethereal tone. Lucia broke through her revelry and made her way toward Dylan Derringer's home base.

Despite the ancient exterior, the inside was quite modern, with new porcelain floors and flat-screen TVs relaying the news for the students. The stairs were built the same time as the building (she assumed in the late 1800s, with the European architecture) for they were quite narrow. The sandstone banister was smooth to her touch. The foyer was empty as she began to climb the stairs.

The tower ascended for what seemed like an eternity. Lucia was quite the runner, but stair-climbing was not her forte. It took her a good ten minutes to get to the solitary door at the top of the tower. Even with the pause she took to look down into the dining hall and other portions of Pearson, Lucia was tired by the time she knocked on the door.

A 1920s radio voice came back through the mail slot. "Who is it?"

"It's Lucia. It's time you open the door for once."

The door creaked open slowly. Lucia stepped inside and saw a skeleton sitting at a desk with a microphone. The bare cranium turned slowly, and the jaw dropped.

Lucia fainted in shock.

"Well, fuck." Dylan Derringer said.

———— ◆ ————

Lucia woke up on the floor and looked back up at the skeleton whose empty eye sockets stared back at her. "Lucia, my dear, have I the story for you!"

"Oh, a story?" She sat up slowly. "Dylan, you're a living skeleton."

"That seems to be an oxymoron, my dear," the John Mulaney-like voice retorted. "So, anyway, how's college? Care for a cuppa? Haven't had a living being in here for a hot minute."

"Dylan, what the fuck do you want?" Lucia pinched the bridge of her nose. "I gotta take care of a sleep problem."

"Sleep? At Gristholme?" Dylan gasped. "*I've* never heard of such a thing!"

Lucia got to her feet and made her way over to Dylan's desk. The tiny room contained one computer, a moderate-sized desk, papers scattered all over the desk, and a cell phone propped up against the computer tower (how Dylan got this, Lucia wasn't sure, considering he was dead). The rest of the room was relatively bland, with a picture of a young man with a woman sitting outside what appeared to be a newly minted Willow Apartment. Both had beers in their hands. There was a restroom (surprisingly) in a closet around the corner and a secondary chair with a thick layer of dust on it.

"Sit," Dylan chimed. "I think this is better than your sleep."

"Well, classes and witch duties don't exactly stop when I sleep, so what is it?"

"Patience, Lucia, patience." Dylan reached for his phone with his bony fingers. He swiped the phone open and pushed the play button. Lucia blinked a few times.

"What?" Dylan said.

"Nothing," Lucia said with chagrin as the panicked voice came over the tiny speakers.

"Mr. Derringer? This is Annabelle. I'm a first year. Um…I know you do the news and stuff…but this is really fucking weird…" A vicious scream came out over the speakers, followed by a dull thud. "My roommate is levitating off the ground, and she's slamming herself into the ceiling." The roommate was crying now. Sobbing to the point of hysteria, another voice came in from the background.

"Annabelle! We should just call Campo. Dylan's not gonna be able to do anything."

"He will help somehow. I just know he will."

The voice of the roommate who was wailing before now screamed in absolute fear. "SOMEONE GET ME DOWN FROM HERE!"

"Dylan, please help us!"

"Dylan, we—"

Lucia's eyes widened in fear. "Dylan, how long ago was this?"

"Well…" Dylan tapped his chin. "Probably twenty minutes ago."

Lucia sprung up from her chair, kicking Dylan's away in the process. He flailed as his chair spun into the far wall. Bones scattered all over the floor as the skull landed crisply onto the seat his pelvis had occupied seconds before.

"What apartment?!"

"I don't find this very humorous, you know." Dylan said, deadpan.

"Dylan, they could be fucking dead, you shit. WHAT. APARTMENT?"

The arms started to crawl their way toward Dylan's torso. "The first-year girls' dorm on the south side, room 213." Dylan's head rolled off the chair onto the floor.

"You owe me," Lucia said as she left the studio.

"You owe me for knocking me onto the floor like a rag doll!" Dylan called out as the door was closing. "Ugh. I wish I still had skin."

Lucia took off, afraid that someway or somehow this tied into the Grimfaern.

———— ♦ ————

Lucia sprinted into the woods from Pearson. From her current position, she would make it to St. Claire Hall (the first-year girls' dorm room) in a matter of minutes. The brush wasn't as thick as the eastern side near the nets. For her this was comforting, because time was of the essence.

The trees whizzed by her, and the path was made clear in the moonlight. Having trekked the woods frequently in search of herbs was also quite a boon, but tonight she was running on pure adrenaline. Lucia broke the tree line and saw a few first-year girls making out behind the building. Lucia almost ran into them as they dived out of the way. The witch threw open the door and ran up the stairs. Busting into the second-floor common area, Lucia frantically looked for a sign to tell her where 213 was. She finally found a placard that pointed to 213 down the hall, realizing she had overlooked it twice.

Collecting herself, Lucia strolled down the hallway to the first open door to keep up appearances. What she saw baffled her.

Two girls sat on the floor trembling, holding each other in fear. Another girl was floating a few inches from the wall. The girls on the floor looked up, mascara running down their cheeks.

"H-h-h-help," one said.

The airborne girl had her back pressed into the wall. Eyes were wide open, and a trickle of blood dripped from her lips and onto the floor. Lucia looked at the girls, then back at the floating friend.

"Hi, I'm Lucia," said the witch slowly. "What happened to your friend?"

"She…" started the first girl. "She…"

"She ended up floating in the air, and now the blood is dripping out of her veins and mouth," the second girl exhaled. "We…we didn't know what to do, so we called the radio station. We don't fuck with Campo—er, Campus Safety."

Lucia nodded, not taking her eyes from the girl floating in midair, pressed up against the wall. "Yeah. I get the sentiment." Lucia took a few steps forward to get a closer look at the girl. "What's her name?"

"Jazz," the second girl said.

"Listen." The witch pointed toward the door. "Why don't y'all get yourselves some water? I'll look after your friend."

"She…she…can we trust you?!" the first girl blurted loudly.

"Yes," Lucia said calmly, continuing to watch for the slightest bit of movement. "I have some medicinal experience."

"THIS is medicinal?!" the first girl wailed. "She's floating off the fucking—" What Lucia saw next haunted her nights until the day she died. After the wail of Jazz's friend, Jazz herself twitched slightly. Her eyes slowly rolled into the back of her head. The head rocked forward in a violent and vicious *snap*. Lucia saw the pieces of her vertebrae sticking out from behind her head. To the girls on the floor, it sounded like her neck had only popped loudly. The white eyes looked back at the friends on the floor and trembled in their sockets. The mouth fell open in a ghastly mimic of a yawning child and exhaled slightly. It sounded like a dull *uhhhhhhhhh* and began to crescendo. The dull tone ascended into a vicious wail that pierced Lucia's ears. Both girls reeled back in horror as Jazz began to shake and tremble horrendously. The blood leaking from her arms began to disappear behind her screaming head…into the mouth of the Grimfaern controlling her like a puppet.

In a flailing motion, the now lifeless corpse of Jazz Carter hurled itself at the girls on the floor, Grimfaern and all. Lucia pulled out her wand and yelled to the girls, "GET TO THE DOOR!"

Both girls crawled as fast as they could, but the Jazz puppet ripped into the flesh of the second girl, who let out her own wail of agony. She kicked back at her pantomime friend. The first kick missed entirely, but the second took purchase. The Grimfaern, with its beady eyes, turned to its lieutenant and smiled. It wondered if Lucia Frey approved of the onslaught. Equal parts horrified and disgusted, Lucia snapped her wand and sent a baleful force of energy toward the arm lodged in the back of the dead girl. The arm inside the girl splintered. To the girls on the floor, their friend's back just exploded open, exposing the carnage of human remains across the interior of the dorm room.

The Grimfaern stumbled back and slumped against the bedframe, clutching its hand in great pain. The lifeless body of Jazz slumped forward and rested on the ground. Lucia tucked her wand away quickly and turned to the now sobbing girls. "Why don't y'all get some water from the fountain?"

They looked up into the eyes of the stalwart witch and nodded slightly. As they exited, crying somber tears, Lucia stormed over to the Grimfaern.

"WHAT THE ACTUAL FUCK IS WRONG WITH YOU?" She flipped open a knife and shoved it into the now molten hand of the monster. It wailed in pain. "NOT FUCKING YET. DO YOU UNDERSTAND? YOU'RE GOING TO EXPOSE EVERYTHING." Lucia looked out the opened door. "Get the fuck back to Nightshade. NOW." She pulled out the knife and kicked the Grimfaern. "Take this mess with you." The Grimfaern picked up the body of the girl in its other hand, looked back at the member of Gredalia, and jumped out the window.

Without making even the softest thud, the monster fled through the trees with the corpse of Jazz Carter.

Lucia pulled out her wand again and went to work. Muttering soft words in Nexian, she began to clean the room. Books, blood, and dirt all vanished in rapid succession. She felt the exhaustion creep into her bones.

As she was finishing up and putting her wand away, both girls walked back into the room.

"Oh! Hi there! I'm Gabby." The first girl smiled at the witch, moving her water bottle to her left hand to shake Lucia's. "Who are you? Have you by chance seen Jazz?"

"We came over for…something? I guess she must have stepped out." The other friend took a swig of water from her own water bottle.

"Probably," Lucia said matter-of-factly. "Honestly, she probably just went for a walk. I'd wait here about an hour or so just to make sure she's okay."

"Sure!" they said in unison and sat back down where they had been crying moments before.

Lucia handed the other friend a bandage. "For your bleeding leg," she said.

The friend jumped slightly. "Oh! I didn't even notice. I must have hit it on the corner of the bed or something. Silly me," she said as she bandaged herself up.

Lucia exhaled in relief and made her way out the door. Into the night, Maester Frey shouldered her trench coat and looked up at the students passing her on the Boardwalk. Couples, singles, and nerds all waved or nodded in passing. Some gave a curt "hi" just to break the tension. As Lucia continued to walk toward her abode, she gave one last look into the night. Key in lock, shoulder into the wood, she noticed Jazz Carter walking back toward her dorm in the amber light of the Boardwalk, with a wicked grin on her face and dead eyes.

Lucia smiled to herself as she watched the Grimfaern go into the night.

The Artificers

RESIN KNOCKED ON the door of the House of IT. It was his off day, and he would rather have been in his house with a beer. However, he couldn't just let this shit slide anymore. Not when it was almost killing his people.

I want to get eyes on this myself, Resin told himself as he stood outside of Darius's house. *The Grimfaern almost got Thorn and Lock. This time, however, Darius and I walking in unannounced* should *give us the upper hand. The question is: Is Darius ready? Lauren seems to think so, but I want to test his mettle to see if she's right.*

Darius was supposed to meet Resin outside of his house. He was fifteen minutes late, and Resin prayed he hadn't fallen asleep.

I could just go into *his house.* He flipped his security keys out of his pocket. *House of IT is just a generic key. I'm sure he'd get a fright though.*

This raid was going to be on Nightshade Hall, which seemed to be the epicenter of the problems. Based on the intel the Artificers had gathered and their previous encounters with the Grimfaern, Resin didn't think it wasn't going to be that difficult, especially with the upper hand of surprise. Resin wished that Lucia was there. Lucia was AWOL, however. Lauren was still recovering at Billings General Hospital, with oversight from Thorn and Lock rotating in shifts. Darius was his only option for backup at the present time.

Resin knocked again loudly.

"Coming," a groggy-sounding Darius called from inside.

"Bro, hurry up. We got shit to do." Resin looked over his shoulder and checked his watch.

"Sup, man?" Darius said. About five feet behind Darius, Resin could see the figure of a beautiful young woman in hardly any clothing. Darius himself was naked from the waist down. "Oh, this is Carolína. Carolína, this is Resin, a buddy of mine."

"Did you forget our…" Resin looked at Carolína, then to Darius. "…arrangement?"

"I didn't. Carolína wanted to see me." Darius chuckled.

Resin looked at Darius and sighed. "What happened to your boy?" Resin said.

"My boy that I hang with all the time? Steve? Yeah, he's been busy lately." Carolína came up beside Darius and nestled into his side.

"Sir, can you come back a different time? Darius and I don't get much time together."

"Carolína, this is something important that we can't necessarily ignore." Resin's voice fell flat. "I was hoping he would keep his schedule somewhat…open until we could deal with what we've got going on."

"What if…he wasn't gone the whole night?" Carolína touched Darius's lower abs. "Please. It's important to me. To us."

Resin looked up at Darius and noticed his tattoo was moving, his eyes glowing a dark purple. Resin exhaled.

"I can certainly do my best." Resin said to the woman, feeling and hoping the lie he told broke through the annoying sexual tension between Darius and Carolína.

Carolína turned to Darius and kissed him passionately.

Resin turned his back, blushing deeply.

It was another fifteen minutes before Darius came out, tightening his belt.

"Lemme guess, you got another quickie in before you decided to meet me?" Resin glared at Darius, without caring if he noticed or not.

"Jealous ass," Darius huffed.

"Nice save too, by the way. I recall a certain man you were swooning over." Resin turned sharply as Darius growled at him, purple eyes violent now.

"Shut. The FUCK. UP." Darius gestured to an open window, with the sound of light snoring emanating from within.

"She's asleep, Romeo." Resin said curtly. "Shall we? We have a non-sexy date with an old building."

"Let's get this over with." Darius's attire was anything but covert. A black tank top with cargo shorts.

"Did you decide you were going to the beach? What's the reason for the athletic tank top?"

"Would you fuck off? I love my tattoo. It swirls, and people think it's hot."

"Dude." Resin put a hand on Darius's shoulder. "I don't give a flying fuck about who thinks you're hot. We have fucking Nexian spawn in a building on campus that could ruin the whole world."

"You don't fool around much at home, do you?"

Resin rolled his eyes. "Come on." Darius snickered and followed Kirkbride.

They were too bunched up for Resin's comfort, but he instructed Darius to wait a few seconds before Darius joined him after his next movement in the trees. It was an old Army tactic that Resin employed in this scenario to make sure that, if he was injured, Darius wouldn't immediately be wiped out or injured too.

Resin seemed to be trembling in the night air when Darius caught up to him after several minutes of their staggered movement.

"I thought you're in the military. Or *were*."

"Yeah, so what?" Resin said defensively.

"Why you sweating, man? What gives? You're supposed to be the cream of the crop."

"I *am* the cream of the crop," Resin explained. "I have awards and accolades from the military. It's just…been a minute."

The pair broke through the northwest tree line to see Nightshade Hall. The decrepit building looked like it could cave in at any moment.

However, this was the place.

Resin took a deep breath and looked up into the lightless building.

"Can you explain—"

"Quieter," Resin hissed.

Darius held up his hands defensively, "Sorry. Can you tell me why this building doesn't have anyone in it, like hardly at all?"

Resin considered while he scanned the exterior of the building. "Yeah, there used to be a lot of classes in here. Problem became that maintenance couldn't keep up. It's weird—Gristholme has a lot of money, but they really didn't *want* to. Therefore, we have this situation: a run-down, shit-ass building you keep up with and put Wi-Fi in for various gatherings and parties. The thing is, no one uses it because it creeps them out. Except the Alphas. Fuck the Alphas."

"Alpha Society? What's wrong with them?"

"Tell you later." Resin's breath caught in his lips as his eyes widened. "Dude, look!"

Darius looked up and saw a ghastly sight. There were a man and a woman fighting in one of the windows. They threw each other, one after the other, against the banister inside the building. Darius looked back and forth until finally the woman went flying, flailing over the edge. There was a thud that echoed as the windows shook. Dust flew out of the bottom of the front door as it came unlatched, swinging open.

I never liked this fucking building, Resin thought to himself.

"Oh. Oh shit." Darius said. He closed his eyes and searched for the necrotic power deep inside of him. He re-opened his eyes, now a deeper, purplish hue, catching Resin off guard.

"Good call," Resin said, not taking his eyes off the man in the window until he disappeared from view. "Nightshade reeks of these echoes from the past. People who died here, murders committed, slayings, trauma—it can all leave a fingerprint, fragment, or residue that we as Nexian users can see. Sometimes, a strong-willed human can get 'visions' or 'communicate' with these fragments and claim that they're mediums." He scoffed and shook his limbs out. "They're only *half* right. Unfortunately, they expose themselves to the Nexian entity. However, we can't linger on that for too long. I need to see what's going on inside."

Resin, in the moonlight, grew in height and took a bit of a slouch. The hair on the back of his neck grew thick, his mouth becoming a pointed snout. Resin looked back at Darius, grinning. "This part never gets old." *SNAP! POP!* Resin's joints and spine contorted in the light of the moon. He was now a full-blown wolf-man. His eyes were a vibrant green and his hands dragged on the ground.

"Come on," Resin said, hand on the door, voice rumbling deep in his chest.

"Right behind you, Ol' Roy," Darius said as he fell in behind him, leaning on the drills he and Lauren had gone through religiously. The wolf was known for his military-style breaching tactics, maneuvers, and room-clearing. Darius summoned the sword and put his hand on Resin's back, tapping twice to let him know that he was there.

Good to see that Lauren trained you well, Resin thought.

Nodding, Resin, followed by Darius, stepped inside Nightshade Hall.

A balcony area was flanked by two sets of stairs, with rooms up top that acted as classrooms or party rooms for students. Bookshelves, now the homes of spiders, were along the walls of Nightshade and underneath the staircase. Cobwebs grew so vigorously that Darius was amazed at how much room they took up.

Resin put his palms onto the ground and scanned the room. Hair bristled on the back of his neck.

Darius gripped his sword tighter, waiting for the first sign of movement other than Resin to come into his field of view.

Resin put a hand slowly to his lips, pointing after a second into the hall. Darius followed his finger to see the woman from earlier, a deep gash in her stomach, with splattering wounds that looked like a shotgun blast. A slash in the throat, with dead eyes staring ahead, hands with tiny cuts in them. She was gasping for air, trembling like an ethereal trout. Darius inhaled slowly, not taking his eyes off the ghost. Resin's muscles tensed. Her mouth opened slowly, and Darius gripped the sword even tighter.

"Got…got…"

Resin growled menacingly.

"Got…got…"

Darius saw out of the corner of his eye a doorway adjacent to the bookshelf, which led into another back room.

Standing in the doorway was a lanky but menacing figure.

"Resin," Darius's voice cracked. "Three o'clock, doorway."

Resin took a quick glance to his right to see the figure in the doorway.

Darius looked back at the seeping wounds of the ghostly woman.

"GOOOTYA!" The rotten breath of the woman snaked through Nightshade Hall. Her corpse slacked before exploding into gore and viscera. Pieces of flesh and limbs caked Darius's clothes and sword.

Darius reeled from the explosion as Resin drove his fist into the gut of the Smiling Man.

The Smiling Man doubled over in pain and staggered back a few feet into the classroom behind it. "We meet again, SCOOBY-DOO!"

Resin roared, spittle flying over his opponent.

"Now, that's *not* polite." The Smiling Man cracked its neck and knuckles. "Even if you are a flea-ridden chuckle fuck."

"Where are you hiding the Grimfaern?!" Resin yelled. "I *know* they're in here."

"Well, that's too bad, isn't it?" The Smiling Man lunged at Resin before vanishing into thin air.

Resin flinched.

Where the fuck did he go?! he thought.

"Helloooooooo! Peek-a-BOO!" Resin heard in his ear before the dull pain of a punch radiated from the back of his head.

He staggered forward, attempting to regain sight by shaking his head.

"Ah, that's such a pity. Here I thought you were *much* stronger than that."

When Resin disappeared into the classroom on the wing of the building, Darius wiped his eyes on the only clean patch of clothes he had. "Fucking nasty, man."

Suddenly, he heard a scraping sound of claws splintering wood.

Through teary eyes, Darius saw a male student standing on the balcony, hand outstretched.

"You didn't even knock? *So rude!*" He was wearing a green athletic jacket, his hair adorned with purple highlights. "The fucking audacity of men these days!"

The student's face contorted as he made his way toward Darius. Darius couldn't see the arm that was dragging along the floor until the student squared up to him at the top of the stairs. Shrouded in darkness except for his blood-red eyes, the man slowly came into view as he made his way into the moonlight that pierced Nightshade's skylights. His arm appeared non-human, at least twice the size and length of his other arm but as black as a piece of charcoal. The talons at the end of the arm were balled into a fist the size of a boulder.

Ah, fuck. Darius thought to himself. *This is not good.* He called out to the student, "What's your name?"

"My name *was* Iman." The student smiled. "Now, I have no name." He roared, bearing his needlepoint Grimfaern teeth.

"Okay, not-Iman," Darius started. "I'm sorry to say, but I'm going to kill you."

The Grimfaern laughed, "I'd like to see you—" Iman gasped as Darius extended his hand, releasing a burst of Nexian energy in the form of a long oozing tendril. Iman coughed as Darius began to choke him.

Darius bounded toward the staircase, maintaining his concentration on the tendril.

The tendril wrapped itself around Iman's torso like a snake as Darius climbed the stairs.

"Funny thing about that, copycat…" Iman let out a groan of pain as the tendril squeezed his lungs. "I have the upper hand now," Darius said.

Back in the side classroom, Resin regained sight only to feel the Smiling Man punch him in the chest. He raised his arms in defense.

"Since when were you able to teleport, Frankenstein?"

The maw opened, and a wheezing laugh rolled out. "The more time I spend here, the better and stronger I feel. Beats not existing in some *hellscape*. But oh? What's that I hear? Seems your friend and *my* friend are having a little tête-à-tête…"

The Smiling Man vanished once more.

Resin growled and ran back into the main hall. "DARIUS! GRIMFAERN INBOUND!"

Darius, focusing intently on choking Iman to death, felt a swift kick in his side as the Smiling Man appeared.

"Now, now," the Smiling Man chided. "Save those tentacles for your browser search history…that's not a nice way to treat my *buddy*."

Iman coughed violently, with dark black blood soaking the floor.

Darius took his sword and swung with all his might at the Smiling Man.

Darius blinked as the Smiling Man disappeared.

Iman, sensing the Smiling Man's disappearance, sent his open palm Darius's way.

Darius couldn't block the slap in time and tumbled over the banister into Resin, who had just left the side classroom.

The pair scrambled to get to their feet as the Smiling Man appeared once more, looming over them.

"The Grimfaern are hungry, boys." The Smiling Man laughed, and his toothy maw oozed blood from the emaciated gums. "I think I know just what to feed 'em."

"Dick cheese sandwich," Darius said as he sliced upward with his sword.

The Smiling Man stumbled backwards as a black ooze seeped from his groin wound.

Seeing the break in the fight, Darius pushed off Resin and dove forward, attempting to seize the advantage.

Resin got to his feet and saw Iman run down the stairs from the second floor. Resin decided to fight Iman while Darius held off the Smiling Man.

The Smiling Man was buffeted by Darius's attacks. His sword sliced through the air and was fueled by the anger building in his chest. The Smiling Man screeched as the ooze left his side, covering Darius's sword in the Nexian's blood.

Darius blinked and the Smiling Man disappeared. He kept his eyes closed and focused. *I'm going out on a limb,* he thought to himself. *However, the magic should bend to the user, at least for a little bit.*

Darius was searching for any major shifts in energy by using his Nexian powers. Suddenly, Darius felt a puff of air from behind him. He wheeled around on the tips of his toes and slashed down with all his might at the air.

The Smiling Man gasped as the neck wound shot black sludge all over the floor.

Darius ran and kicked the Smiling Man with a burst of Nexian energy, sending the Smiling Man into the wall by the door.

The Smiling Man slumped forward, apparently unconscious.

Darius slowly approached, placing his blade on the neck of the Smiling Man. He stood guard while Resin fought.

"SMILING MAN IS DOWN!" Darius yelled. "YOU GOOD?"

Resin howled, "I shouldn't be long."

Iman laughed and squared up to the wolf.

In the time that passed, Resin and Iman were duking it out. Resin would launch a blow, Iman would deflect. Iman would kick, Resin would block. The back and forth concerned Resin greatly.

This is supposedly a newer Grimfaern, Resin thought while he lashed out with his claws. *If Darius and I can't stop the Smiling Man and a new Grimfaern, what about the ones that have had time to develop new powers?*

Resin feinted when Iman threw an uppercut.

Iman, cocky that he could kill the wolf, was now off-balance.

This is my chance! Resin thought. Resin took his full strength and plunged his pointed claws into the chest of Iman. The loud, saturated squelch echoed throughout Nightshade Hall.

Iman's body landed with a dense thud on the floor.

Resin stood panting over the dead Grimfaern, blood sprawled up his torso and arms.

Darius relaxed his blade at the Smiling Man's throat and nodded at Resin. "Okay then, let's get out—"

The Smiling Man drove his claws into Darius's side, and Darius cried out in pain.

Resin ran and slashed at the Smiling Man, who released Darius to block Resin's attacks.

Darius dropped to his knees and put a hand on his side, wishing he had listened to Resin about his choice of clothing.

"TIME TO EAT, MY CHILDREN!" The Smiling Man laughed once more. "DINNER IS SERVED!"

A rumble careened through Nightshade Hall, emanating from the classroom that Resin and the Smiling Man were previously in.

"RUN!" Resin cried.

Darius struggled through the pain and followed Resin out of the hall, looking back just in time to see the swarms of Grimfaern gnawing on the limbs of a lifeless Iman.

Lucia

THE SMILING MAN LOOKED toward the second floor, laughing before collapsing to his knees. The blood dripped from his worn gums. The dark black blood was beginning to dry, but the gashes in his body were still painful.

"Can you give me a hand here, or am I supposed to do this on my own?" The Smiling Man coughed.

Lucia Frey stepped out from her viewing spot on the second floor and scoffed, "You're a Grimfaern, heal yourself." She walked across the balcony and stood at the top of the stairs. "Rob Horn trusts you to lead this army, and you can't even heal your own wounds? Give me a break."

The Smiling Man seethed through his gums. "It isn't so much a matter of *can't* as *speed*." He grimaced as Nexian magic began to stitch up the bleeding wounds. "Are you going to get this lot to sleep, Maester? Is that why you watched the fight, or are you only here to heckle?" The Grimfaern continued their feast with sounds of tearing flesh and slurping.

"I'm here so I might as well. You're probably too tired from a fight with a half-Nexian and a wolf-man. I'm glad I got to see this mysterious Nexian user in action. His powers are growing, from what I can tell."

The Smiling Man squinted at the witch, searching for a hidden meaning in her tone. "The psi-girl told you about the battle, eh? We should have been there, Frey. *WE* wouldn't have let the insolents get away."

"Well, you just did. Right now. Just out that door." Lucia pointed. "Nice job, fuck nuts." She drew out her wand and began to speak in

Nexian, slowly speaking the words to send the Grimfaern into a slumber before they rose again to take on the world.

This should hold them until Rob is ready, Lucia thought to herself as the power built up in her wand. *They just ate, so they'll be compliant to a deep slumber in addition to the spell.*

She released the spell and watched light green wisps descend over the well-fed monsters.

Snapping to a position of attention, the Grimfaern finished the final pieces of their feast before heading to the bookcase and descending to the Gredalia Council chamber, where they would sleep like bats up in the ceiling.

"Oh, dog?" Lucia called down to the Smiling Man.

The Smiling Man looked up at the witch, attempting to hide his frustration and resentment. "Yes, Maester Frey?"

"Be sure to not let the door hit you in the ass on the way out."

The Smiling Man made his way to the bookshelf to let the Grimfaern into their cavernous home.

"Fucker," the Smiling Man muttered as he pulled the book down to trigger the hidden door's mechanism.

When the Smiling Man and the last Grimfaern were out of sight, Lucia descended the stairs to clean up the very violent mess left around the hall. Books, furniture, and various odds and ends were scattered about the place. The broken door needed to be fixed as well.

I can't take any chances of the water spell not working or some rogue Nexian discovering the damage done here, Lucia thought to herself as she lifted her wand. *Thus, the role of second in command of both Gredalia and the Artificers is truly revealed: Hell's janitor.*

She felt the buildup of Nexian energy in her body as she flicked her wand to and fro. Floor tiles that appeared to be overlooked with age returned to their rightful places. Splintered pieces of wood lifted into the air and stitched themselves back into place in the wall, chair, or desk they came from. Lucia flicked her wand toward the remaining pools of blood, bone, and viscera from Iman and watched as they lifted into the air, swirling around in a circle like a laundry spin-cycle before vanishing into thin air.

She received texts from both Resin and Rob while she was finishing her cleaning.

> *Robert Horn: Frey, nice report about the Smiling Man. It seems that he was, at the very least, able to fend off some rogue Nexians. Thanks for the heads up. Please return to the water treatment plant tonight for another round of contamination. I won't be joining you, but the plan is almost ready to be launched. This 'test' serves as a nice reminder of that.*

> *Resin Kirkbride: Lucia! Darius and I gained some insights on the Grimfaern. Meet soon w/ other Artificers? Please respond.*

"Goddamnit," Lucia huffed. *It never fucking ends with those two,* she thought to herself, feeling the annoyance build up as she sent broken glass and forlorn wood back into their places before moving into the classroom.

The classroom itself was a nightmare. The Grimfaern had come up through the floor, creating a hole the size of a compact car. Tile and other flooring components were thrown about, caking the desks in sealant and blood where the creatures clamored out of their nest.

She noticed that her anger hadn't subsided as she mustered the strength to return the floor to its natural state.

Lucia allowed herself to feel the emotion, in a surprising drop of her stoicism. It all washed over her: the tears, the exhaustion, the backstabbing, the pseudo-clandestine operations, the attempts to play each side's number two, the jaunts to the water treatment plant to keep herself and other Nexians safe…

"No," she said aloud, feeling the last pieces of tile fall back into place and exhaustion creep into her bones. "I can't think like that, not now. I've got a job to do for Gredalia."

Lucia wiped her face and made her way back to the front doors.

She stepped into the night air, continuing her trek south.

The Boardwalk was illuminated with its usual soft amber glow, but Lucia decided to stick to the tree line. She preferred the darkness when pondering the futility of her emotions and the cascade that was to ensue. Both sides, she dangerously wagered, were out of their element. Gredalia wanted to take over the world, and the Artificers wanted to protect it.

But what do you want, Lucia? Her thoughts crashing through her reason like an ocean at high tide. *What is it that* you *want for your life, Nexian kind, planet Earth?*

She shook her head and pinched the bridge of her nose. *What good does any of this do,* she countered, *except drive me to the brink of madness?*

Lucia took a left, walking next to the House of Campus Safety and the House of Counseling Services. She looked into both buildings, seeing only the dispatcher at the Campus Safety desk who was looking at her computers. Counseling Services was as dark inside as she felt internally.

"How easy it must be," she said aloud, "just *existing*. Living a normal life while, outside your measly consciousness, there are great forces working to kill or save you." Lucia felt the sting of resentment growing and the return of the tears on her cheeks. She rarely got emotional like this. When she did, it was particularly difficult to stop, which caused her to grow angrier the longer it lasted.

Lucia walked past both houses. She felt the drive to get home more than she had ever felt it before. Crossing the Boardwalk, keys in hand, Lucia got to the front entrance of the Moon's Loft. She rested her head on the door, feeling the weight of the world rest on her shoulders. They bowed under the weight, but she managed to turn the key in the lock.

The door creaked open.

Lucia stepped inside and took stock of the place she had called home since she was seventeen. The bustling café was now a silent tomb of memories.

She walked in the darkness and ascended the stairs. Her boots grew heavier and heavier with each step.

I'm so, fucking, tired. She rubbed her eyes. *I'm so tired of this bullshit.*

Lucia barely opened her door before falling in a heap of exhaustion onto her floor. Gideon, her trusty houseplant, extended several tendrils to gently drag its maester toward the bed.

Lucia snored, the soft echoes of her lungs assuring the plant that she was getting the rest she finally deserved.

The plant pulled back the covers and gently laid Lucia into bed. Two tendrils tucked the covers under her feet, arms, and chin, creating a soft cocoon. Gideon pulled back to return to its resting place underneath the bed, content that for once it was able to take care of the young witch to its fullest potential.

The Artificers

RESIN SCANNED THE ROOM and pondered. The faces that met him displayed various expressions: some nervous, some resolved, some just plain stoic. He knew that he had to be the leader they needed in this moment. Lauren had returned after several weeks in the hospital due to her injuries. Lucia looked downright exhausted. Darius had summoned his sword and was twirling it slowly as the tattoo shifted on his arm. Lock looked like he had gone through a bad night of partying. Thorn looked resigned to not fully knowing what was going on. Resin ran a hand through his hair and looked down the table.

"Gredalia is moving." He paced back and forth. "The Smiling Man, Brent, and Olivia have all waged attacks on us recently. What's going to stop them?"

"Us." Lucia said slowly, pensively.

"*Us.*" Resin pointed to Lucia. "She's right. We're going to have to move to the offensive. Which is downright scary." Darius and Lauren nodded. "Gredalia, from what we know, has several members here on the campus. We've talked about this before. We have profiles on Brent and Olivia. Are there any others we're missing?"

Me, Lucia thought to herself.

"Not that we know of," Darius chimed in, putting his sword on the table. "Wonder if they have any fuck buddies running around."

"It's likely," Lauren said with a sigh. "So, we know who they are. We have the location of their hideout. What are we waiting on?"

"Well, considering the fact that they have a legion of Grimfaern in the place, I thought getting the jump on them would change something." He threw up his hands, resigned. "It seems like their powers are growing and evolving. The Smiling Man can now teleport, which is different from my first encounter with it."

Thorn piped up, "Lock and I almost got canned, Darius and Rez almost got nerfed by them. It's dangerous as hell to go in there without some kind of plan to deal with the beasts. Even with a plan, you're *fucked*."

"I don't want any of you to die," Lock chimed in.

"Me either," Lucia said in a monotone voice, rubbing her temples. *I truly don't,* she thought to herself. *Y'all are nice people. However, there's a new world order to build.*

"I've got a plan for that." Resin cracked his knuckles. "We're going to advance on Gredalia when winter break comes. I believe that students like Iman, maybe even Olivia and Brent, are Grimfaern. How many are there? Well, that's to be determined. We can conclude this from what Darius, Lauren, and I have seen: students morphing into Grimfaern or having Nexian powers. I wonder if Brent and Olivia will be staying on campus. I can check the student log and see. They should be submitting those requests within a few days.

"We'll draw them out in some way, shape, or form," Resin continued. "I suggest breaking up into teams. Thorn and Lock, Lauren and Darius, me and Lucia. We can possibly tail Brent and Olivia, with a group launching another assault on Nightshade. The Smiling Man is by far the strongest among the Grimfaern, but he can be beaten. I think that with such a large group of the students gone and large scales of movement—like cars leaving, buses, etc.—the 'Gredalia Council' that the Smiling Man kept referring to may be using this time to launch their 'new world order.'"

"I like this so far, but you realize that Olivia and Brent are students, right? They'll want to go home to their folks," Lock said.

"Maybe. We're unsure of their home lives as far as I know, but they won't want to go home if we antagonize them," Resin said. "They want us gone, right? But that's not all." He crossed the room to a chalkboard next to where Darius was sitting. An image of the chapel and a circle that was supposed to represent earth were already drawn.

Resin picked up a piece of chalk from the tray underneath and started to draw arrows going from the chapel to the world. "I think they're looking to use these entities as sleeper agents. Bear with me a second here. Grimfaern are shape-shifting creatures. We have confirmation they're disguising themselves as students. Why?" He drew over the arrow on the chalkboard to bolden the lines. "They're going home for Christmas break. One thing I noticed when Darius and I were in Nightshade is that the Smiling Man *commanded* them. Well, what if the Smiling Man's order, code word, or cue was the *exact* thing needed to trigger an act of global terrorism, the size of which no one has ever seen, because *everyone* around you could be a walking bomb should enough Grimfaern arise. If a handful of the Grimfaern, disguised as students, go home for holiday, then they are the bombs placed, waiting to be detonated…"

As Resin continued, Lucia could feel a cold sweat coming on and her focus drawing inward, Resin's words fading out. It was the thing she feared the most: sitting in the room where it happened. The moment when Darius, Resin, Lauren, Thorn, and Lock all became her enemies. She didn't honestly know what to do. She wanted to save herself and tell Rob Horn what was going on, but to what end? What did it matter that the Artificers, relatively weak compared to the Gredalia Council, were trying to overthrow a new organization of terror? She would be secure in her place in the new world order. What did it matter that Resin was out of his league? She should save herself. She should totally save herself without question…

Lock slammed his fist on the table in frustration. "This is *ABSURD!*"

This snapped Lucia out of her deep thoughts, Darius out of almost falling asleep, and Lauren from picking at her cuticles with a knife.

"We're banking on a lot going right. The students must be gone, but some of them are monsters. They leave, which is what *GREDALIA* wants and Gredalia *is still here*. What does it *fucking* matter, Resin?!"

"The point is, Lock, that we need to have our heads on swivels more than ever. Someone you bump into in the cafeteria, a late-night hookup, a buddy from football—all of them could be Grimfaern or a member of Gredalia. We can't risk being clumsy here. Also, if we provoke Gredalia *enough* to keep them here, then maybe their plans will shift. If these *are* sleeper agents that can shape-shift, anything we can do now to maybe take one or two of them out would be extremely beneficial."

"At the point of inaction," Lock seethed through his teeth. Darius noted how his hands seemed to glow a light blue.

"It doesn't do us any good, brother, to get angry," Thorn said, with a reassuring hand on Lock's shoulder. "If anything, Resin is trying to keep us all safe."

Like a Labrador at the heels of its master. Lucia felt the annoyance rise and fall within her. *Excuses, excuses, excuses. I'm glad I'm not completely blind and haven't bought into Resin's false beliefs. He does so much to "protect" them, but at what cost? Blind servitude? I know my stance with Rob: Help me to help you. Resin can't even keep his own flock under control.*

Lock tucked his head and clenched his fist.

Lauren placed one of her knives on the table. "Rezzy. We are fighting a battle in which we do not *truly* know the odds. An assault of any kind needs to be calculated, which *you've* done, but the Grimfaern aren't just going to keel over. We are going to have to draw them out. Let's do *just* that. Let's each of us make an assault on Gredalia. Here. Now. We've got…" She checked her watch and sighed. "Three weeks until winter break. We have classes, and you have to work. We can gain even more insight on Gredalia. Let me trail Olivia, let Lucia observe in the coffee shop. Let's get Darius into high-volume places with his IT job and see what we can find. Thorn and Lock have the football field and other class-rooms too. We're resourceful. We must manage our assets."

The room collectively nodded, and Resin said, "Yeah, I believe that's a solid plan." He clapped his hands to add a finality to the decision. "Okay! So we're going to do this?" Everyone chimed in with agreement. "Alright then, be safe everyone. Let me know if you see anything out of the ordinary." Resin made his way to the other side of the hall while Lucia and Darius remained seated. Thorn, Lock, and Lauren exchanged farewells with everyone and made their way to the door. Resin grabbed a cup, a tea bag, and a teapot from the cupboard.

Lucia leaned back in her chair and closed her eyes, pretending to drift off to sleep.

Resin came back, noticed Lucia's "sleep," and sat on the chair closest to Darius.

"I know this is scary, Darius, but I really think that we're going to be okay," Resin said after he brought his cup of tea back to the table. "We have never faced an enemy like this before. It's usually situations with the societies being asshats to the students or parents needing to be thrown off the trail of their child's death." He took a deep sip. "This is something next-level."

"Seems oddly conspicuous, don't you think?" Darius had his arms crossed and leaned into the table. "Why would they be so careless? The Smiling Man told you that Gredalia was making a 'new world order.' Doesn't that give away the plan?"

"He seems pretty stable, right?" Resin shook his head, disgusted. "Coming from another space and time, warped by some fucked-up magic, and bad dental work would make anyone demented. I think, personally, the Smiling Man is so confident in his abilities and those of Gredalia that there's no other outcome *but* winning. I think it could have also been a slip of the tongue. Either way, they're wanting to commit mass terror and we need to stop them. I just wish everyone wasn't so tense." Resin got up to return his cup to the kitchen.

"There was a lot of tension. They know a war is coming." Darius's sword vanished in a hue of wispy purple smoke. "It's a diabolical plan: shape-shifting terrorists."

"By my assessment, they could thoroughly destroy the essence of humanity. The Grimfaern are shape-shifting entities that can morph into anyone so long as they have a directive and a picture."

"Okay, but one thing I'm lost on here… The Nexus and the manifestation of it into creatures, how does it gain consciousness enough to take commands?"

"Okay, here it goes. Nexian creatures like Grimfaern are fey creatures, basically what we consider to be 'demons.' Fey creatures are typically your forest spirits, minor deities, etc., etc. Grimfaern are perversions of these creatures. They come from the "ether," or the Nexus of the spiritual world…"

"So, we all just get reduced to this ether? There's no after?"

"There's energy. Good, bad, magical, unfiltered energy," Resin answered. "The Grimfaern come from this Nexus. For example, if Gredalia summons energy from the Nexus and brings it here, it manifests. This manifestation, this drawing from the well, so to speak, is how the Grimfaern attain bodies. Of course, it's likely that Gredalia can shape them to look however they want, but the Grimfaern likely on-command assume the shape of whomever they choose. They're amorphous. Their fluidity poses a huge problem, because then it's possible they assume the shape of a student, go home in place of that student, and then on a command word they trigger. This triggering implodes the modern world. Imagine your elected official is a Grimfaern. It's disastrous to wake up one morning, have your caffeine, and see that your elected official ate half their cabinet or parliament."

Darius exhaled loudly. "Well, that fucking sucks."

"It's everything." Resin sat up in his chair and looked down at the table, gathering his thoughts. "You think I don't stay up late thinking about this stuff? I walk around at night alone, waiting on people to need me, and all of a sudden this falls into my lap."

"How long have the Artificers been around dealing with all this shit?"

The wolf rubbed his hands together. "Lucy and I were the first two. We noticed some sporadic Nexian activity. Our powers grew. She took her mastery test, and I got the Wolf's Mark…" Darius now noticed Resin's own tattoo, a Norse depiction of a wolf, peeking out from underneath his three-quarter-sleeved T-shirt. "We found Thorn, Lock, and Lauren in their first year here on campus. Lauren was already Sundered, but we almost lost Lock and Thorn in the Rendering. We showed them the Hall of Ancients for what it really was, and now they know how to get in." Resin stood by the sink. "I never fully understood my responsibility until this came up." Darius cocked his head at this. "But I persevered, and I'm still alive. It's what we do." He sat the cup in the sink and turned to the young man. "I'm off tonight, whatcha got going on?"

"I'm gonna call up one of my love interests and see what's gonna please them tonight." He smiled a wicked smile, and his eyes turned the familiar dark-purplish hue.

"Well, have fun," Resin walked back toward Lucia. "I gotta wake her up. You don't have to hang around."

Darius got up and waved goodbye to the wolf and the witch. He saw that Carolína had texted him, wondering if his bed needed warming this evening. The smile that hit his lips as the autumn air broke into the doorway was one of the last he would ever smile. Had he known, he would have taken a moment longer to soak in every moment.

However, he did not know, nor would he ever.

———— ◆ ————

Thorn, Lauren, and Lock made their way back to the frat house. Beta House was somewhat in disrepair, as it had only two true members in its ranks. The door was slightly ajar due to the lack of concern from its members about whether their shit was stolen or not. The boys didn't care that Lauren was skeeved out by the way they kept their house. In fact, Lauren was too infatuated with Thorn to care. He had stayed with her in the hospital while Lock went to class and took care of the house. It had been a long recovery, but these three knew how to handle themselves.

They stepped across the threshold and wondered how everything was going to play out. Lock threw his jacket onto the couch haphazardly and sighed, stretching toward the dilapidated ceiling.

"I'm going to bed." Lock sighed, followed by a yawn. "Don't knock the walls too loudly, okay? The dust falls on me and I wake up."

"Fuck you, man," Thorn said with a laugh. Lauren hugged Thorn tightly and laughed with the group.

"We need to get some rest before the school week tomorrow! And *don't* forget your assignments. Both from Resin and class." Lauren's eyes twinkled as she looked around the room. "This place is a shithole and a half."

"We intend to fix it up," Thorn said solemnly.

"Eventually. That's what summer training is for!" Lock threw up a peace sign and closed his door, turning in for the night.

"You good?" Lauren looked up at her lover and patted his chest.

"I have a really ominous feeling about all of this." Thorn looked down at Lauren, standing a foot taller than her. "I feel like Resin is usually on his game. But now? Now it feels like we have nothing. You called him out on it a little bit, and I love you for it. However, now we sit at another impasse, not knowing what the absolute hell is going on. There are still members of Gredalia out there?"

"And Olivia and Brent are really strong…" Lauren winced at her healing injuries.

"I hope this works out." The tension in his shoulders caused them both to worry.

"We will be fine, my love." She resigned herself to the most common phrase known to man and took the hand of her beloved. They walked hand in hand up the stairs to Thorn's bedroom, speaking phrases lovers knew so well. The night entangled them in the throes of intimacy and sang them to sleep shortly thereafter.

Lauren stretched and threw on a bra that she had on the night before. She knew too well that this wouldn't be the last time that she would be doing this, and that comforted her greatly. She patted Thorn's head and smiled deeply, admiring the scrappy face and the physique of the man. He was a lot to look at. She had to fight off the cheerleaders (including Olivia at one point) to get remotely close to him. In the end, Lauren was glad that Thorn chose her, especially after she knew that Olivia was part of Gredalia and could have poisoned him.

She drew her blades and tested their mettle in the morning light. Supple yet deadly, just the way she liked them. Strapping them onto her back and one on her side, she stood in the sunrise, which crested through the windows and cast a shadow onto the floor. She went into Thorn's closet and pulled out a dress, threw on a pair of slip-on shoes, and finished getting ready.

She chose to go natural and without makeup, pondering what the day would hold. She bent over, giving her love one last goodbye kiss, and made her way downstairs. She looked in the cupboards and sighed at the breakfast options. There was one molding banana with not much shape left before it would become absolute slime, baking soda, beer, and a light box of cereal. She resigned herself to going to the school cafeteria.

As she checked her watch, she noticed how late she was and worried about the possibility of missing another stats class. She rushed to the armchair, grabbed her bag, and made her way to the Boardwalk and south campus. Lauren smiled in the morning sun as students made their way to their 9:00 a.m. lectures. Pulling her earbuds out of her satchel, she connected them to her phone and hit the Boardwalk, getting lost in her thoughts. She looked up and noticed the students jaunting about. With a quick pat of her knives and a nice deep scan, she noticed something odd.

A student's face shifted, just ever so slightly. Right beyond her field of vision but enough to be clear, Lauren saw a student's face contort into one of deep sunken eyes and a sullen mouth. She felt her breath catch in her chest. The Grimfaern. Lauren typed a quick text to the group chat, but before she sent it noticed another student, then another, all beginning to have contorted faces.

It was beginning.

Thorn and Lock

MIDMORNING, Thorn and Lock made their way to the school cafeteria, both knowing that they were absolutely going to be late to their classes. They were in different majors but the same classes (political science and history respectively, with minors in health sciences), and with football practice it was easiest for them to be on the same class schedule. It only made sense. The boys were bickering about miscellaneous plays and finals they didn't want to deal with when they got the text from Lauren, a couple hours after she composed it.

Guys. I think they're on the move. The students… Some of them are not students at all, but Grimfaern.

They exchanged glances and headed on into the cafeteria, suddenly wondering if they would get another full meal again.

Resin responded a few minutes later: *Shit. Well that's not good.*

Followed by Lucia: *An understatement if there ever was one. We need to execute our plan quickly.*

Darius sent back a few heart emojis, to the chagrin of the boys. They both grabbed plates of odd-looking muffins and cereal, sitting down at one of the tables in the dining hall.

"I've got to text them back…sumfinguh," Lock said as he shoveled food into his maw.

"We can monitor the football team? See if during lifting there's something off about them…" Thorn took a bite of cereal and gagged. "Shit. This tastes like literal grass."

"It's the new vegan option. It was literally on the dispenser." Lock chuckled.

"Regardless, we thought we had time…and now?" Thorn shook his head. "This keeps getting worse and worse."

"And we still have finals to deal with also."

"Really boyo?" sighed Thorn, his face incredulous.

"I only seek to help." Lock raised his burly arms in defense.

Thorn checked his watch and cringed. "We're gonna be really late."

The boys got up hurried to the conveyor belt located outside the dining facility. They placed their trash on the line and started to run for class.

The boys made their way to Watson Hall in a brisk walk. Ascending the building's ancient stairs, the boys ducked into the back of their food science class as the haughty Professor Catalina came in. She scoffed at their almost-late arrival and went through the roll-call list. She crossed their names off the list and began to lecture.

Thorn sat his phone on the desk and continued to scratch in his notebook. Lock was drawing in his notebook, wondering if there was really a difference between good and bad carbohydrates when he felt his pocket buzz. It was a text from Brent.

Lock looked over at Thorn, noticing how intently he was listening to the teacher's absent-minded ramblings. He waved. Thorn didn't respond. He gestured. Thorn was otherwise distracted. He looked around, seeing the beautiful women in the class sitting around him. He sighed, knowing what he had to do. Lock mustered up every bit courage and farted as loudly as possible.

To his dismay, along with that of the class, it was not just a simple bit of broken wind. It was more vicious than that, accruing peaks and valleys in sonic structure during its flight. At one point, Lock was afraid he had ruined his pants. He finished in two quick puffs and looked up at the professor sheepishly.

Catalina only held up a finger. Her face was the color of a beet.

Lock grabbed his items and made his way to the door. No one dared laugh. Thorn checked his phone as his friend walked out. He felt a slight pulse in his hand as the notification dropped down.

Yo look what I got from Brent!

Another text vibration.

Lock. Bring Thorn and meet me after lifting near the cliffside on south campus. I need to discuss some things with you.

Thorn scanned the room and saw that the teacher had her back turned, and no one else was looking toward him. He typed a quick response. *Bring your A game.* Sent.

Lock looked at it and sent back a thumbs up.

Thorn grew more worried as the seconds passed.

When he stepped outside, Thorn listened to the news on the campus speaker systems about the young man who "almost defecated in his class seat" and rolled his eyes. Dylan Derringer had flies on the wall everywhere. He should have known this would be no exception. Looking up to the campus around him, Thorn took in the fall day.

Autumn had started to wither through Gristholme and the plateau a few weeks prior, but today it was truly a marvel to behold. The parts of north campus that were deciduous were trying their best to hold onto autumn. Crisp leaves crunched under hurried feet as students milled about to class. Some took photos with cocked legs and spiced lattes in their hands. The air was soothing and not musty, and it wrapped around the body like a weighted blanket in a cozy fireside library nook. Thorn was thankful the season was almost over, because the Geese were not doing as well as they had hoped. The Gristholme football team had lost to Billings almost every single time over the years. It was only once in a blue moon that Gristholme could seal the deal. They were supposed to just stretch and warm up today for practice and then go over the game plans for the big game on Saturday.

Thorn took one of the side paths and checked his watch. He assumed Lock had gone back to the house to change before heading to the gym to lift, because their practice started thirty minutes after their 10:30 class ended. He scanned the Boardwalk and decided to take the path south instead of grabbing a coffee first. Pulling out his protein shaker bottle, he shook up his pre-workout. Sipping as he went, Thorn looked out for what Lauren had referred to. The students he passed looked relatively healthy and normal. The only anomaly was one student puking on the 'walk, but he honestly didn't care. It seemed to be just another day for the students of Gristholme.

He continued south, hands in pockets, and walked with a purpose. He felt the pre-workout kicking in, and his bones began to shiver with anticipation and the caffeine. While deep in his thoughts, Thorn felt a shoulder aggressively graze his. He turned back toward the source and noticed a very pale-looking individual with grey eyes, lengthy and lithe.

"Sorry," Thorn said, rubbing his shoulder tenderly.

"The fault was mine. I should have mentioned something to you, Mr. Gisalt."

"Mention what, exactly? Also, how do you know my name?" Thorn questioned.

The reply came back stoically. "It's my responsibility. I work in Student Affairs and know every student on facial recognition. Thorn Gisalt. Beta House." He turned away and continued walking lithely up the path.

"What the fuck?" Thorn turned away, sensing that time was running out. "What did you want to tell me?!"

The student ignored his call for more information.

"Jesus CHRIST!" Thorn shook his head and continued to his practice.

———— ◆ ————

The Gristholme Athletic Building, often referred to as the GAB, came into view fifteen minutes later on the southeastern portion of the plateau. Thorn loved watching the sea roll while deadlifting. However, this wasn't his day but a team lift day. He had to check in with his coach and figure out what his workout was going to be. He felt a vibration in his pocket and saw Lock's name appear on the cell-phone screen.

Hey, you here yet?

Thorn sighed and texted back. *Yeah, just walked in, why?"*

Brent is side eyeing me like crazy. Think he wants to fuck me?

Lock, seriously?

A few seconds lapsed between the replies as Thorn watched the basketball players working on their conditioning drills.

Brent was glaring at Lock.

Okay I'm sorry. For real though he's being weird.

Gotcha.

The GAB had anything and everything one could possibly want in a workout building. Occasionally, Lock and Thorn enjoyed the pool after a long day's lift session. A sauna was nestled into the locker rooms outside the pool area for everyone to partake. Thorn and Lock frequented it often.

The GAB was another piece of Gristholme that Thorn cherished profoundly. It was his equivalent of the Moon's Loft for most. It was a place to put on headphones and disappear into the throng of the student body. No Gredalia, no Artificers, just weights, pulleys, and sweat. He made his way to the reception desk, scanned his student ID, and proceeded down the stairs to the weight room. After throwing his bag into a cubby along the wall, he grabbed his headphones and selected his lifting playlist. Coach O'Flannery was along the wall with a clipboard. Thorn made his way toward him.

"You looking ta come 'round here looking like an absolute wreck?" His Irish accent crested the air. "Figure you'd be at least somewhat present- able for an outing about the plebeians."

"Coach, what's my workout?" Thorn sighed, annoyed at O'Flannery's beratement. *I guess the linemen don't get a simple stretch day, huh?* Thorn thought to himself.

"Five sets of ten reps for burpees, four sets of ten reps for deadlifts..." He droned on for a few minutes before looking up at the young man. "Any other questions?"

Thorn shook his head.

"Good. Lock is about with the lineman. Be sure ta holler if you have any questions."

"I will."

He finally was able to put on his headphones and disappear into the void that was the gym.

———— ◆ ————

The day went on and muscles tired out while the sun set over the water. Thorn eventually rested his weights on the racks. Wiping sweat from his brow, he nodded to Lock as he shuffled over.

"Okay, so have you seen Brent yet?"

"I thought you were tracking him."

"No! I lost him. I could always ask Coach..."

Thorn caught Lock's arm to keep him from moving. "No. No you will not. This could end up being deadly."

Sighing, Lock resigned. "Fine. But I really do think it's not as big a deal as you would think it to be."

They both retrieved their bags from the cubbies, and Thorn put away his headphones. Lock shouldered his ruck. He changed his gym shoes and wiped his arms down with a towel from shoulder to wrist. "Whatcha think's going to happen, Thorny?"

"I think we're gonna end up seeing Brent's powers," Thorn said solemnly.

"I thought we already knew Brent's powers…" Lock said.

"Firsthand." Thorn groaned.

"Oh. Shit," Lock said, embarrassed that he had missed the point. "Here I thought it was going to be how Lucia and Resin found us: We were in the wrong place at the wrong time, and our powers manifested."

"No," Thorn said. "I think this isn't anything like how we were found, Locky. I think Brent is looking for a fight."

"Gotcha."

The boys made their way outside and sensed the air. They felt a strong pull. Exchanging looks, Thorn pulled out a small stone and held it in his hand. Lock cracked his knuckles and blue energy trickled over his body. "Let's do this."

Thorn nodded and they followed the path toward the southern cliff-side. Along the south paths where students used to hide their underage drinking and illegal "funny" cigarettes, there were several ramshackle huts the school still used. One of them was the groundskeeper shack in which Lucia kept some of her witch's herbs. Students never saw the groundskeeper, who often moved around during the nighttime. Strangely enough, his hut was never locked. Students went in on dares and pranks but found only a bed, a coffee pot, plants, and a table. It was here that the boys found Brent, sitting at the table, hood pulled around his ears on his faded zip-up sweatshirt. He was poised, and both hands were on the table, folded.

"Sup?" The short burly man scratched his bearded face.

"Not much." Thorn said. He felt Lock tense up. "We're here. You're here. What do you want?"

"I'm here to parley, not fight." Brent started.

"About?" Lock took a step forward, blue energy moving up and down his arms.

"I want you to join Gredalia and tell us where your stupid hideout is."

"Our hideout?" asked Thorn, confused.

"Don't play games with me. I know that there is a band of you hiding here on the campus. It's obvious. First, some of you break into Nightshade, trying to infiltrate us. Then, some of you attacked me and Olivia. Then you break in *again* and you almost kill one of our members. Not the best member, but still a member, nonetheless. That's blood drawn, boys. And we of the Gredalia Council do not stand for this bullshit." He kicked his chair back and it busted against the counter of the hut.

Thorn and Lock both pulled back.

Thorn ran his palm on the stone and a sickle appeared in tingling energy. Lock's eyes changed to a dark blue, and whisps of blue energy swirled around him.

"Is that your answer?" Brent's fist clenched on the table.

"Fuck your stupid club." The sickle-wielder squared up.

"We're not joining." Lock's voice boomed out.

Brent's body began to change shape and contort. His eyes sunk into the depths of his head and his teeth grew forward into dangerous, needle-point fangs. He howled viciously, and the boys launched into their attack. Thorn's sickle scraped across the floor, drawing sparks of lightning into a bitter uppercut. Lock's energy pulsed out from his hands, and he began to float off the floor.

And then…they all froze in their places in the groundskeeper hut. Lucia Frey turned away from the window of the hut and walked north toward her home while the boys were locked in suspended animation from her Nexian magic.

Lucia

LUCIA FREY WALKED NORTH following the events at the groundskeeper shack, wiping her wand. She nestled it back into her holster and sniffed the air. She noted with contempt that she had to leave Brent in a bit of stasis, but it wasn't Brent. Not the Brent that she knew when he first joined the Council. Brent was selected as the test dummy for Operation Twilight. Rob had requested that one of the Grimfaern be tested, and Lucia chose Brent to be the human sacrificed to the Nexian monsters when they first came into the world.

The experiment had not gone as planned. First, Brent fought against Rob's request, causing an unnecessary brawl between the members of the Gredalia Council. Lucia was finally able to lock Brent into a stasis spell, rendering him unable to move. The Grimfaern dropped down from the ceiling and ended Brent's life. The goal of the sacrifice was to see how quickly the Grimfaern could change, now that they had been acclimated to Earth. All present members of Gredalia (Rob, Lucia, Olivia, and the Smiling Man) were satisfied with the Grimfaern's abilities.

Second, the new Brent-copy threatened to change while in class, so Lucia had to monitor him with quite some annoyance. Finally, she had to make sure that he didn't detonate while in his apartment and added mood spells to make sure that the Grimfaern didn't snap. This would ruin their plan to put the first round of students (twenty in total) out into the world for the holidays. These students would leave right after break started. Lucia knew the plan and knew she had to make rounds to check up on them, run a coffee shop, feed info to Dylan…but she was worn out. She didn't want to do it anymore. She wanted to retire up to the apartment and have Gideon hand her ingredients for the different potions she wanted to concoct in peace. Between Resin's demands and Rob's, Lucia was sick of everything in her sphere of existence that measured up to "world ending." They wanted it done yesterday.

Well, that just wasn't how things worked.

She hated the way in which she had to double cross both the Council and the Artificers. She respected each of their endeavors. In all honesty, she really did. It had gotten to the point that it was just business. Business, business, business. She wondered if this was how it really all had to go down. Her heart sank when she thought about her double-crossing coming to light.

In true Lucia fashion, she shoved these feelings and thoughts deep down into her soul and carried on, making her way to her next task. She had a date with a young skeleton.

———— ♦ ————

Lucia ascended the stairs of Gristholme Tower one step at a time. It didn't pay to rush someone who didn't eat, but she knew that Dylan would be going dark between seven and ten in the evening. She checked her watch and realized she had a few minutes to spare. Her coat brushed the railing and her boots echoed with soft *clicks* along the walls. Reaching Dylan's door, she rapped on it three times.

"Hold on, my plug-in baby!" Dylan's 1920s-announcer voice echoed through the mail-slot. The door swung open, and a cigarette-smoking skeleton sat in the chair. "You wanna go on a date with me?"

"I date women."

"So do I. Come on in!"

Lucia walked into the small newsroom and smelled patchouli and orange ginger. "I seriously hate your aroma combinations."

"I did it for you, Lucy baby! I did it for you." He patted the seat next to him.

"What's up, Dilly?"

The skeleton's features softened, with the corners of the eye sockets tugging downward with concern. "I gotta ask you, Lucy. This is not exactly what I wanna bring up when I see my favorite air-breather. In fact, I don't wanna be the bad guy here."

"Fuck. Send it."

"What do you do when you sneak off at night?"

"Sneak off at night?"

The skeleton nodded. "I see you, my love. You walk the sunken Boardwalk, gathering and following up on news sources for me. When do you sleep? Is it caffeine that drives you forward?"

Lucia just raised her hands in active lack of knowledge. "I just do it 'cause someone has, to and there's only one life you get to live."

"This is true," the skeleton sighed. "But within that one life, remember to *live*. Look at me!" He rattled his bones. "Don't wanna end up a bag of bones like me, spewing news into a microphone till time immemorial."

"Ever think about going into podcasting?"

"They'd love me, but everyone has a podcast."

"Except you!" Lucia laughed.

"They're definitely fun to listen to. No question about that." He cracked his knuckles. "Gimme a second." Dylan blinked and shook his fingers as if his arms had fallen asleep. He grabbed his microphone and crafted the words from the air like a wordsmith.

"Alas, Gristholme, it's that time again. Time again to return to your homes, where your childhood bedrooms beckon you. These bedrooms are probably time capsules and odd shrines that your families have kept up in the event that you dropout, fail, or just return home! Not to worry, Gristholme. It's the best possible thing they could do to you besides driving themselves deeper and deeper into debt to make sure you get a job in a field you may or may not go

to school for. It's shameful, really. Shameful, shameful, shameful! But this is the bedtime story my mother used to tell me many years ago, and it always stuck. So, I wanted to pass it on to the young first-years still deciding on their majors! I hope your travels are safe as you go home, my lovelies! The DFAC has decided to provide you with some sacked lunches, as winter hours will begin Saturday after the football game! Good luck, Geese! Best those Bee-devils and bring home the Rivalry Cup!

There's nothing else to report, other than finals on the horizon. The weather tonight is an ombre sky with possible snowfall on the horizon. Clouds are heavy and ready to burst! With that, we will close the night out. Good night, Gristholme! Be sure to snuggle deeply in your beds. Finals begin tomorrow!"

Dylan pushed the microphone away and shut off the record button. "This is what I really want to ask: Are you safe, Lucy? It's no secret that you're dabbling in the arcane, clearly, as you're talking to me and don't seem fazed at all. I sense trouble in your soul, though. Believe me, Lucia, if you get too deep into magic, you'll lose your soul." He lit up another cigarette and propped his feet on the console mixer. "I don't want you to be gone, doll. I want you to be existing in the world. This campus needs you. Fuck, *I* need you. You're a good air-breather, and your talents in journalism would go to waste if you were gone."

She took Dylan's hand and soothed him softly. "Dilly, I promise I'll be here. Okay? There's just a lot going on, and Rob is asking a lot of me to keep campus running."

"Isn't that what his technicians are for? Or grounds people? Maybe even the maintenance staff? Why are you working for the head of Campus Safety?"

Lucia scanned the room. She took a deep breath and then divulged info that she had kept close to her chest for years. "Rob Horn and I have a working agreement. I have honed my powers, giving in to the arcane and becoming a Maester." Dylan groaned. "And Rob is going to help me in return."

"That doesn't end well, Luce." Dylan rubbed his bony hands against his skull in frustration. "You're smarter than that!"

"You don't even know the half of it," Lucia scoffed.

"The half of it?" Dylan shook his head. "It's the classic trope, Lucia! You think you're getting ahead, but all the while the other entity is just *draining* you of your incredibly brilliant powers while they sit on their laurels. *Please* don't go through with whatever it is he's making you do, and listen to me!"

"Maybe." Lucia sighed. "It won't matter when I'm at the right hand." She stood and made her way to the door. "I gotta go."

"Lucy, what have you done!?"

She smiled at Dylan, "Okay bye, Dylan, love you!"

"Lucccccciiiiaaaaaaaa!" *FWOMP.* The door closed as the skeleton called out to his informant.

Lucia rubbed her temples and checked her phone. Radio silence. No one was missing their respective boy…or boys, thinking about Brent, Thorn, and Lock in their frozen states. It was a bit of relief in an otherwise annoying bout of tension.

She descended the stairs and felt the vibrations echo off the walls as her heels clacked on the steps. A few minutes later, she stepped out onto campus, with the giant doors closing behind her with a click. The moon was ominous, as was the crisp air, but for Maester Frey, it was the status quo. She made her way toward south campus once again, taking the path along the coastal shoreline. She mused about the entangled lines between her allegiance to Gredalia and the Artificers.

She continued onward, making her way toward the deep pines off the Boardwalk and First Years' Trail.

Lucia plunged into the thick trees and found a spot where the pine needles created a soft bed under her boots.

She leaned up against the tree, took a deep breath, and bitterly wept, allowing herself to feel the emotions she had repressed through exhaustion, sleep deprivation, and moroseness. Her legs slowly gave out from underneath her, and she landed softly on the ground.

Pawn. She heard Rob's soothing voice echo in her head.

Minion. Resin's voice seemed calm at first but grew menacing to her.

Tool. Rob's voice once more, growing in malice.

Expendable. Resin's voice shouted in her mind.

Lucia wept not for her "friends" in the Artificers. She did not weep for her co-conspirators of Gredalia. She wept for herself and her position as a pawn in the games of two powers.

They had sent her all over the place without regard for her well-being. Never had Resin or Rob actually reached out to see how she was doing. She was like the proverbial hamster in the hamster wheel, generating power for not one but *two* operations. Lucia needed Rob Horn's ability to remove the implant in her arm so she wouldn't become a silvery whisp of her former self and a member of Alpha Society.

Her place in the Artificers was out of a prior life and friendship with Resin. Breaking away from Resin would create alarm; she would be the rogue witch with the ability to turn people into Nexians or Nexian users. Resin would naturally see her as an enemy. It was just easier this way.

Rather, it *had* been easier.

Now, she had created Nexians and summoned them. Commanded them and served as their lieutenant.

As the tears fell, Lucia felt the burning inside her stomach. Shame crashed like an ocean wave reaching its crescendo. Once the wave subsided, hatred grew within her. She hated Rob for dangling her around like a puppet, throwing her to and fro with the strings of her Alpha implant. She hated the Artificers for not respecting her powers, particularly Resin and Darius.

"Oh god, Darius," she sighed and looked up to the stars. "I never should have Sundered you."

Lucia sat on the ground and wept for a long time. So long, in fact, that the night gave way to the day, and the sun crested over the horizon, reflecting off the cold sea.

When the tears finally stopped, Lucia Frey got up off the ground. The fear, tiredness, and paranoia fell with the pine needles. Rising was an anger and hatred that burned deep and furious: the scorn of the abused. The resentment of the creator ashamed of their creation.

Resin

RESIN OPENED THE DOOR to his house. It creaked as he stepped inside, and the air was stale. He didn't like the way that the air sat in his home.

A thought occurred to him then: Check the War Room. He sprinted up the stairs and threw open the door to his sanctum. Hyperventilating, he surveilled the scene, slowly drawing in all he could.

The window was open, to his surprise. The room was a total wreck, with his tackboard down on the floor and papers sprawled across the floor like a drunken night at the Gristholme frats. He tried to take stock of the room but immediately darted for his locked desk. He fumbled with his keys, which were shaking in his hands, and he opened the drawer. Within, he found his dad's lockbox, the journal of the Almost Doctor (an arcane Dr. Frankenstein that Resin fought solo when Resin first became the Fenris Wolf), and other items and artifacts Resin had gathered in his time at Gristholme. These arcane artifacts were some of Resin's most prized possessions.

Nothing taken, Resin thought to himself. *Just a scare tactic, it seems.*

He pushed the drawer closed and locked it.

Resin howled, hoping to scare whatever had broken into his house out of hiding.

CREAK.

Resin shot up directly with the realization that the intruder who ransacked his room was potentially still in the house.

Claws began to form out of his hands, growing slightly longer than they did last time. He grew a little taller and felt his shoulders and chest flatten out, acquiring fur and muscle along them. His clothes ripped a little, but it was the last thing on his mind.

His tread softened instantaneously, and he used it to his advantage as he pressed forward into the cold depths of his house. The lights were still off and the air heavy with anticipation. This wasn't the first time Resin had to deal with a scary situation (numerous students trying to ambush him, Nexians popping into this plane of existence, wolves trying to cut him off a hunt, and many more annoying instances). It would most certainly not be his last.

Inching his way along the landing, his ears flicked continuously. Like radar, he was looking for the slightest misstep from his invader. He looked down the hall and saw the shadowed figure glide through his bedroom, from left to right, disappearing to the right.

Resin sniffed the air.

It smelled like a Nexian entity.

Resin crept toward the bedroom with caution. The palpable fear was beginning to edge to the back of his tongue, marking the way in which he was responding to the stimuli. His light tread and long stride carried him along the floor with ease. Passing pictures of scenic views that he visted, Resin shook off his emotions and focused on one: survival.

CREAK!

Resin stopped. He looked down at the floor and saw that he had stepped on a board. Looking toward his open bedroom door, he saw shadows dancing behind his headboard with flailing movements. Long tendril-like whisps for hands grasped toward the ceiling as if the entity was drowning. He slowly lifted his foot off the board.

No noise emitted from the board he had stepped on.

Whatever made the creaking noise was coming from inside his bedroom.

Resin took a deep breath to steady his nerves, feeling energy coursing through his veins. The shadows continued to flail in an anguished fashion.

Resin crept up to the door of the room and paused.

Take a deep breath, Resin thought. *I have to clear the room.*

He counted to three before kicking the door open the rest of the way.

He jumped in and roared, trying to scare whoever was inside his house into submission. The cackle came slowly, dryly, from the corner.

"Really coming on strong there, boss."

Resin turned toward the sound and felt rage building up within him. He roared again, spittle flying out toward the Smiling Man.

"Grow up!" He tsked. "Resin, my canine friend, you knew this was gonna happen! You saw this coming. You sat on your laurels instead of attacking. Now Gredalia is coming down on you! It's soon, chief." The wicked grin barely moved. "We're gonna detonate our sleeping Grimfaern inside these students and we're gonna wreak havoc upon the world." The Smiling Man's claws began to grow as well. "Boss is gonna want me to end you so that the head is cut off the snake. I don't want to, naturally, so I'm going to ask you once to join Gredalia."

Resin's wolf form started to growl, but it continued to evolve and shift until it was a deep and hardy chuckle. "Smiling Man," Resin started, "you're a fool."

Resin sprang off the floorboards and launched himself toward the sickening figure.

"Fuck all," said the Smiling Man. Pulling his hands back quickly and crouching, he launched himself toward the young wolf. Their claws connected; blood splattered on the floor as the Smiling Man received a blow to the stomach. Resin pushed back and extended himself to full height. The Smiling Man reeled back and launched in for another attack. Claws connected with Resin's shoulders as the Smiling Man latched his large teeth into the wolf's shoulder. Resin cried out in pain and felt his own blood beginning to trickle out.

The Smiling Man spat a tear of flesh out of his mouth. "Come on, Resin. That's the best you can do?"

Resin squared up and dropped his hand from the wound on his shoulder. He cracked his neck, staring intently at his opponent.

"You're a *fucking* wolf!" the Smiling Man continued. "The Fenris Wolf incarnate. You completed the Sundering *and* the Rendering, and *THIS* is the best you can do? Show me. Show me *RIGHT NOW!*"

The Fenris Wolf began to glow a deep shade of green. The Smiling Man extended to his full height, back on his hind paws, arms outstretched. Resin took a deep breath, picturing the Nexian word for *burn* in his mind, just as his dad had told him. Feeling the peak of his inhale, Resin propelled the green energy from his chest in a laser-like beam toward his opponent.

The Smiling Man staggered in pain, as his attempt to dodge was in vain. Green blood plastered the wall behind him.

Resin took a step forward.

"That's nothing." The Smiling Man spat blood onto the floor. "I know what you can do. Fight me, coward!" The Smiling Man dipped as Resin sent another wave of green energy at his closet. The door frames splintered, leaving a gigantic sear mark in the wood of the house.

The Smiling Man ran toward his stairs, trying to make his way back into the rest of the house.

Resin held his wound as he ran into the hallway, feeling great exhaustion take over his body. Resin expected to see the Smiling Man on the stairs, making his way down the banister and off to somewhere in the house.

Everything was silent once more.

Resin walked slowly along the upper floor and called out in guttural speech, "I would *never* join Gredalia! Your boss is going to die, along with the lot of you, for trying to release the Grimfaern upon the world. That's why Ragnarök happened the first time. My father told me—"

"Your father *LIES!*" The voice of the Smiling Man echoed inside his house.

Resin clenched his fist. *Shit. I gave him too much info.*

"Tell me, Resin. Did you ever wonder how I came to be? Do you know the story of the Nexian Frost?"

"Yeah." Resin bristled, annoyed that the Smiling Man was trying to distract him. "I thought we were fighting!" he called out as he started to make his way down the stairs.

"*Shut the FUCK UP!*" the Smiling Man called back.

BOOM.

The loud sound caused Resin to flinch as the foundation of his house shook. *The basement.* The sound came from his basement. He quickly analyzed how he could get down into the basement without being cornered by the creature. Resin guessed he could break through the floor with his arcane energy, but he would probably land on something he didn't want to.

"The Nexian Frost was the attempt to hold the Old Nexians hostage after Ragnarök. Here on Earth, this was your Ice Age. So, I slept. I slept and waited, until one day our leader pulled me from the ice. He searched for me because he had researched the perfect team. That team is *here*, Resin. We will bring about a new age of peace and we will establish what humans have failed to: a true golden age." Resin crept over to his living room, guessing where he could break through and land. He got up onto the sofa and took a deep breath, feeling the reserve of energy inside him building.

"You could be part of the Council and make things how you like them. Want a continent?" Resin could tell he was in the basement, being as close as he was now. "We can *give* that to you, good sir." A chair scraping along the basement floor and slamming into the wall to Resin's right made him jump a little. "This is null and void though if you turn this offer down." *This would be their equivalent of an entry exam,* Resin thought. He stretched and focused his energy into his legs. "Well? What's your ans—"

Resin sprung from the couch, doing a front flip in the air. He directed the energy in a sudden burst to his legs, aiming for the floor, hoping to break through. The strength of his powers caused the floorboards to shatter as he propelled himself through the structure. *FOOOMP.* He felt a weight make contact with his legs.

As he collided with the concrete floor, he tumbled over the weight and into the cluttered basement. A pipe of water burst where Resin fell through. He looked up from where he rolled and saw the Smiling Man in a pile of floorboards. Green blood leaked into the basement combined with the water.

"Good job, Fenris." It coughed blood into the pooling water. "I never would have thought…you could kill me."

Resin pushed himself up, despite the wish of his bones to drop back into the water. He shuffled over to where the Smiling Man lay. He grabbed the Smiling Man, pulling him up and out of the water. He looked intently into his eyes. "I will never join you fuckers." With a rapid motion, Resin snapped his neck. Releasing the body, Resin made his way quickly to find the water shutoff valve associated with the burst pipe. Within ten minutes, he was able to shut off the water to that specific pipe and call the water company to temporarily postpone his service, as he was leaving on an extended business trip.

He grabbed the body of the Smiling Man and carried it by the broken neck upstairs. He threw it onto the kitchen floor. Dragging a reclining chair, he placed it on top of the body. He then returned with a second reclining chair and put it on top of the body as well.

"Fucker." He spat on the chairs.

He made his way up the second-floor staircase slowly, gasping in pain as he went. Walking down the hallway, Resin had half a mind to burn the place down. It didn't serve him anymore, and he wasn't sure how the property would be settled. However, he recognized the need for it one day, if he survived the impending battle.

He turned into the war room and made his way for the closet. Digging behind some old boxes, Resin grabbed his rucksack. Inside was a few days' supply of clothes, a couple of knives, a substantial amount of cash, important documents, and other necessary items. He turned and went toward the desk, grabbing more of his sensitive items. *Bvvvvvt. Bvvvvvvvvt.* He pulled his phone out of his pocket. *Lauren. Bvvvvvvvvt. Bvvvvvvvt.* He hesitated but answered on the final ring.

"Hi, buddy! How are things going?"

"Lauren, Gredalia is moving."

"Fuck. Are you okay?"

"I got ganked by the Smiling Man. He's dead though."

"How did you kill him?"

"Snapped his neck. I'm getting ready to come to campus now."

"Oh, shit. Well, take care and be safe! We will see you soon!"

"Okay, Lauren, bye."

Resin continued to pack his things. He emptied out his desk. Resin patched the wound on his neck and shoulder with some gauze and medical tape he kept in his desk. He had to get back to campus.

He swept through the room once, twice, three times to make sure that everything important was in his rucksack. He shouldered it with a wince.

This fucking stings, Resin thought to himself, *but there's no time to heal with magic. I need to keep moving.*

He stretched deeply, wincing. Resin sighed, feeling exhaustion grow within him as he made his way back down the stairs. Kicking the chairs off the Smiling Man, Resin grabbed him back up by the scruff of the broken neck again. He dragged the corpse to his Jeep and threw it in the back, slamming the door shut.

Resin didn't bother to cover the body because the need to be covert was over.

He locked the door to his house as rain clouds rolled overhead, beginning to release the first few drops of atmospheric tears. He looked up into them, feeling the prickle of bitter cold pierce through his skin. He recalled his dad's words of wisdom and spoke them out loud: "Bitter winds and rains envelop the soul, but my body withstands them all. I embody them, allowing my mind to recognize them, accept them, but I do not become them. I am stronger. I am resilient. I am greater than the forces that strike against me."

His gaze made its way in the direction of the school. Resin felt the embodiment of his fear pulling him ever-nearer to his potential demise. Resin exhaled with finality and got in the car, flicking on the radio to listen to Dylan Derringer banter about winter break coming so quickly.

———— ♦ ————

Resin wiped his hands on his pants, as the towel from his emergency car kit had tumbled off the cliffside. He knew even if he were being watched, no one could see the burning item that was tumbling to the cold waters. Looking at the clouds rolling in, noticing the way in which the rain was starting to form into snow-ice crystals, he checked his phone. He saw that Lauren and Darius were on their way to the Hall of Ancients to meet him for a very quick meeting regarding what had happened. He would tell the others to get filled in from these two. His temporary accommodations would be the hall. It was a place he could slip in and out of quickly without much notice. He was going to start a deeper analysis of the Grimfaern.

As he drove north, he thought about how dead the campus was becoming. Finals were in full swing, and only a tiny amount of the student population was still on campus. Resin was thankful for times like these when the students went home. It was a nice reprieve from the constant onslaught of the students discovering how to be adults. During break, Resin's emergency calls would cut to a quarter of what they had been. He would be able to just work and enjoy the snow falling. He would often just walk around to the buildings, trudging as he went with his waterproof boots.

Now was Gredalia's time to act. Less students, more time for Gredalia to move around, more time to plan and execute an attack against the Artificers. Resin turned quickly along the roads and sped a little through Gristholme's shops, giving a half-hearted wave to a student as he passed the Moon's Loft. The streets were starting to accumulate snow, and he was thankful that his house would stay at a steady temperature. Sure, he was a little worried about the pipes, but he could always go back once a week and check. Worst case, he would file an insurance claim.

Around a few bends in the road, he allowed the Jeep to take the twists and turns as the vehicle was designed to do. The Jeep tucked into the snow, splashing the accumulated particles here and there with the movement of the tires. Resin felt confident as he pulled into the driveway behind the Hall of Ancients. He parked the car and went to the back. Opening the tailgate, he picked up the corpse and carried it inside. Still holding onto it by the neck, he pulled out his key chain and looked for the dark, rusting key for the door to the Old Tree. He pulled the door open with his free hand and walked inside.

The Old Tree was groaning in pain as the young wolf stepped inside. "Have you brought me something?"

"Yes. This is the Smiling Man. He just recently attacked me, so I decided to kill him."

The Tree's eyes moved slowly in Resin's direction. "Smart, young Fenris Wolf. Very smart indeed." A bark-crusted maw began to open at the base of the tree. Resin allowed his wolf form to take over, swinging the dead body and throwing it toward the amber-colored mouth of the tree. The Old Tree began to consume the corpse, crunching its bones. Green liquid began to ooze at the base, making the tree look ominous and powerful.

"Is this one of the Grimfaern?" the Tree spoke with its mouth still full of the Smiling Man's limbs.

"Quite possibly. He's been around before the Nexian Frost, apparently, so I didn't know if he existed prior to the Grimfaern?"

"So it says, eh?" The tree croaked with laughter. "I am feeling the effects of light restoration. Thank you, Fenris."

"No problem, my Old Tree." Resin bowed. "Was it enough to sustain you indefinitely?"

The Tree shook its leaves, or rather, what leaves it could. The branches extended into the ceiling and pulses of blue light thrummed through the branches, going into the house.

"I'm not sure. Tell me of the outside world. What's happening around us?"

Resin sighed and crossed his arms. "Well, Grimfaern have been assembled to harm the rest of this world."

The Tree paused, considering what the young steward was saying. It seemed an eternity passed before it finally spoke again. "Can you stop them?"

"I think we can. I have a witch, myself, a vampire, and three humans with Nexian powers who have been fully Rendered and Sundered."

The Tree chuckled at this. "Quite the accumulation of various talents!"

"So it would seem," Resin said. "My Tree, is there anything you can give me? Anything that could possibly stop the Gredalia Council, the ones who are trying to bring about the end of humanity as we know it?"

"There may be something," The Old Tree pondered. "It will take time, however. A ritual must be performed before you can utilize the new abilities."

"I may have time, but not much of it. I just need to talk to a couple of the members of my group." Resin felt the anxiety build up in his chest. Making time between everything that was going on felt like an impossible task.

"I anticipate your return, Fenris Wolf."

Resin nodded. "I value your wisdom and insight, my Tree." He bowed and turned to leave. He lingered at the door, waiting for the Tree to say something else, but it seemed to fall asleep shortly after they finished speaking. Locking the door, Resin turned into the Hall, deciding to unpack before the others got there. Thirty minutes passed before he heard the door open.

Darius and Lauren stepped into the hall.

"Shit hit the fan," Resin said as he was changing his bandages at the table.

"Fuck." Darius sat down at the table. "What do we do?"

"We prepare to attack." Resin's eyes were on fire. "We are going to launch our assault within the next forty-eight hours."

Darius and Lauren

RESIN SAT DOWN and began to plan with Darius and Resin. "I saw the Smiling Man again. He asked me if I wanted to join Gredalia."

"You could have joined them and blown them up from the inside," Darius quipped.

"Why didn't I think of that?" Resin sighed.

"Because of your pride, wolf boy." Lauren patted his shoulder.

"Anyways, I'm thinking you guys need to lead the assault on Olivia. If you can take out Olivia, we can potentially flush out her leader. We still have no idea who that is."

"Okay." Lauren went to one of the coat closets and grabbed a heavy rucksack. She shut the closet after grabbing two long blades without hand-guards. She threw both over her shoulders in an X pattern across her back.

Darius summoned his blade, twirling it a few times before making it disappear again. "So, we're gonna go kick Olivia's face in, then what?"

Resin sighed and looked at the both of them. "I really don't know how to explain the next part, guys. We're gonna have to find these Grimfaern and take them out. We may not survive this at all. I will contact the others and get them here so we can assemble properly. Have you heard from Lucia or the boys?"

They both shook their heads.

"*FUCK.*" Resin ran his hands through his hair and threw his bandages away. "I'll get working on this. You guys see if you can find Olivia."

"Resin, she has those psychic powers. Any recommendations there? It hurt us last time."

"Psionics are difficult to deal with. Y'all got the jump on her once, so she will be suspecting any traps. I would try and get her cornered somewhere. She won't have anywhere to go, so you'll be able to finish the job. I would particularly stay out of Nightshade, but monitor it to see if she leaves or goes in."

"You're telling me," Darius started. "Not to mention she could have gotten stronger since the last time we saw her."

Resin nodded. "I trust you guys. You can do this."

Lauren continued to strap on blades, her face showing bitter resentment, fearlessness, and bloodlust. "Would be better with you there, but we'll make do."

"You don't think you can heal quickly so that you'd be able to join us for this fight, do you?" Darius made his way toward the door, nodding to Lauren as if to accept their fates.

"I have to heal up, but I'll join you guys. If you succeed in killing Olivia, come back to this hall. I'm gonna be here resting up." *Shouldn't have said that,* he thought. *The Tree needs me to be alone.*

"Sounds good, Resin. I know this is lame, but I hope we all make it through this," Darius said, looking afraid.

Smiling, Resin touched two fingers to his head and moved them forward in a mock wave. "Godspeed, Artificers. See you on the other side." As Lauren and Darius set forth into the snowy night, Resin slipped away to the Tree's nook where he would begin whatever the Old Tree had in store for him.

Darius tucked into his coat and looked out over the campus.

"The students aren't going to see us at all?" He looked down the Boardwalk toward south campus. "It's just odd to me that we can brandish swords, kill monsters, and cast magic, yet the students have literally no idea it's happening."

"It's the fucking water, dude." Lauren said. "Remember?"

"Still, I never would have guessed." Darius set forth toward Nightshade once more, hoping that Olivia wouldn't be too hard to follow or find.

"Do you think we're going to die?" Lauren's face was stoic. It wasn't a question for her but for Darius, to see what his thoughts on the odds of dying were.

He looked at Lauren with a concerned frown. "I don't know, to be honest. Why not risk death to live? I'd rather have this freedom now and fight for my existence than be struck down by some otherworldly creeps."

"I agree." She fell in step with Darius. The snow was coming down faster than before. "Darius, I have a feeling that everything is going to crash around us."

"Let's hope not, dear. I have a date next week."

"You're a horn dog."

"I like to think of myself as a passionate lover, thank you."

The pair was approaching Nightshade Hall. Crossing the Boardwalk, Darius noticed how dead the campus was. He saw one student walking north into the woods. They looked feminine in form, but he couldn't really tell for sure. Was this Olivia? He nudged Lauren and pointed in that direction.

"I don't think it's her. It's too risky for Gredalia to be moving out in the open like that with the Artificers as their main threat. It was surprising in and of itself that Resin was attacked by the Smiling Man."

"This shit is fucked." Darius kept looking over his shoulders to see if they were being followed.

"Did you bring your keys?"

Darius looked up at her with stark fear. "Shit."

"You didn't bring your keys?!" Lauren hissed as they approached the door. "What the fuck, man?"

"It's been a stressful-ass day today, okay? I got ripped by the boss, and

I forgot to sneak the keys out of the office."

"I thought you worked remotely."

"My point exactly. The keys are at my house."

Lauren rolled her eyes as they made their way across the campus to Darius's house. The pair arrived in less than ten minutes. Lauren waited outside while Darius made his way up the stairs and snagged his work key ring. Returning downstairs, he held up the keys to the vampire. The pair returned ten minutes later to the door of Nightshade Hall.

Darius looked at Lauren, exhausted.

"Lauren, didn't Resin say to just stake the place out?"

"He did." She paused, taking careful consideration of the situation. "However, there's only so much inaction I can take."

Darius smiled, "Ah, fuck yeah! Let's go."

He laughed as they entered Nightshade Hall.

The remnants of the battle with the Smiling Man were gone. Everything looked like it had been repaired, from the flooring to the lights on the wall.

Lauren took a deep breath as she inspected the scene. "You and Resin did a rough number on the Smiling Man, didn't you?"

"Yeah…I don't understand what's going on here." Darius looked puzzled. "It was a bloody scene. Even the dead Grimfaern is gone."

"Maybe we should have listened to Resin," Lauren drew one of her blades.

"Maybe." Darius continued to look around the room. The skylight was clean, the staircase was clean, and the hallway to the side classroom was clean. The only thing that stood out in the room was the bookcase along the wall.

Lauren noticed the bookcase as well. "Hmm…I wonder." She walked over and started tugging on all the books on the bookshelf.

Darius summoned his Nexian-infused blade, black mist billowing off the blade and into the room. Lauren's form writhed, and her fangs popped out longer than before. She looked somewhat feral, an absolute monster of the Nexus. Her heightened senses allowed her to be even more dangerous than she already was. The vicious stance she positioned herself in freaked Darius out. Lauren tugged on the correct book and watched as the bookshelf swung open on hinges.

Darius breathed in deeply, feeling the Nexian power echoing through him. Suddenly, he felt a pain in the center of his forehead. His eyes were opened as he looked toward the ceiling, feeling a rush of understanding surge through his consciousness. Lauren looked back and saw him locked in place. Knowledge coursed through him, and the universe itself unraveled and built itself back up inside his mind.

Darius looked at Lauren, who saw shades of blue swirling inside of his eyes, then looked to the floor and nodded to Lauren. "She's here."

Lauren drew her other sword. With both swords pointed forward, she made her way to the stairs, Darius quickly on her heels. Descending the staircase, the bookcase wood gave way to stone and rock, showing two paths: one to the right and one to the left. Lauren made her way to the right, based on where Darius had nodded upstairs.

A few minutes later, the pair entered a large cavern. The stone altar appeared before them, with bars inside parts of the cavern walls. They looked like cages.

Darius held his sword up defensively. Lauren's arms returned to their normal position, her face still contorted.

"Where is she?!" Lauren hissed.

Darius took a deep breath to steady his nerves. His sword moved to the side, still defensive and ready for Olivia's attack.

Lauren stepped forward in front of Darius, blades still down, looking around. She scanned the ceiling, the floors, and the altar, yet there was nothing. She made her way over to the cages when a flash caught her eye.

Lauren dodged and did a backflip as a bolt of purple energy crashed into the cages. The metal bent inward.

She landed and extended herself to full height. "It's about fucking time."

Lauren looked into the eyes of the crazed woman. Her hair had grown out to cover her face. Her eyes were bloodshot, with the corners starting to become a purplish-maroon hue. Her mouth was open, cracks in the lips revealing severe dehydration. She held no blade. Instead, her hands were glowing vibrant shades of orchid-purple and were contorting and twisting as she walked. "We were occupied otherwise."

Lauren shot a look at Darius. He was looking at Olivia.

Lauren returned her gaze to Olivia. Suddenly, the sound of a large object echoed through the air as Darius's sword barely missed her head. "Darius! Dude, what the fuck?" Lauren felt her blood pressure rise and panic start to take hold. She backed away.

"Darius, please enlighten our guest that it takes an invitation to come into our sanctum." Olivia laughed.

Darius squared up with the blade pointing at Lauren. The black mist rolling off the tip sent a shiver up her spine. She stepped back, and Darius advanced. She looked at Olivia, who started to laugh.

"You're all pathetic. Really pathetic. It's not hard to surmise what was going on. When you first attacked us, we couldn't just sit by and let you carry on. That's why I decided to possess Darius by way of a latent possession spell that I could activate whenever I wished." She looked at Darius fondly. "Bless his heart. Quite the powerful Nexian. Sad that we had to annihilate his free will. He's quite spirited. Is he by chance an Aries?" Lauren felt her face morphing into the vampiric form she rarely showed.

"I'm gonna fuck you up, Olivia."

She raised her hands in annoyance. "Okay? Am I supposed to be scared of this? Do I look like I care?"

Lauren raised her swords. Looking at Darius, then Olivia, she took a deep breath.

Darius only had time to inhale before he felt his sword hand falling through the air. He blinked and let out an unholy wail. Blood began squirting across the floor as he writhed.

Olivia recoiled as Lauren sliced into her side with one of the blades. Lauren felt the blood of Olivia's ribcage course out onto her blade. She followed through, slicing Olivia in the stomach.

Olivia doubled over in pain as Lauren rolled behind her.

She dropped one blade, two-handing the shaft of the other, and swung for the fences. Olivia dove out of the way, rolling over the altar.

The vampire advanced, picking up her second blade. Olivia, getting tired of Darius's wailing, sent him into the wall. Lauren watched on in horror at the way the psionic girl could attack her puppet without any care for his well-being.

Darius collided with the wall of the cavern. His head smacked the stone and a sickening *crunch* emanated from his body.

Lauren stood on top of the altar, looking down on her quarry. Olivia was waiting and launched a wave of purplish-pink energy at her enemy.

The vampire took the brunt of the hit, causing her to go flying back over the altar, tumbling end over end. She finally found her footing and sprung back up.

I have to get out of here, Lauren thought. *Resin needs to know what's going on.*

Olivia closed her eyes and sensed the room. If Darius had been awake, he would notice that upon her forehead was a third eye protruding from the skin. It flicked left and right, searching, looking.

Olivia could foresee only so far into the future. What she saw there wasn't too troubling. Either Lauren would escape and live to fight another day, or she would be dead upon the floor. It didn't matter to her either way. She knew as one of the higher-ups in Gredalia that the Grimfaern students were beginning to mobilize. Olivia knew that it would be only a matter of time before Gredalia found out who these people were, with or without Darius. She knew that, if Lauren was in it, then Thorn and Lock were as well. How many of them were there? She closed her third eye and waited for her quarry.

Lauren, knowing it was either death or life, decided to make a break for it. She reached into her jacket and pulled out a pen. She reared back and lobbed the pen off over to her left, Olivia's right. Olivia sent a bolt of psionic energy at the pen, causing it to fling violently into the cavern wall.

Lauren bolted for the altar, ascending the steps boldly.

As she appeared over the top, Olivia turned. Lauren's hand was behind her head, throwing her left-hand sword end over end. Her opponent reared back, sending a blast of psionic energy toward the blade. The energy caught the hilt of the blade, sending it spinning.

Olivia's eyes widened as the blade sliced deeply into her own shoulder.

Letting out a wail of pain and trying to hold it in place, Lauren took the pommel of her other sword and swung with all her might.

THWACK! It connected with Olivia's temple.

The enemy's eyes began to roll back in her head. The staggering feet, the swaying body, and her limp hands all became bricks as Olivia sank to the floor, subdued and unconscious. Of all the futures she had seen, Olivia had thought this one was the least likely to occur.

Lauren ran. She sprinted toward her blade and picked it up. Darius's was next to his bloody hand, where it had fallen at the beginning of the fight. She picked up her pace and ascended the stairs back into Nightshade Hall.

It wasn't long before Lauren was violently knocking on the door of the Hall of Ancients. Checking the time on her phone, it was now 0100 hours. She hoped Resin's insomnia was in her favor tonight, as now was not the time to idly sit by. A few moments passed, Lauren nervously glancing over her shoulder in fear.

The lock finally turned as a somber-eyed Resin looked upon the face of his friend. Noticing the sword in her hand, his mind immediately wondered if Darius had been slain.

"We've got big problems," Lauren told Resin, in a huff of breath. "We're down Darius."

"How did they get him?"

"That's what we need to talk about."

On the Wintry Plateau

RESIN AND LAUREN LOOKED out the window of the Hall of Ancients. The snow was picking up, with the tiny crystals descending in a waltz. Resin got up after several moments and made his way to one of the cabinets. He opened it, revealing a decanter with an amber liquid in it. "This was made by my dad, I guess. Back in the seventies, he said that he and his buddies hid this in here when they came to their reunion. The liquid inside is whiskey. However, whenever the whiskey hits your lips, it changes to your favorite drink's flavor." He poured a shot and took it. "Hell yeah, mint juleps are heaven." Walking over to Lauren, he offered her the same glass.

She poured herself a double shot and took it in one swig. "They got Darius."

"I know." Resin shook his head in disgust.

"If Lucia had been there, she could have done something." Lauren rubbed her temples. "He looked possessed, mind-controlled, or something. I feel like Lucia could have knocked it out of him somehow. He kept attacking me, so I cut off his hand and left him behind. He's a traitor. It didn't feel right though, even if he did attack me."

Resin gave her a long look then. "I know, buddy. I'm concerned we lost a member. The boys aren't back yet, and we're missing Lucia. It's all gonna be okay though. Gredalia won't win this."

"Resin!" Lauren slammed her hands on the table. "We have no fucking idea if the students they're going to deploy are gone yet! We don't even know how many are in their party. What do you propose that we *fucking* DO?! You're our leader goddamnit! ACT LIKE ONE."

He sighed, "Okay. Fine. I'll show you something that may be able to help us."

"Okay?" Lauren looked around the walls of the hall.

He sighed. "I was afraid of this moment."

Lauren looked concerned and said, "What are you talking about, Resin?"

Resin got up and made his way to one of the locked doors in the wall.

Lauren got up and followed.

"My dad gave me this power…" Resin appeared flustered as he spoke. "But it comes with this…*tasking*." His shaking hands turned the tumblers in the door handle. "I have to keep *this* alive." He opened the door, the hinges creaking. Lauren's jaw dropped in horror, as the World Tree was glowing a vibrant green color.

"The World Tree is part of the Nexus. It's the first implantation of the Nexus in this world." Resin rubbed his temples. "The task of the Fenris Wolf is to keep the World Tree fed. It has to either be entities like the Grimfaern or Nexian users like us, but this is what I must do." The tree kept crunching as Resin walked near it. "I fed it the Smiling Man, but it was the first thing it's had to eat in a while. The Tree said it was possible for it to give me a new power, but I have to spend time meditating in front of it. Time is the *last* thing we have right now."

"Resin…" Lauren took a few steps back. Around the pulsing room, she saw the Tree's leaves obscuring pictures depicting how the Nexus had sent the Tree through the universe until it landed here, among other things. "This is fucked up. Were you going to feed us to this tree?!"

"No." He looked at her calmly. "I would honestly feed Darius if he went rogue. I wasn't certain if he was going to be a true asset to the team." He stared back up at the tree. "I guess I was right to not trust him." Lauren made her way up to his shoulder and patted hesitantly.

"You didn't know, Resin. It really couldn't have been seen." Lauren recoiled as green blood splattered her face from the World Tree finishing its meal, bones crunching in its maw. She swiped at her cheeks, smearing it all over in frustration. "Do we have to watch it finish eating? I really don't want to be covered in blood after my encounter with Olivia."

"Yeah, we can go."

The pair made their way back into the main chamber of the hall. "I really think we're just going to have to make a stand." Resin rubbed his chin. "Either that, or we go after the Grimfaern waiting to board whatever mode of transportation they're going to use to execute their plan."

"Now you decide to lead." Lauren laughed and sat down at the table. "If we go after the students, won't they know? Olivia is still alive, Darius… Brent? Are we missing one?"

"The Smiling Man is dead." Resin paced back and forth. "We don't know where Lucia or the boys are. They're going to want to protect their own interests, so they're going to focus their manpower on the Grimfaern to make sure we don't hinder the big plan." He sighed. "I wish *we* had more manpower. Have you tried calling the boys?"

"Straight to voicemail." Lauren huffed. "So that means we're going to have to divide. Do you want to take the Grimfaern, and I take Olivia?"

"Olivia almost got you twice." The wolf went to the large windows and looked out onto the falling snow. "I think it's time I spoke to her and we settle this once and for all."

The vampire pushed up off the chair. "I'm wondering how I'm gonna find these students."

"The bus stop. If I remember correctly from work, the remaining students are going to be bussed out tomorrow, or rather…today, at zero nine hundred hours." He crossed the room back to the table. "I really think that the worst thing we can do is blow our cover, but then again, everyone on campus who drinks the water unfiltered is drinking the metaphorical sports drink. So, what do we have to lose?"

"The world, our lives, the list is kinda endless there, Resin."

"Well, the good news is, at least we will die trying, am I right?" He grabbed his seat and reached under the table. A map was produced, yellowed and crinkled around the edges. Lauren sat down next to her friend and began consulting the map as well. Resin had drawn a plan of attack during the night after the Smiling Man died. "This is the layout. I'm thinking we each take a patch of the campus. Unfortunately, the bus stop is going to be the split." He pointed to the north. "I have a feeling you're going to have to take north sector, mostly because of the fact that the kids were all staying in Willow Apartments, and they're going to be leaving for the bus stop tomorrow." He pointed to the south. "I'm going to draw Olivia here. I'll head to the House of Campus Safety, cross-reference the student contact list, and get her number. I'll make my stand on the Boardwalk or at the chapel." The wolf nodded to the vampire. "Hopefully, no one gets caught in the crossfire."

"When do you want me to head over there?"

"Let's go at zero three hundred hours. Olivia will come. I guarantee it."

"What about Brent? And where are Lucia and the boys?" Lauren was pacing at this point. "Resin, I really don't like this. They haven't even texted."

"I know. It sucks because we lost Darius too." Resin left the map on the table. "We're going to win. I'm sure of it." His smile seemed to be more fake than Lauren liked.

Lucia Frey walked the Boardwalk in solemn silence. Looking up into the night, feeling the moonlight on her face, she wanted nothing more than to end it all there. She hated these organizations and their pettiness. She wanted to kill them all. It was getting old fast. She wanted to finish school and run the coffee shop. She wanted to learn more things about her ancestors and magic and maybe even start a witches' coven of her own one day. She couldn't do that with all this business of summoning the Grimfaern from the Nexus to take over the world. It had seemed like a good idea in the beginning, but her priorities had changed. She had been used, and she wanted to make them *all* pay for treating her so poorly.

She came to a halt in the middle of the Boardwalk. Looking to the stars, she took one final, slow, deliberate, deep breath. It was the last moment she would be safe for a very long time. In their twinkling spheres of ambiguity, the stars seemed to provide her a little bit of comfort. They had been there during her worst times. In her best times (which seemed few and far between ever since she met Rob), they provided guidance. She assumed Resin felt the same, but she had to distance herself from her former friend.

My allegiance to Resin and the Artificers was bad enough when I sent the Smiling Man to attack Resin in order to test the Smiling Man's worth to the Council. Lucia pondered this, allowing herself to be engrossed in the twinkling orbs in the sky. *I am still unsure how I kept it all from the rest of the Council. Maybe they have always known I was unsure of where to step or who to align myself with. They gave me the berth of a true Maester, and I took full advantage of it.*

She slowly raised her wand toward her celestial guardians, feeling tears streaming down her face and starting to freeze on her cheeks. The Nexian phrase sat on the tip of her tongue. It began to burn, the anticipation and the fear keeping her in the moment. Against her will, she felt the words spill out of her in the guttural drawl of the Nexian tongue. "*Galdonbrök.*"

Lucia felt the pulse of Nexian energy leaving her wand, releasing the spells she had placed around campus.

First, the Grimfaern would be awakened from their slumber. Second, Brent, Thorn, and Lock would resume fighting. Next, she would begin to correct her mistakes.

BZZZZZT. BZZZZZT. Lucia's phone went off in her pocket, but she deliberately ignored it.

Wiping her hand on the inside of her coat sleeve, sheathing her wand, she made her way north.

———— ♦ ————

The stasis spell began to release its hold on the fighters in the groundskeeper shack. Brent launched himself into Thorn, scattering tools and propelling Lock through the wall of the hut out into the snow.

Lock dusted himself off and got to his feet. He started to move his hands in a circular motion, with green energy beginning to form from the Nexus. His eyes began to glow green as the energy built up.

Thorn's sickle swung up and caught Brent in the throat. It found purchase, and Thorn quickly pulled the enemy into Lock's line of sight. Lock hit his pinnacle of energy and sent a beam propelling into Brent.

Brent caught the brute force of the blow, which sent him flying out toward the cliff. Smoldering, Brent stood up, extending his arms in a motion to antagonize the boys.

"COME ON!" He wailed. "THIS IS THE DAY YOU DIE, BOYS."

Lock, with eyes still glowing green, began to run around the building. Thorn felt his sickle glowing with electricity and walked out slowly. The boys picked up speed, descending upon Brent.

Brent, snorting, squared up, and waited for Thorn and Lock to attack. He flexed, and two additional arms dropped down.

Thorn flanked him on the right while Lock went head on.

In a seafoam light created by Lock's magic, Lock sent a flare to Brent's left, which flew over Thorn.

Brent's eyes followed the light as a magical dagger of light-blue energy went plunging toward his side.

Brent caught the blade with one of his free hands, to Lock's disdain. Brent followed through with punches, sending Lock the edge of the cliff.

Lock let out a wail and screamed, "THORN!" before tumbling beyond the safety of the Great Net.

Thorn yelled as the tears fell. Adrenaline rushed through his body and the world went silent. Thorn instinctively sent his sickle through the air with all the rage he could muster to avenge his friend. Brent sent an arm up to catch the blade, but it cut through his palm, severing several of his fingers. He wailed and clutched his hand.

The sickle careened toward the cliffside, still spinning.

Thorn ran toward Brent, yelling as he charged. His hand outstretched, Thorn channeled the Nexian energy to call the sickle back toward him.

The sickle spun in place when Thorn willed it back toward him.

The sickle reversed its spin, spinning in the opposite direction, and headed back toward Brent.

A squelch echoed on the cliffside as the sickle lodged itself into the back of Brent's upper arm.

Gripping the handle, Thorn sliced downward and felt the flesh ripping against the steel. Brent's lower left arm was gone.

———— ◆ ————

Resin stepped out of the Hall of Ancients, throwing on his leather jacket and exhaling. He didn't like the feeling of the air. It was too ominous for his comfort. Looking up and down the campus, he spotted no one.

This shouldn't have been a surprise to him because of the time of year, but not even a campus security vehicle could be seen. No animals were roaming around. It was just Resin and Resin alone.

Shouldering his rucksack, he made his way south. The snow was accumulating to the point of immobility, and Resin really didn't want to have to hop back into his wolf form. He wanted to progress without any kind of delay, for the last thing he needed was a block in this plan to save humanity.

He crossed the Boardwalk after five minutes of hard trekking. His waterproof boots came in handy as the snow piled up around his ankles and calves.

He continued to scan the campus for any sign of movement, but so far, nothing. Not even footprints in the snow.

He looked for the familiar signs of his people. Still nothing.

Resin's adrenaline began to kick in as he trudged through the snow. Thankfully, a few minutes later he hit the main road and jogged as best he could to the House of Campus Safety. As he approached, he noticed the security vehicle was gone.

Who's on shift right now? Resin wondered to himself. He couldn't rightly answer.

He opened the door and expected to see the familiar face of one of the dispatchers (tonight it would be Holly), but she wasn't there. No one was.

Panic began to take root in Resin's soul as he used his key card to scan into the door, leading back to the familiar kitchen and break room that was like his second home. The lockers were off to his left in their own separate room. Within, he identified his locker, Kasey's locker, Trev's locker, Meghan's locker… Nothing seemed in its spot. He went to the lockbox full of keys and checked to see who was on shift that night. Kasey's keys were gone, as well as Trevor's. Trev often took his home to keep his belt squared away, but Kasey?

Resin shook his head and ran back to the switchboard where the dispatchers normally sat. He couldn't find the Campus Safety vehicle's keys. Perplexed, he checked his watch. 0345. He was cutting it close to the arrival of the bus.

Resin paused as he typed away on the switchboard computer. He pulled up the winter contact list for the first week of December. He took a picture and sent it to Lauren. Next, he pulled up Olivia's phone number from the student directory. He dialed it and got up out of the seat in the office. Continuing outside, Resin threw on his jacket and once again picked up his rucksack. He hit the call button on his phone.

A few rings later, a feminine voice picked up.

"Meet me at the chapel." Resin's voice did not waver.

"Aren't you going to propose first?" Olivia responded with snark.

"I propose your death," he retorted.

"Good. I'm already there." *CLICK.* The line went dead.

Resin felt his phone crush inside the palm of his hand.

It was the beginning of the battle on the wintry plateau.

Lauren trudged through the snow, cursing Resin for his wolf abilities to navigate such difficult terrain. Her combat boots were picking up more snow than they were deflecting. When she scanned around, she saw a mass of students gathering outside of the Willows. Her eyes grew wide, and adrenaline carried her forward.

Sprinting as fast as she could, Lauren pushed onto the main road. Looking over her shoulder, she saw the mass of students heading to the bus station. She steadied her breath, anticipating the fight that would occur. It was a *fuck-ton* of Grimfaern, enough to wipe out the northern residential dorms if they detonated.

Lauren felt her form shifting: arms lengthening, teeth becoming more acute and sharp. Her eyes became adjusted to her surroundings, and she smelled *everything*. Her own claws extended out as she rounded Counseling Services. Her plan was to ambush them. If things went her way, which they typically did not, she would ambush the last Grimfaern of the pack. Her intent was to use their momentum to knock the others off balance and gain the advantage. The worst part was that she would have to climb the Counseling Services building to get into the best position.

She launched herself up into the air, using her claws to begin the climbing process. She could feel the sinews in her arms strain as she pulled herself up. Arm over arm, hand over hand, Lauren scaled the building.

The snow was beginning to come quickly. Even under the semi-cover of night, she was exposed with her neo-gothic attire like a spotlight on a lonely car in an empty parking lot. Lauren took a deep breath and slid down into the snow banked on the slanted roof. She felt her bones reverberate with cold. In dire situations, she could stave off the effects of the environment (cold, heat, etc.) but not for too long. She waited in the cold for her targets to come to her, like a spider in its web.

Praxis

RESIN FELT HIS BODY begin to shift as he walked south. The lights on the Boardwalk were illuminated against the dark sky, and the snow was accumulating more quickly. He was afraid whatever battle was going to take place was going to happen soon.

The snow was drifting across the Boardwalk as the wind picked up, much to Resin's displeasure, but he held fast. He was ready for this battle with Olivia. For most of the fights the Artificers had, he was tucked away behind the safety of either his job or the Hall of Ancients. Now, he was in his element and the element of his people. The weather and his breath in the air were more than enough to bring about the drive he needed to remain focused.

It took him a shorter amount of time to reach the chapel than he expected. If not for the water, the students would have seen the wolf-man stalking across the campus in the fog of snowy winter.

The fight for the world was upon them.

Resin walked up to the chapel, took a deep breath, and opened the door.

Inside the sanctuary, the ornate ceiling of stained glass appeared less vibrant in the early hours of the morning.

Resin took note of the pews and the multiple portions of the chapel that had religious iconography placed for easy viewing. Upon a deep inhale, the air tasted bloody to him.

He looked along the red velvet-like floor.

DRIP.

He raised his head slowly. It was coming from the altar.

DRIP.

He felt his whole body beginning to tremble.

DRIP. DRIP. DRIP.

In a *WOOSH* sound, blood began to spill out of Darius Crosbane's lifeless body. Hanging from the ceiling by his neck, the man's entrails were slowly unraveling themselves from the deep slice in his stomach. Resin sprung off the carpet, dashing to the center of the chapel. He was just about to make it to his former friend when a magical barrier launched him and the pews around the chapel. The wolf pushed up with his arms to look at Olivia walking through the barrier.

"He's dead, *Rezzy.*" She laughed. Snapping her fingers, Darius's vertebrae protruded out of his neck with a visceral tearing of sinews. His eyes rolled back in his head as a death groan spewed out of his lips. "Darius was caught away from you and now…he's my puppet." She leaned back, her back arched to look toward Darius. "It's fun to play with your food, no?"

"Olivia," the wolf grumbled, "give up, now."

"Nah. No, I think I'm good. Better yet, we have some talking to do, you and I." She lifted her hands slowly. Resin felt the energy surrounding him as he began to rise off the ground. "I would like you to take note of how Gredalia is *not* fazed by you and your—"

Resin kicked a pew toward Olivia, who was distracted by her handiwork. A sharp *crack* of the pew against Olivia's jaw sent her reeling across the chapel and through her own barrier. Splinters of wood shot in multiple directions. One particularly long piece pierced Olivia's leg, and she let out a wail of pain.

The wolf hit the floor, making a mad dash toward his enemy. He tasted iron on the insides of his cheeks.

"I don't give a *FUCK* about Gredalia!" He reared back his foot, as if to kick a soccer ball. One foot landed beside Olivia's body. The other, aided by Resin's wolf-like abilities, kicked the psionics master with immense force.

Toes connected with teeth as Olivia's face contorted to Resin's wolf paw. He felt a sickening *crunch* as a few of her teeth fell out of her mouth. He reared back for a second attack, but Olivia was prepared.

In a wave of psionics, she sent a pulse of energy down upon Resin. It slammed him into the floor once more.

Olivia yelled and sent another blast into Resin, propelling him across the floor. The carpet flew up from its stapled location as he went tumbling end over end.

He collided with the door, pushing it open with the force of impact. He rolled outside in the snow.

Olivia got up, wiping the blood off her lip, and progressed through the broken pews and disheveled carpet. She felt her power building in her hands. The wisps of energy from the Nexus built in spirals amongst her fingers. She took a few more steps, her body swaying from the kick to her teeth. The psionics master spat out a few more teeth. She wiped her mouth again, staggering to the front church door.

Resin pushed up off the ground again, feeling his body quiver against the cold and the cuts in his skin. He looked up to see Olivia walking toward him, with energy growing around her. His eyes bugged out of his head, and he started to scoot away from the entrance. The wolf begged and pleaded for his body to lift itself, but he felt exhaustion creeping in. Crawling around the corner of the church on his stomach, he pushed himself up and started to stagger deeper into south campus, hoping and praying against all odds he would have the resources to combat this skilled fighter.

Olivia stepped out into the brisk air, rounding the corner, following the blood trail of her big-game kill. The energy building up pushed into dangerous levels where she wasn't going to be able to control it.

She cracked her neck and continued to follow the blood. When the trail ended around the second south corner, she paused and cocked her head. The trail ended and not a single footprint in sight…

WHACK! Resin smacked her on the back of the head with a forceful punch.

He sighed a heavy bit of relief, but as Olivia laxed, she released her energy, sending Resin up into the snow-filled sky like a balloon with its string pulled free.

———— ◆ ————

Thorn sent his sickle deep into the skull of Brent, beating Brent multiple times as blood shot up into his eyes. He relinquished his grip on the sickle as the monster slumped to the ground next to him, dead. Tears fell from his face as he began to process the loss of his friend.

Walking toward the edge, he looked down and saw only the crags and juts of the rocks below.

He cried.

Lock, his best friend and companion, was dead.

The sheer horror of the cliff face became even more brutal as he realized that the Great Net had been removed. Students who attempted to take flight and leave the earth would now plummet to their demise, stripped of the potential for a second chance. Lock was likely lost in the vicious waves, his body breaking and bending in the current as he drowned. Grief began to consume the living along the edge of the cliff.

Thorn looked over the churning waves as the pain came from his chest. He heard a crackling sound, like a large wave crashing against the rocks.

Thorn felt a pang in his chest, right where his sadness emanated from, and saw the blood soaking through his shirt.

He gasped, stumbling forward, stopping a few paces from the cliff-side. Turning, he looked to see what the cause of the blood was.

Lucia Frey stood holding a pistol. The smoldering tip produced wisps of fine, grey smoke that extended up into the snow-covered trees. She slowly lowered the pistol and sighed.

"Lucia…" The blood shot out of his lips as he called out to her. "Why? Why would you do such a thing?"

She remained silent as the winter winds blew in the early hours of the morning.

Thorn blinked and drew another breath as the witch's second bullet sliced open his intestinal wall.

He coughed up more blood as Lucia walked forward and pushed him over the cliffside.

Thorn tumbled downward to the craggy depths below to join his friend inside the sea. He said a prayer to his Sundering patron as his skull connected with the brine.

Lucia threw the pistol over the cliffside and turned back to the north.

That's three down, she thought.

She realized several things as she made her way toward north campus.

It wouldn't have been easier to kill both the Council and the Artificers over time. Resin and Rob were very similar in the way they do business. Rob was gung ho about taking over the world, but it would eventually bite him in the ass. You can't control Grimfaern, despite what he had told her many times. They're Nexian creatures; they lacked true morality.

Rob saw an in, making himself into a hybrid version so that he could be a more grounded version of the Smiling Man. Then, he attempted to use his power to control the Grimfaern and make them into ticking time bombs. He would use his link to their minds to detonate the Grimfaern out in the world.

This was her chance to fix the Rob issue for good.

Resin and the Artificers were also perversions of the natural order.

Rendering and Sundering shouldn't be allowed in mortal bodies. Lucia had basically become a perversion of herself.

Her grandma wanted to continue the legacy of the witches that lived on the plateau. It wasn't a bad sentiment, but she decided to continue the bloodline knowing the terrible secret: the magic that human Nexian users had shouldn't be in a human vessel for too long. It corrupts, spreads, and decimates. It even destroys the psyche if it gets too wild. That's what might happen to the Artificers and those in Gredalia if they survive and get older, eventually to linger on into perversions like the Smiling Man.

Lucia would have to fix all the mess that she created. She would go out, track down the Grimfaern student copies, and destroy them. She should have stopped them and never Rendered or Sundered anyone, but if she didn't go with Rob and figure out his plan, she would have lost herself to the Alpha implant. She couldn't afford that at the time.

With the Artificers it was a similar mistake: She had to keep her cover active and alive, or else Resin would get suspicious.

She looked at her arm, where the scar of the implant lay.

I have to fix things, even if the implant stops me. I must try, she thought as she took one last look out over the ocean.

Lucia continued northward, itching to tackle Olivia and Resin.

◆

Olivia pushed herself up to her feet, the blood now freely flowing from her nose. She was panting heavily, most of her strength sapped from her during the final blow dealt to Resin. She swayed, feeling the world spinning. She sank to her knees, and snow began to accumulate on the cuts and tears of her outfit. She wiped her nose on the back of her hand, then spat onto the ground violently.

Looking up to the sky, she saw the stars faint twinkle against the modern backdrop of the streetlights along the Boardwalk and the postmodern lights illuminating the buildings around campus. She felt the tears descend from her cheek, knowing she wouldn't be long for the world. She inhaled as a hand grabbed her hair, drawing her neck to be exposed.

Olivia tried to grab at her hair, writhing around, but a spell bound her hands to her sides.

"Is this how it happens?!" Olivia yelled out. She strained against the hand holding her head in place. "I DON'T WANT TO GO!" Lucia drew closer. "NO GODS! NO GODS PLEASE NOOOOOOO!"

Lucia's wand smacked Olivia's neck right below her chin.

"Olivia," Lucia whispered, "I fucking *hate* your guts. Killing you is more satisfying than coffee, and I love coffee more than life itself."

Lucia uttered the Nexian command that turned her wand into a knife that was able to cut through bone.

With a simple slice, the body hit the ground first, peppering the snow with crimson. The head, blinking, noticing the familiar face, attempted to speak and mouthed the name of Lucia Frey.

Lucia let Olivia's head hit the ground a few feet from the body. Steam began to rise from Olivia's remains as Lucia cast a decompose spell on the corpse.

With the back of her overcoat to him, Resin confirmed a creeping suspicion that had been in the back of his mind when he was unable to contact Lucia: His old friend had switched sides.

He climbed down the tree as quietly as he could some five hundred feet away from Lucia. Attempting to avoid any noise whatsoever, the wolf made his way to the east, running counterintuitively into the light of the science commons.

Resin dropped to all fours, bounding north along the plateau's eastern edge toward Route 13 and the bus stop, hoping to help Lauren.

Lauren hid outside Counseling Services and waited for the students to make their way to the bus stop. As they drew closer, she felt her pulse quicken and her muscles tense. Her claws clacked against the brick building. Her breath formed on the air in short bursts.

Through the swirl of snow, a figure appeared. As the man came into focus, she saw that it was the head of Campus Safety, Rob Horn. Rob's attire was a winter coat with snow pants and thick black boots. His moustache quivered in the breeze as fifteen students with bags in tow were buffeted by the wind and snow. He called out to them over the wind. "Y'all wait here. Don't go anywhere until the bus shows up! There are dangerous people that have been reported along the plateau. The snowstorm came in from Billings just this morning, which is why the head of Campus Safety is here." He gestured, palms open to the students. "I'm sorry it's so cold. I've been told the bus will be here in the next five minutes, so it won't be too much longer until it's arrived."

FIVE MINUTES! Lauren sighed. *How am I going to defeat fifteen Grimfaern in five minutes?!* Some of the students made quiet comments to Rob, who in turn addressed the crowd around him.

"Kapura has a great question! Yes, the bus *will* arrive. I know in the past we have told y'all to brace yourselves for a longer delay. This time, however, there isn't going to be a delay. This is the truth. I called the bus driver myself, and they should be here shortly. Take care! I need to run inside my office really quick, and I'll be out to see you off!" Rob turned and left for the Office of Campus Safety. Lauren's ears piqued as she listened for the latch to close. She drew her claws across her chest, breathing slowly.

CLICK.

With fangs out, she opened her eyes and launched herself from the rooftop.

The first student she descended upon cried out in pain as Lauren ripped open the sinews of their neck. Blood shot everywhere. Students two and three cried out as they saw their friend go down. Expecting the mutation of the Grimfaern to begin, Lauren chopped at the Achilles of both students, dropping them to the ground. Two quick stomps on the face like a game of Dance Dance Revolution squashed their startled cries. The twelve remaining students broke off into groups of six, running away. Lauren descended upon the next six, with her assassin-like abilities spraying more muscle and blood about. Claws dug into the flesh of two students. The vampire pulled back and felt the entrails of the first-year spill out onto the ground. She then flipped in the air, kicking in the throat of a girl. Another slice through the air felled another two. The final one of the first pack took a second to run down, but Lauren took two big bounds and sliced through the neck of the sixth student. She felt the satisfying crunch of their chest cavity caving in.

She turned back to the other six, who began to scream loudly and break off in different directions.

She made her way for the northernmost group, who began to run up the Boardwalk, when she heard the roar of a wolf. Resin cut down three students who had tried to break away to the south side. He ripped off an arm of one, bit into the throat of another, and pounced on the third. More carnage and blood flew into the early-morning snow.

Lauren jumped into the air, feeling her arms contort into taut wings. Her wings carried her for almost fifty yards before descending upon two female students who were huddled together and crying.

She bit into one while holding the other by the throat.

"PLEASE LET ME GO!" cried out the student as Lauren lifted her into the air. "I CAN'T SEE YOU BUT PL—" The neck snapped with one quick squeeze by Lauren, and the carcass fell to the ground. The final student, now looking at both Resin and Lauren, stood their ground. Their body contorted and shook until the familiar sunken features of a Grimfaern began to come to light.

"This is it!" Resin yelled from behind Lauren. "Flank it! We need to keep it from going north into campus!"

"You got it!" Lauren jumped into the air again as Resin charged it from the front. The Grimfaern laughed at the Artificers as they closed in.

"You're too late, little ones." Its smile grew, exposing an array of vicious teeth. "It's already done." The Grimfaern's head bowed, pointing to Route 13.

Resin and Lauren both turned to see the bus rolling away from the entrance to south campus. The bus was half occupied, with Rob Horn as the driver.

Rob smiled wildly, closing the door with a wave at the pair.

"FUCK!" Resin yelled, making his way to the bus stop as a bolt of necrotic energy pierced his side.

"Resin!" Lauren turned away from the Grimfaern and saw a billowing cloud of energy shoot over her head. She scanned the Boardwalk and saw a young man walking toward them. His entrails skittered along the ground, making his movement even more impressive. Sunken eyes, now enraptured in Nexian energy, were violently purple against the man's pale skin. His sword was out into the open, his hand was outstretched toward Resin. He lowered his hand, finding a spot along the hilt of the sword and came to a defensive stance. The illusion created the appearance of a perfectly healthy human torso. Veins bulged in Darius's body with reeking necrosis and the energy derived from it. He extended to full height, now standing almost as tall as Resin, and gave a deep hearty chuckle.

"Surprise! A gift from Lucia Frey," the demon goaded the Artificers. Raising his sword to eyebrow height, he charged the wolf. Resin let out a roar, brandishing his claws in the early morning light. Lauren turned back to the Grimfaern, who was bearing down upon her in the light of dawn.

In the Cold, Cold Night

DARIUS'S SWORD DESCENDED upon Resin with a hefty strike. Resin deflected it, driving his claws forward.

Behind him, Lauren let out a shriek and jumped over the dead students, slicing Darius's scalp with her claws. Darius yelled out in pain as Resin's claws pierced his side.

Darius took the opportunity to draw Resin close and slashed across his back. Blood splattered across the ground in an array of crimson droplets.

The wolf stumbled back, howling out in pain.

The vampire's feet hit the snow, and she launched herself onto the back of Darius.

He attempted to shake Lauren off, like a human trying to escape the succinct precision of a wasp defending its home.

Lauren held on with one hand, reared back, and stabbed at the left eye of the demon. Her talons made their purchase as black ichor shot out of the sphere that was once the eye of Darius. She dug her talons into his neck with her left hand and made her way to his right eye when he caught her arm and threw her off his back.

Darius squared up to Resin, who was breathing heavily. The sleek sword suddenly disappeared, and the man raised his hands. "Resin. Let's be reasonable, my friend." The vocal inflection did not sound like Darius: a discordant and gravelly voice rumbled from Darius's throat. The body looked the same, but the eyes were that of the Nexus finally collecting their prize.

"I don't want to kill you or the lovely Lauren here. I just wanted to… merely distract," Darius said. "It's just business, sir."

Lauren got to her feet and charged Darius once more.

"Business for your new master?" Resin grunted.

"Correct." Darius contorted a little, with wings sprouting out of his back. "My Rendering and Sundering were…flawed. With the help of Lucia, I assumed a new patron, one who isn't afraid of the mortal plane of existence. Rather, they thrive in it." The wings grew to a larger span. "I've been instructed to kill you, along with my fellow compatriot here, and return to our base."

"I'll burn you alive, Darius," Resin cried out. Lauren felt a pang of confusion and fear as she squared up to the Grimfaern, who had dealt her a few blows.

She was now bleeding due to a deep cut in her leg.

"I'm a hellspawn, deary." Darius ascended into the dawn with a few flaps of his wings. "I don't burn."

He plunged at the wolf, his features contorting into those of a demon.

Resin roared and sent a green blast of energy up into the air. Darius dodged it with grace. Resuming their fight, the pair slashed and hacked at each other while Lauren swayed.

She looked at the Grimfaern, who was now bleeding profusely, and summoned her swords. She crossed the pair of them, feeling her final bits of energy pouring into micro-focus as Resin and Darius grew closer to her.

Lauren shook in the quick breeze of winter. She closed her eyes, projecting her senses out into the world. She could feel Darius and Resin moving around her. Her blades sang silently against the cold. The breath that she took separated her and the Grimfaern by one stride. He sprung off the ground in flight above Resin as Lauren launched herself forward.

The slicing and tactful balance of the blades honed by the master made the blade sing in the night. Sinews, tendons, and bones protruded from the skin as the howl permeated the night. The Grimfaern's remnants plastered Lauren in a gothic spray.

Lauren stood and shook herself off as the Grimfaern hit the ground.

She swayed and dropped to her knees, feeling blood soak her pant leg. The cold soothed her despite the danger that Darius still posed. Resin felt Lauren hit the ground behind him. He could smell the blood of both Darius and Lauren beginning to flow freely.

Time slowed. Resin felt his soul shake as the words of the World Tree echoed in his mind. Secret, hidden words that were meant for a time of danger. Spoken in the Nexian language, he began to recite the words out in the snow. Darius was on the ground, clawing at his injuries, trying to heal himself as quickly as possible with his sword at his side. He dug into the powder to try to kick himself away from Resin and his chanting.

Resin continued to mutter the words, time around him slowing even further. Resin felt the connection he had established with the World Tree as well as his own Nexian energy.

The Tree groaned in pain as Resin uttered the final words of the spell.

Darius continued to shimmy away, attempting to escape. Pain was visible across his face as his chest cavity was pierced by the wolf's clawed foot.

Resin said the Nexian words one last time.

Darius began to implode while the words lingered in the air. He yelled out in pain as his bones began to snap. This continued with his torso and legs until his head was all that remained. The demon eyes flashed before the crown of his head folded onto his chin. He evaporated into the wisps of air as Resin delivered a seismic punch, using the World Tree's energy to send Darius back to the Nexus.

The concentration and rage of Darius's scream rang in Resin's ears.

Resin sank to the ground, feeling the toll of the Nexian energy in his exhausted body. It was then that he noticed Lauren.

He crawled over to where Lauren was.

Resin looked at Lauren, who was bleeding out of her leg.

He ripped a chunk of his shirt and began to tie a tourniquet around her upper thigh. Hands trembling, he called an ambulance.

Twenty minutes later, as he noticed the cherry lights rotating on the ambulance, Resin began plotting how to locate Rob Horn and Lucia Frey.

———— ◆ ————

The bus sped away down the plateau.

Rob Horn, pondering the elation of his resignation letter on his desk, considered how he was going to send out the ten Grimfaern he was able to save on the bus. Some would go to each continent, but he wasn't sure which would get the most. As he drove, he continued to plot.

He wondered if Darius would be able to finish the job.

Rob looked out through the windshield as the plateau rolled away behind him.

Laughing to himself, he hit the bottom of the plateau. Turning left, he picked up speed as he navigated toward Billings. It was a few hours north to the next major airport, and his phone indicated that, with the snow and accidents, it would take even longer.

He looked in the rearview mirror. The ten students were asleep.

"Thank the gods," Rob said, relieved that he didn't have to attempt to lull them to sleep before their big show.

Rob situated himself as he drove, looking at the winter sprawl before him.

The students, situated low in their seats, shifted in their slumber.

One, however, was wide-eyed and awake.

Lucia Frey looked out the window as the bus full of Grimfaern sped off toward an unknown destination.

LUCIA FREY WILL RETURN IN THE SECOND
BOOK OF THE GRISTHOLME TRILOGY,
GRISTHOLME: THE RENDERING

Afterword

GRISTHOLME WAS FIRST *GREYMOORE* the podcast, when I was a senior in college, working as a security officer.

I recorded a podcast, like any senior in college tends to do, because I thought it would make me cool if I started one. I also liked to think I could tell a good story. Troy didn't think so, snickering as he left to go make his rounds about campus. My supervisor, Greg, listened to a little bit of the first *Greymoore* episode and said: "What if you made it into a book?"

A book? I thought to myself. *Am I capable enough to write a book?*

"What the hell?" I said. "Worth a shot!"

Five years, a deployment, and a pandemic later, with a few false stars and money invested into the project, this is the result.

My hope is that it was a solid read for you, and that it left you wanting more stories about the Artificers and Lucia Frey. Soon, I'll finish up the prequel podcast for your consumption and maybe some musical accompaniment. What can I say? I love this story and its characters. By sharing them with you, I want to provide an escape, even just a little bit of one, in these wild times. Growing up as an only child, I absorbed stories of whimsy and fantasy because they held magical qualities. *Harry Potter*, *Lord of the Rings*, *Charlie Bone*, *Pendragon*, and *A Series of Unfortunate Events* all shaped my storytelling.

When I got older, it morphed into Stephen King, Ransom Riggs, and Douglas Adams.

I say all of this to give hope to the person who is sitting in their office chair, break room, or classroom, considering writing the next great novel. You *can* do it. If I can do it, you can do it.

See ya at the movies!

Acknowledgements

THERE'S AN INFINITE NUMBER of people to thank for this project. I could not have completed the book without them. (Spoiler alert: you, the reader, are one of them too!)

First, I'd like to thank God for giving me the strength to see this project through when there were many times that I asked what the hell I was doing.

Next, my loving family, Crystal, Felix, Mom, Dad, Jake, Grandma, Grandpa, and the rest of the "herd": Thank you, guys, for always bending an ear while I talked about my wild ambitions to craft a piece of literature. Your time in listening and contemplation means more than you know. Particularly Crystal, as I went down rabbit holes and convinced you that I was a badass for being a fledgling author. Love you dearly! Hope I made ya proud.

To my friends, service members, and coworkers: Thank you for not telling me I was crazy for my wild concept of a novel. Hope you enjoy the result!

To my publisher and editors, particularly Emily, Clair, Catherine, and Devon: Thank you for believing in me and my story! It was a pleasure to work with you. I appreciate your patience in the stark learning curve that comes with writing a novel. Let's get to work on book number two!

To Mat: Thank you for the most badass book cover in the world. You are a master at your craft.

Special shoutouts to Dan Herdman, Greg vonFreymann, the Campus Safety Team at Kenyon College, Mike Harris, Jay and Heather Colo,

Maria Miller, Jon Nouse, The Zest fam, Josh Stidham, Hayden Frazee, Spencer Chajkowski, Justin Louderback, the Banner of the Silver Claw, Steve at the WarpGate, the Fat Dog Vinyl crew (especially Phil Hicks), Phillip Floyd, Lydia Taylor, and the Dibles. Thank you all for your kind support and words. It means more than you'll ever know!

To the people who instilled a love of reading in me: My parents, Grandpa Byers, Grandma and Pa DeWitt, Aunt Jan, Mrs. Whittney, Mrs. Kirkpatrick, Mrs. Schwartzentruber, Mrs. Justice, Mrs. Pursel, Mrs. Von, Mr. Lubera, Mrs. Scarazza, and Poz: I cannot thank you enough for your tutelage. I would not have been able to write this book if it weren't for you fueling my desire to read and write. Hopefully, I made ya proud!

To the musicians and authors I look to for inspiration: I couldn't have written *Gristholme* without a slew of artists to jam to. There are several big names, but I would be amiss if I didn't single out the big inspo.

First and foremost: Annie Clark of St. Vincent. I couldn't have chased this dream without watching your Masterclass on finding your voice amid the world. I took your lessons to heart, and my hope is that this is reflected in the text, as well as dashes of the macabre and dark academia.

Second: Dave Grohl and Foo Fighters. Thank you, guys, for keeping me alive. I wouldn't be here today if it wasn't for you and your beautiful music.

Third: twenty one pilots. Josh and Tyler, thank you, guys, for also keeping me alive and showing me that you can take past trauma and turn it into something grand. I hope to make Ohio proud, just as you do.

Fourth: Goose. Another amazing band among the masses who keeps it real with their beautifully crafted jams and unique talent. I envy your passion and strive to embody it daily.

Fifth: Jon Bellion. Another artist who I strive to be like. Thinking outside the box is a lost art. You showed me how to do that with your approach. Blessings to you and yours for this!

Sixth: Quinn XCII. The man. The myth. The chill dude. Mike, you rock, dude. You are the soundtrack to my life, and let's see you drop a track for the movie! I'll be calling.

Seventh: Death Cab for Cutie. Wouldn't be on this earth if it wasn't for you! Thank you for also keeping me alive and being my life's soundtrack. Love you!!

Eigth: George Watsky. You taught me to constantly chase one's magnum opus, as well as to follow your own path towards that goal. Thank you for being a constant source of inspo, and if you'd like, would love to have you on a track for the movie as well!

Second to Last: To Stephen King, Leigh Bardugo, Frank Herbert, Lemony Snicket, and Douglas Adams. Wouldn't be writing if it weren't for y'all! Many thanks and returns.

Finally, to you, the reader: Thank you for extending the reader's trust in this new author. It means the world to me. If you like the book, please share it with someone! Tell your friends, tell your enemies, neighbor, dog, cat, what have you! Please leave us a review on Goodreads and Amazon. Cheers! See you in book number two.

About the Author

L.J. BYERS IS AN AUTHOR, musician, podcaster, soccer fanatic, avid Columbus Crew supporter, movie nut, coffee connoisseur, fisherman, reader, music lover, vinyl collector, army veteran, Ohio enthusiast, ocean supporter, songwriter, father, and significant other. He is in two bands: Longstrider and Attic Sunsets. He lives in central Ohio with his loving family, both human and animal: Crystal, Felix, Adylade, Ozzie, Magic, Maggie, and Marceline.

He can be found on TikTok: @LongstriderProductions, wherever you find your music as Longstrider and Attic Sunsets, and wherever you listen to podcasts as *Gristholme*.

QUESTIONS? COMMENTS? EMAIL L.J. AT:
LONGSTRIDERPRODUCTIONS@GMAIL.COM

THE *GRISTHOLME* WRITING PLAYLIST:

Motion Sickness- Phoebe Bridgers
Emily I'm Sorry- boygenius
I Put a Spell On You- Nina Simone
A Lack of Color- Death Cab for Cutie
Your New Twin Sized Bed- Death Cab for Cutie
Why Worry- The All-American Rejects
Die Wiating (2020)- Beck
Los Ageless (Piano Version)- St. Vincent
Notion- Tash Sultana
If You Run- The Desert Sessions
Aselestine- Yo La Tengo
Get Out of Town- Melody Gardot
Sister, Do You Know My Name?- The White Stripes
Burn the Witch- Queens of the Stone Age
Ohio Honey- King Serpent
No Surprises- Radiohead
No One Knows- Olivier Libaux
Little Monster- Royal Blood
60 Feet Tall- The Dead Weather
Northern Attitude- Noah Kahan & Hozier
Sinnerman- Goose
Bet Against Me- Watsky